the Lastling

the Lastling

BY

PHILIP GROSS

Clarion Books
New York

Clarion Books
a Houghton Mifflin Company imprint
215 Park Avenue South, New York, NY 10003
Copyright © 2003 by Philip Gross
First published in Great Britain in 2003 by Oxford University Press.
First American edition, 2006.

The text was set in 12-point ITC Clearface.

www.clarionbooks.com

Printed in the U.S.A.

Library of Congress Cataloging-in-Publication Data

Gross, Philip.
The lastling / Philip Gross. — 1st American ed.
p. cm.
Summary: Having traveled to a war-torn area of the Himalayas with
her uncle to hunt exotic game, fourteen-year-old Paris befriends a
lost twelve-year-old Buddhist monk and a young yeti, from whom
she learns about humanity and friendship.
ISBN-13: 978-0-618-65998-2
ISBN-10: 0-618-65998-6
[1. Survival—Fiction. 2. Yeti—Fiction. 3. Conduct of life—Fiction.
4. Himalaya Mountains—Fiction. 5. Hunting—Fiction.] I. Title.
PZ7.G902Las 2006
[Fic]—dc22   2006002973

MP 10 9 8 7 6 5 4 3 2 1

Contents

1
The Girl in the Ice

There was a hiccup—a hitch, some bomb alert or something fouling up the flight paths—and suddenly the airport lounge was full. People were piling in around the monitors and under the departures board. They were staring, swearing in a dozen different languages, as names above them flickered, rearranged themselves but didn't change. *Kuala Lumpur . . . Anchorage . . . Honolulu . . . Chiang Kai Shek, Taipei . . .*

When she was small, Paris used to search until she found her own name—*Look, me—Paris!*—but that was years ago, before she'd even *been* there. She still noticed, of course, but these days wouldn't say.

Beside her, Uncle Franklin had stopped. He looked round sharply, putting out a hand to keep her by him. "Is there a problem?" Paris said.

"Don't worry. It won't apply to us." He said it with his usual cool assurance, but he was tense—the way he was when something thwarted him. "Wait here," he said.

It was easy to track Franklin's path through the crowd—that shock of gloss white hair, carried high, so striking on a man who wasn't old. He went straight through. She could see the eerie way queues parted, families separating from each other naturally to let him through. He didn't need to speak or push. Her uncle had . . . authority. Already he'd located someone in a uniform, and they were talking, with their heads together. Paris saw the moment when the woman spoke into her mobile phone. Someone more important would be on his way. Paris recognized the routine: A hitch . . . and Uncle Franklin fixing it. But in this crowd, even he might have a little wait.

Paris dumped her bag down. She and her uncle were two of a kind. She hated waiting, too. The thought crossed her mind, but only faintly: What if Uncle Franklin can't fix it? Now, of all times, when it mattered. They were on a schedule, with people to meet. Important people. This was *not* a holiday.

A party of Sikhs pushed through, with all the men in smart blue turbans, all the women bossy, bickering, and slow. There were dozens of them, with a lot of dolled-up, big-eyed children, meek and silent: one huge family. *Great!* thought Paris as they settled down in front of her and blocked her view.

Just off to one side was a fountain—a stainless-steel water feature, rather, with several tiers of waterfall shimmering down. She guessed the hissy splashing of it was meant to keep people calm at times like these. There was a steel lip round the side, and Paris climbed up on it—the kind of thing people slapped their kids for doing. But Paris was fourteen, and no one, *no one* was going to slap her. Nobody had dared try that for years.

She couldn't see Franklin where she'd seen him last. Just wait, wait. She looked down. In the shallow, choppy water, people had thrown coins. A few banknotes, even, were lying there, turning to mush. But it was the waterfall that had caught her eye. The water didn't *fall,* exactly, but sheeted down smoothly, in a streaky film, on a surface of stainless steel, so that it was a mirror, warping the bright lights around her. People in saris and sweaters and business suits became abstract colors, neon flickers; and as she watched, the fat white fish of a plane wobbled slowly past the airport window. Only one thing was still: her own reflection, staring back at her, blurred and distorted, like those bodies they find in a glacier from thousands of years ago. It was motionless but almost moving . . . as if . . . as if, she thought, that frozen girl might step out of the ice and start to speak.

"Paris!" It was Franklin, almost shouting. He'd had to come back and find her, and he'd nearly lost his cool. Paris spun round, and for a moment her foot slipped and she nearly fell. But she had a skateboarder's judgment, and she caught herself. She jumped down and went pushing toward him, through the crowds of people, all so same-ish in their different ways. People the ordinary rules applied to.

Not her—not when she was with Uncle Franklin. "Come on," he said. They were on their way.

2

The House of the Snows

A journey," said Shengo.

A journey. As simple as that. Later, Tahr wondered whether there had been something in the way the old monk had put on the water for tea—done it himself, instead of telling Tahr to. Or was it the way he had taken the bowl in his hands, watching the butter dissolve in a swirl on the greenish liquid—all this in more than usual silence?

A journey. Had it come to Shengo *then,* some message in the patterns on the tea? People liked to think that this was how his "leadings" happened—the people who climbed up from the village hoping for a bit of a blessing or advice. If they wanted to think it came by magic, well, Shengo would sigh to himself but wouldn't disappoint them. As they left, though, Tahr would sometimes catch the twinkle in his eye.

Tahr looked now, but his master's lined face didn't give a clue. Even with years of practice—maybe nine of his twelve years, in fact—Tahr often could not make out what was going on behind those eyes. *A journey.* For all he knew, the old man could have been planning it for weeks. With Shengo, you never could tell, and Tahr didn't expect to be told. Shengo was his master, even if he was something like a father, too. If he said "a journey," they were going on a journey, and even Shengo himself might not quite know why.

Not that this had ever stopped Tahr from asking. But now, for some reason, he didn't dare speak. The voice of a crow came through the window of the hut, up the hillside beneath them. Then all of a sudden Shengo smiled.

"Aren't you always nagging me to *move about?*" he said. This was a joke. The monk was so ancient, so much like a bundle of sticks in a blanket, that sometimes as he watched him at his meditation, Tahr would wonder whether those old joints would ever click and crack and move again. Shengo grumbled when he walked, but he moved lightly.

"Aren't you always pestering me with questions?" Shengo went on. "'What's on the other side of the mountain?' 'Where do the birds go when the snows come?' Do I ever have a moment's peace from it?"

"Sir . . ." Tahr lowered his eyes. This wasn't fair. Shengo was teasing. Tahr asked a question like this once a month, maybe. Asked it out loud, that is. What Shengo knew, in the way he seemed to know things, was that this kind of thought was in Tahr's mind most days. Especially lately. Time and again, he'd find himself staring out of the small window when he should be meditating. Or he'd let the goats stray slightly, so he'd have to scramble up the hill to fetch them back. But *a journey* . . . There was something about the words that made Tahr's heart beat faster. This didn't sound like the usual trudge down-valley, followed by the trudge back with a sack of rice or barley meal.

Shengo laughed. "You're allowed to be pleased!" He ruffled the fuzz on Tahr's shaved head so suddenly that Tahr was startled. At once, Shengo made himself brisk again. "Come on, get packing," he said. "We leave . . . almost *now*."

"What about the goats?" said Tahr.

"Untie them."

"But . . . they'll stray."

"No matter."

This was it. In any conversation there came a point where Shengo said, "No matter." Beyond that point were reasons, but Tahr would have to put up with not knowing.

Strange, then, that this time the old man spoke again without Tahr asking. "A life . . . ," he said slowly. "There is a life . . . on the edge." His hand made a little rocking movement that made Tahr think of a boulder dislodged on the hillside that catches on a ledge and teeters, so that even a gust of wind could make it fall.

A life . . . on the edge. Shengo's brow wrinkled as he said it, as if he, too, was hearing the words for the first time. Then he turned away. There was a shadow, like tiredness or strain, in his face. You might even say "hurry," were it not for the fact that Shengo *never* hurried. But he turned away, as if he did not want young Tahr to see.

The way went scrambling zigzag up the hillside. It wasn't a path. Downhill from the hut there was at least a dirt track, worn by Shengo's own feet in his long years there—more recently by Tahr's, too. The steps were worn deeper by the people from the valley; they came up as pilgrims now and then, to leave a bowl of food or a handful of flowers by the stone hut with peeling patches of red plaster on the wall.

Red: the deep red, almost dried-blood red, of holiness. . . . Shengo's eyes would glitter some nights as he told Tahr tales of a great *gompa,* home to fifty monks and fifty gold Buddhas. In his mind's eye, Tahr would see the high red halls and gateways, the many-storied ramparts clinging to the mountain. It would be a *dzong,* a fortress, if the Way they followed hadn't been a way of peace. Whether Shengo had actually been there, Tahr was not sure, because each time he told it, the details would change . . . even down to the number of Buddhas. Still, the old man had dragged up a bucket of bright red mud to plaster on the wall that overlooked the valley. It was cracked and peeling now, but it seemed to be saying that their hut was a little *gompa,* too.

When the visitors came, Shengo sat with them, and rarely spoke. Some never even came inside. It seemed to be enough for them that he was *there,* the old monk in the red hut. And it pleased them now to see that a young monk, young but with the same shaved head, was up there, training with the old one. They loved it when Tahr greeted them three times—first in ordinary language, then with a blessing from the sacred texts, in Pali, then in a scrap of the English—*good afternoon thank you I beg your pardon*—that the old man taught him for some reason, maybe just to pass the time. Sometimes the bowl they brought would have bright yellow sweets made of honey and milk, so sweet they made your tongue curl. Shengo would leave these, as if they were Tahr's by right.

The hillside was steep, but Tahr went at it like a dog let off its lead. This was his place—and for the first half hour they climbed, he was at home. Far above, the skyline was jagged with rocks and a few thin pines. That was farther than he or anyone with any sense would venture. Here, though, there wasn't a boulder that he didn't know; he knew the fresh patches of green for the goats, he knew where there might be wild honey in a thicket. Most of all, he knew it from just scrambling, for the sake of it, while Shengo's back was turned. Thinking back, he realized that the old man turned his back quite often, knowing that a boy would need to play. And even when he caught him at it, sometimes the monk would watch a little before calling him down.

Tahr: That was Shengo's name for him, the name he gave him when he found him, a thin kid, no more than a toddler, who had lost his people and his name somewhere. *Tahr:* The shy wild sheep of the mountains, good at melting into the hillside when you so much as looked at them . . . then reappearing high up on a thin ledge with no way you could see for them to get there, unless they had wings.

As they climbed now, the old man went slowly. Tahr had to stop himself from pushing on past him. That would not be respectful. Instead, Tahr took the shortcuts, little gullies in between the boulders. He kept out of sight, scrambling up behind an outcrop, ready to surprise his master, waving *Look at me! Up here!* Except that when he jumped out and looked down, there was no Shengo. No, he was level with Tahr—a little higher, even—trudging with his head down, and he didn't turn.

Below and behind them, the valley opened. There was the roof of their hut, very small now. Beyond it lay the green of the fields, line upon line of thin terraces scratched from the slopes, plumped up after months of rain. There were a few clumps of darker green, where trees still clung, in places too steep to farm. There were the heaped stone walls of villages, and smudges of smoke in the air. The farther down the valley Tahr stared, the more the world sank into haze.

When he looked back, Shengo was almost out of sight above him, and Tahr had to put on a burst of speed to catch up. Before he reached him, Tahr was out of breath. And the old man? Climbing, slowly climbing, with his tireless, nonstop, steady step. *Hey, that's not fair,* thought Tahr, and he nearly called out. But he knew the old man would not turn. He'd smile and trudge on, while his novice learned his lesson. In some way, though Tahr could not put his finger on it, Shengo was not playing this time. Something was driving him on. Tahr wiped the cooled sweat from his forehead and from then on kept his head down, moving at a steady pace, with his eyes on the track.

All his life in the hut, Shengo had told Tahr stories. It was what he did when the child was ill, frightened, or sad. Some nights Tahr couldn't sleep; some nights he just pretended that he couldn't so he could say, "Tell me a story." He loved the ones about the lamas of the old times, who would stride across the mountains, covering a week's trek in one night. They used to go barefoot across snowfields and glaciers, hardly leaving a track in the snow, wearing only their everyday robes. "Why didn't they freeze?" Tahr would ask, and Shengo would make a gesture like a furnace burning, as if they'd had a fierce heat inside them, stoked up by the powers of their minds. Experienced hunters or herdsmen who'd tried to climb the same way in their furs and boots might be found the next day frozen rigid to the ground.

When Shengo told tales like this, his eyes glinting in the yellow flicker of the butter lamp, Tahr would picture a blizzard on the high peaks, almost a whiteout, except that in the middle of it moved a shadow, a man-shaped space where snowflakes melted instantly, an inch from the lama's skin.

I suppose they don't sweat, either, Tahr thought grumpily. *Or get blisters.* Even now he could feel where his thick felt soles would start to rub him. Pity that Shengo never taught him how those lamas did it. "No matter!" he would have said if Tahr had asked him. *Well,* thought Tahr, *it matters now.*

The skyline they had been toiling toward was within reach—one last push and. . . . No. Beyond the rise it rose again, as steep as ever. Five minutes later, he couldn't even spot where his skyline had been. *No matter,* huh! Tahr was aching in unusual places, and they weren't even out of sight of home.

Shengo sat on a stone. Without a word, he held out a battered khaki flask, and Tahr slumped down beside him. "Thank you, sir," he said, the way the old man liked him to. English was the language, Shengo used to say, to be polite in—though not much good for praying or for buying rice.

The water was *wonderful.* Tahr took a deep swig. Then he

raised his head and looked around and saw a greater wonder still.

From the hut, the slope above had always seemed like one half of the world. (The far side of the valley was the other.) Now Tahr could see that their hillside was just one rib of a larger hillside, which was rucked and folded like a robe—a robe wrapped around the shoulder of the mountain. Below them there was not just their one valley but three, four, five valleys, folded in the mountain's side. In each of the creases, reaching higher up than they were now, was the dark green of pine forest or the paler green of oaks, slightly orange this high, with a hint of autumn—all made paler by the wisps of cloud that hung around the hillside, wandering in and out of the trees.

This was the world! Tahr's heart was thumping, but it wasn't from the climbing. All those days he'd found himself gazing out of the window of the little hut . . . This was what he'd been looking for. The world! And it was big, big, big. . . .

Downhill, the valleys vanished among foothills; then there was just distance, fading into a gray green haze. Without thinking, Tahr was on his feet, spreading his arms like the wings of the lammergeier, the great mountain vulture he saw sometimes, so high it was almost out of sight. Those wings never flapped, just angled slightly on the currents of the air, and the bird would sweep out over miles of valley. With his arms spread, Tahr turned slowly through the whole arc of the view, feeling as free as the vulture must. Imagine it: Just tilt your wings and you are heading . . . *anywhere*.

From behind him came a gentle chuckle, and Tahr turned

to see Shengo with those little laughing creases round his eyes. "Oh, little bird," said the old man, "I wish I had your wingspan. Who knows where you're going to fly one day."

There was something in his voice that made Tahr look at him again. Back home, Shengo was the master, and he filled the tiny hut with his presence. Out here, on the mountain's shoulder, he looked tiny. Tiny, and old, and fragile. Now he held out a hand. Tahr helped him to his feet, as gently as those times when *he* had fallen over as a little child and Shengo had helped him. He'd never scooped him up in his arms the way Tahr had seen fathers in the village do—but gently, courteously, offered him his hand, as if they were equals. Sometimes young Tahr wondered what it would be like to have a mother who would put your head against her soft, warm shoulder, rocking you to sleep. His cheek seemed to remember the feeling, though his mind did not. Then just as he felt sad, he would catch the old monk looking at him in that kind and anxious way, and Tahr knew he was loved, after all.

Tahr pulled at Shengo's hand, and he came upright with a little sigh. "A little higher," Shengo said, and glanced up the ridge behind him. It was as steep as anything they'd climbed that day—grit, rock, and scree, a few stunted juniper bushes. Here and there along the skyline something else peeped over, shocking white—a glimpse of the place where, even in the hottest summer, it is always freezing. The house of the Snows.

For a moment, Tahr quailed, and Shengo saw it. He gave him a nudge. "Spread your wings again, little bird. You go first, and show an old man how to fly!"

———

At last, there were the Snows, so bright that Tahr shielded his eyes and looked away. Some while back, toiling up the ridge, he'd given up hoping that they would get anywhere ever again. They would be climbing forever, that was how it felt . . . and oddly, once he thought that, it felt easier, at least a bit. Now they came over a rise, and suddenly the ground stretched round them in hummocks and dips. Here and there was a patch of melting snow, but mainly there was bare rock, gray but with splashes of orange and yellow lichen, all as smooth as if they had been worn that way by constant use. In the dips between the rock, a few pools of dark water lay as still as ice . . . which perhaps they were. Tahr felt the cold breath of the Snows on his face.

There was a clatter, like a little rockfall, as a flock of blue gray sheep took fright. They poured over the edge of the rise like long grass in the wind. Then they were out of sight.

The line of snow peaks faced them, piled together in a solid wall. There was no way through, and as for habitation—not the slightest hint. Tahr knew all about snow: a few weeks now and the showers would come, and first the tips of the ridges, then gradually lower, would turn white, till it was lying all day and not melting just above their hut. He knew, too, that there were higher mountains not far off, behind the mountains he could see. From lower down the valley he would have seen those white crests as a backdrop all the time, but up near their hut the steep sides closed in round them and only a certain color, like a brightness in the dark, dark blue of some clear nights, gave a sign that there were glowing wastes up there.

But nobody lived there. Nothing human could.

Shengo had stopped beside him. The old man's face never showed much, but now Tahr saw a shadow in it that might just be doubt. "This way," he muttered. Yes, he was worried. What if this time he was wrong? He'd had one of his leadings, Tahr knew—but what if he'd misunderstood it? However they worked, those odd sure thoughts that came to him sometimes, they didn't come in words he could explain. Still less did they arrive with maps. For the first time, Tahr found himself thinking that his old friend *was* very old. What had he meant by "a life . . . on the edge"? It hadn't made much sense. Tahr had seen old people in the valley going slightly crazy, slightly vague. That couldn't happen to Shengo, could it? Tahr didn't like to think. But the thought came back: If it did . . . ? If it did, would he know—would *either* of them know—before it was too late?

"This way," said Shengo, and they went on.

Then they saw the shelter. It was tucked behind a boulder, for a little protection from the wind, and could almost have been a random pile of stones itself, apart from the flutter of a ragged prayer flag above the door. *Om . . . Mani . . . Padme . . . Hum* . . . the letters spelled out on the wind, the same sounds he and Shengo chanted every day, but up here they felt different—here, where there was no one to hear apart from sheep, a flock of birds . . . or at best the *yeh-teh,* the Mountain Spirits who were said to roam the Snows.

A life? On the edge? Did somebody live here? If so, maybe that was the life Shengo meant. So they wouldn't be going any farther. This morning, Tahr had wanted an adventure. Now that he'd seen their way barred by the mountains, and felt the breath of the Snows, he thought: *If this is it, then that's a relief.*

But there was no one in the shelter, and Shengo showed no sign that he'd expected anyone. "Is—is this it?" Tahr whispered.

"You are doing well, very well," said Shengo—a gentle way, Tahr knew, of saying no. If he'd dared, he would have asked, very carefully: *Shouldn't we go home now? Come back in the spring, maybe?* But one look at the old man's face told him what the answer would be.

"Time for something to eat," said Shengo. They hunkered down out of the wind. A few flat stones had been hauled up to form a roof, and inside the shelter it was almost warm. Shengo opened his bag, and though the food was only cold *tsampa*—"Thank you, sir," said Tahr—they both went at it like a feast.

There was a clunk as Shengo put the flask down between them. He did not speak. Outside, the prayer flag flickered and whispered, blown to shreds by years of snow and wind. Now that they'd stopped, Tahr felt the moisture chilling on his skin. He needed to move . . . but as he poked his head out of the shelter, he saw that something had changed. Half the peaks had vanished, and the rest were darkening, as gray clouds rolled up out of nowhere. Almost at once, Tahr felt slight prickles of snow.

The darkness moved across them, and so did the cold. Tahr shrank against Shengo, and they crawled backward into the shelter, as far in as they could go. He'd seen sheep on the hillside in crevices; sometimes you could stumble on a boulder cave and find it one packed mass of the quivering beasts. Tahr and Shengo crept back into the tightest corner—out of the snow and wind—but the cold of the sunless air pressed in after them. Shengo pulled his thick wool cloak around them, tucking the edges in and under. Just feeling the old monk's body, frail as it was, next to his was a comfort to Tahr. "Don't fidget," said the old man, but not sharply. "We must save what warmth we have."

"Those lamas you told me about," Tahr said, "you know, with their mystic inner heat . . ." If Shengo was ever going to teach him the trick, now was the time.

The old man smiled. "Hah! So you *do* listen." He tucked an extra fold of the cloak around Tahr. "When you are Enlightened, you come back and teach *me!* Just be calm. Breathe . . . breathe through the cloth, like this. . . ." Then he was silent, and the wind groaned in the cracks around them. Sometimes the sound of it was muffled by a swirl of snow, sometimes it would ease a little. Then Tahr looked out, and there was a small drift of snow blocking half of their entrance. Outside, the bluish ground was lighter than the sky. "We'll be snowed in!" he whispered.

"No matter. It will keep us warm." The flurries came and went, and in between it was a little lighter, but only a little, and never for long. Tahr's left leg went to sleep, and when he moved it, pins and needles bit him till he cringed with pain. "Wiggle your toes," said Shengo, just like any parent anywhere. Gradually, Tahr began to notice that the sky was darker all the time.

"No matter," Shengo said. "We are better in here for the night." There was a pause.

16

"Please, excuse me, pardon me for asking," Tahr said, "but . . . what did you mean by 'a life . . . on the edge'?"

In the dark, Shengo's face was not even an outline, but Tahr thought he felt the warmth of it, turned toward him in this dreadful place. "We eat a little *tsampa*," Shengo said, as if that was the answer. "Then we get some sleep."

3

Iron Dragonfly

"Tell me a story," Tahr said, as he used to years before. With something in his stomach, he felt somehow safer. But sleep . . . ? He'd always loved to hear Shengo's tales of lamas, gods, and demons, or the story of how Shengo had found him, lost and walking nowhere, in the valley, and had brought him up to the red hut for safety, until someone came to claim him . . . but no one ever did. Sometimes when they went down the valley, village women would sneak a chance to lay a hand lightly on Tahr's shaved head. *Poor thing,* they must have been thinking, *up there with that dry old man . . . without a mother.* But in his own way, Tahr knew, Shengo cared about him as a father would. Shengo knew when the boy needed the comfort of a story, and he never minded, even if it meant the same tale again and again.

"Tell me about when you met the Mountain Spirits," Tahr said, though he knew every word in advance. How Shengo had gone to raise a prayer flag high on the mountain and there, just where the snow was melting, was a line—no, three lines, two big, one small—of footsteps in the snow. That moment gave Tahr a thrill . . . when they were safely down the mountain. Now, no sooner were the words out of his mouth than he wished he hadn't asked.

"Oh, them . . ." The old man must have felt him shiver. "They do no harm. They just want us to leave them alone."

"But they're Spirits!" Tahr said. "Nothing can hurt Spirits, can it?"

"What makes you think that? They have bodies. They leave footprints."

"But they're . . . *big?*" said Tahr, and shuddered. *Yeh-teh* . . . great red-haired shaggy mountain monsters, that's what people in the village said.

"Oh, they were a long way off when I saw them. They seemed small, up there against the snow. Besides, they won't be up here this late in the year. They're not silly. They're sentient beings—like us. They feel the cold!" When Shengo put it like that, Tahr wasn't sure whether to feel relieved or disappointed.

"I'll tell you something else," said Shengo after a pause. "Something I've never told you, and—and I wouldn't want you not to know it . . . after I'm gone." Outside, the prayer flags muttered in the wind. "My old water flask." He tapped it, and it gave the dull clunk Tahr knew well. "Have you noticed the word on it?"

"Some letters," Tahr said. "It—it looks like English. Not a word you've taught me, though."

"Clever," Shengo said, approving. "And observant. Some of the letters are scratched off. It says 'H.M. Property.'"

"H.M.?"

"H.M. was a king. The king of England. I worked in the house of his District Commissioner. And then later . . . I was in his army for a while."

"*His army?* But you—you are . . ."

"Shengo. The name means 'sergeant'—a kind of soldier. I wasn't always in robes. I didn't grow up in them like you."

Tahr was staring at him, though he could not see him in the dark.

"No matter." Shengo's voice went on. "The whole world was mad then, mad with fighting. Whatever I did, I'll pay for it in my next life. Maybe I'll be something peaceful, like a snail."

"What—what was it like?" breathed Tahr. Shengo, the monk, a soldier! Should he be shocked . . . or interested? If he was interested, was it right to ask? "Tell me, please."

"We should be saving our breath," said Shengo. "But I will say this. . . ." He wrapped the cloak tighter round them. "I met people who were gods and titans then."

In his mind's eye, Tahr saw the old monk's precious painting of the Wheel of Life. At the top, the gods lived in a land of peace and plenty. Down one side were the titans, mighty but ambitious, always rivals, always locked in strife. On the other side were people and, below them, beasts, and then the hells, which the worst souls had to pass through before they could start ascending. And in the last part of the Wheel . . .

"I also met some who were Hungry Ghosts."

Tahr stiffened. The old man had lifted the words from his mind. Just then the wind leaned harder on the walls of the shelter. The Hungry Ghosts. Tahr had seen pictures of them, half funny, half dreadful: pot-bellied creatures always rushing about to fill their empty stomachs . . . but they couldn't. There was food, but they could never cram enough in through their tiny, tiny mouths.

At the thought of it, Tahr's stomach rumbled. "Ah!" said Shengo. "I saved something for you, my small hungry ghost." Under the cloak he passed him a little cube of something that Tahr's fingers recognized. He slipped it up to his mouth, and the sweetness of the yellow honey-sweet tingled on his tongue.

He made it last, fighting the urge to bite it, and letting it melt through his teeth. By the time it was gone, he heard the old man breathing very peacefully beside him, maybe deep in meditation, more likely asleep. Tahr sat still, trying to follow him, but there was something, something itching inside him. The thought of Shengo as a young man . . . as a soldier. . . . Yes, it made his heart beat faster. He wanted to know. And also he did not want to. The word "soldier" brought a chill, a kind of numbness to his brain.

Instead, he pictured the Wheel. The gods in their garden by a flowing stream, and the Buddha with them playing on a lute. Sweet music, yes, but the words of the song were to remind them: Nothing lasts forever; even gods can fall.

And then, as his mind began to wander, there were the wind voices outside, and they were the sad, greedy wailings of the Hungry Ghosts. *Please,* thought Tahr, *don't let me need to go for a pee in the night;* then, cold and cramped as he was, he was slipping asleep. That seemed the safest place to be.

Bright light—sunlight—came in through the entrance of the low stone shelter. Tahr opened his eyes. He was stiff and aching. But it was a new day and they were alive—not frozen into blocks of ice.

At least, he was. Shengo was not there. He must have shifted very carefully, bunching the cloak up next to Tahr in the place he had been, not to disturb him. Tahr sat upright, wide awake in an instant.

All round, there was tremendous silence. Last night's wind had gone. Then, very softly, he heard the familiar throaty sound—half muttered, half sung—of Shengo, chanting.

Tahr poked his head out. There was the old man, perched on a boulder—and around him was a whole new world. Last night's snow had been soft, the first of the year, and it had not settled. Every boulder, every blade of grass, was lined with snow down one side, and as Tahr watched, the sunlight touched it and the white turned to clear drips. The hummocky ground was melting into patches. Only the mountain ridge beyond was bright, invincible white.

"Good." Shengo looked up, briskly. "Now we can move on." Tahr groaned. "We have to," Shengo said, and Tahr saw that he meant it. "We must get to the pass before the next snow comes." There were stray clouds waiting in the clefts between the peaks, where the pass was. Tahr would have to take the old man's word for it. Even as he looked, the mountains seemed to shuffle places. A trick of the cloud, he knew, but they were never quite in the same place when he looked again.

The ground rose slowly, and as they gained height, a low cloud came down to meet them. Soon they were in a thin bright mist. In it, the dips and rises seemed like small hills, and Tahr kept close to Shengo. If they lost each other here . . .

Once, the old monk stopped and hesitated, as if he'd lost the direction; there was weariness and worry in his face, and Tahr reached out to take his hand. Then there was a low *cronk* far off—far, but coming nearer, until suddenly a raven came over their heads, so low they could have touched it. Shengo led them on, the way the bird had gone.

And then the miracle happened. One last push up a stony rise, and suddenly the mist thinned. There was deep blue overhead. As the clouds fell away around them, Tahr saw they were there, at the pass, a shallow dip between two slopes of rock and snow. Ahead of them, a whole new world fell open.

It was a wider, more complicated place than Tahr had imagined, even from the wonders of the day before. There were valleys, deeper and greener than the ones they'd left behind. Beyond that . . . higher mountains, brilliant white against the sky. Ropes of white waterfalls came twisting down through steep forest and, once, the still glint of a slate blue lake. Shengo's yellowish lined face beamed for a moment like a child's—first at the huge view, then at Tahr. He clapped his hands: "There! That was worth a few blisters, wasn't it?" And they laughed.

Then the cloud came down, as if a minute's vision was enough. But Shengo was sure now, striding downhill with a purpose, and Tahr felt like skipping down beside him, down toward the tree line, where first bushes, then a few thin pines, found footholds on the scree. As they lost height, they came out of mist, and the deep green of the rhododendron forest came to meet them. When he heard the thin *chee!* of a bird, Tahr knew he was back from the realm of gods and spirits, back in the world of ordinary living things. He picked a blade of grass, stretched it between his thumbs, and blew a raucous happy screech like a peacock's call.

Shengo emptied his pack out. There was only hard bread and little *tsampa*—but they were going to taste good. "We had enough, you see?" said Shengo. "We must be nearly there." He caught Tahr's eager look.

"Where is *there?*" Tahr said.

"Ah . . ." That he could not say. *Could not or would not?* Tahr would think much later, thinking back on that day. *Couldn't say because you didn't know what was coming? Or because you did?*

"Look," said Shengo in the sunlight. "Have some of these before the bears get them." In the cracks of the outcrop there were berries—red, tiny but sweet. "Not too many, or you'll be sick." As Tahr ate, Shengo walked up to a rocky bluff and gazed across the valley. After a while Tahr heard the soft, endless sound that had run through his life like his own heartbeat: Shengo's *Om Mani Padme Hum.* . . .

Then there was another sound, faint but all around him. For a moment Tahr felt queasy, as if he'd eaten a really bad berry. Then he was stiff and sweating. He got to his feet without wiping his red-stained hands and lips, and as he scrambled up toward Shengo, the sound came clearer. It was a thick, steady clattering, far off, as if he was hearing it from years, not miles, away. The old man's face was very still now, watching something far below them in the valley. Tahr followed his gaze . . . and saw.

Way down, something was flying, slowly, following the bot-

24

tom of the valley. It kept just over the tops of the trees—moving forward, stopping, hovering. It was gray green, plump at one end, long-tailed, like a dragonfly, but that choppy rattling sound was man-made, made of metal. A dragonfly of iron.

"Helicopter," said the old man softly. "Why here?" Tahr had felt his body go rigid with fear. His breath came in jerks, and he was struggling, with small wheezing noises. Shengo put his hands on both his shoulders, turning Tahr's gaze toward him, away from the valley.

"Breathe," said Shengo firmly. "Look at me . . . and breathe." He did not let go. Gradually, the breathlessness began to ease a little, as it usually did, once he had calmed down. But these spells did not usually come on as suddenly as this. The old man watched him carefully, with concern in his eyes.

"What's in your mind?" said Shengo.

Tahr shook his head. There was a smell, the smell of smoke and burning. He'd been choking on it—that and the sound. The sound of *helicopter* felt so close and loud, it seemed to get inside his ribcage, in his lungs. It hurt.

"It's all right. It was long ago now. You were very young. . . . The soldiers came."

"Soldiers? You said *you* were a soldier. . . ."

"Not then. This was long after I had taken robes. Soldiers came to your village and. . . . Do you remember?"

Tahr gazed into his mind, gazed harder than he had ever done in meditation. The memory he'd almost had was fading; it left a terrible emptiness, a burnt smell. Tahr thought of a scroll that he'd knocked against a lamp when he was first with

Shengo. They had opened it, and there, in the middle of the writing, was a scorched hole with crisp edges. He shook his head.

Shengo let his hands rest on Tahr's shoulders a little while longer. "We must go on," he said.

"Not there. Please." Tahr felt the breathlessness again. "Not that way. Not down there, with . . . it."

Shengo looked down at the valley bottom, where the helicopter seemed to have returned, for now, to base. He looked at Tahr who was still shivering. Then he glanced up the valley, where the hillsides closed in, steeper, darker green. "We could go a longer way around," he said. "It will be harder."

Without looking up, Tahr nodded. He hung his head, ashamed to be afraid.

"You're a brave boy," Shengo said. "I was afraid, too, up there on the mountain. I was proud of you."

They moved on, silent, and the forest closed around them, muffling all sounds but its own. A woodpecker burst out of the branches near them, with its laughing call. The hillside was steep and getting steeper, and there was no track: they threaded through undergrowth and boulders, ducking branches, using roots as handholds when the ground slipped away at their feet. It took all his concentration, and slowly Tahr forgot to be afraid.

Strangely, the old man seemed happy. Tahr could not understand it. *Almost there,* he had said, and now Tahr had sent them miles out of their way, on difficult ground, and yet. . . . Sometimes Shengo would stop, to take a breather, Tahr thought, but when he caught up with him the old monk was listening to the woods around him, a smile on his face. In the sheltered rhododendron glades it was still late summer, and there was an occasional flash of purple as a big late butterfly zigzagged through the leaves. Once Shengo caught Tahr by the arm and pointed; out along a branch there was a rustle and a shudder, as a big rusty brown animal paused and turned its pretty foxlike face to inspect them. And the birds were singing as if this might be the last great day of the year.

Very slowly, though, the world was getting colder. Tahr hardly noticed it at first, with his eyes on the slithery ground at their feet, but there was no sunlight in between the bushes anymore. There wasn't a layer of gold in the tops of the trees. It was hours now since they'd left the outcrop, and the sun had shifted. At the same time, they were going deeper in: the sides of the valley leaned steeper toward them, till they started to see the treetops opposite through the trees around them. There were places that the sun might not have reached all day.

Another thing: There was a sound, everywhere—not the helicopter but a deep and steady *husssh*. Every now and then Tahr glimpsed white among the leaves—white, white and black, where a narrow river rushed between the stones. First time, it seemed a long way down, then it was closer, not so much running as throwing itself down a staircase of falls. The sound grew louder, and Tahr began to feel a coldness in the air that made him think of snow.

Then they were standing on the edge of it—a ledge of black rock that the waterfall seemed to have cut straight through. The ravine was just two arms' span wide, but out of it rose a slight mist with that snow feel in it. This was glacier water, still just at the point of melting, and when Tahr peered, he saw it running fiercely, a strange milky green.

What now? He might have called to Shengo, but he would not have heard him. The old monk was edging his way along the ledge, and when Tahr looked, he wished he hadn't, because there was the answer to his question, at the old man's feet.

It might have been put there for them, or for someone else who came this way. A log. A smooth log, fallen from somewhere above and resting perfectly across the chasm. A log bridge, its surface slick with spray.

Sometimes, as a change from sitting, Shengo did walking meditation. Half a pace at a time, putting each foot gently down before easing his weight forward, he would move with his hands cupped in front of him, his eyes lowered. Once around their little *gompa* took an hour. And now he was out on the log—the same pace, the same concentration. Tahr laid down his bag and watched, hardly daring to breathe, as the old man made the crossing, turned, and then crossed back again. Shengo gave a slight bow, smiled, and beckoned.

There was no saying no. "Come on, little mountain goat," said Shengo. "I've seen you jumping round on ledges half as wide as this." He paused. "It is the only way."

Very carefully, Tahr stepped on the end of the log. Once he put his weight on it, it was okay. The log didn't wobble. If it had been lying on the ground at home, he could have done it backward, with his eyes closed. He tried to tell himself that. He took a step on, and the sound of water rushed up. Tahr clutched Shengo's hand.

Shengo loosened his fingers, very gently. "I can't keep your balance for you," he said. "Fix your mind on a point. I will be right behind you." And he touched Tahr's shoulder lightly, so he could feel it was true.

Then it was half a step, half a step—shifting his weight slowly—as the water noise roared round him. Tahr was halfway—*Just one jump,* he thought—and the lightest touch on his back reminded him. One point. One breath at a time.

He stepped off onto the ledge, and the old man stepped off beside him. Tahr grinned, feeling as light as if he'd lifted a load from his back.

Then he remembered. He *had* taken a load off his back. His bag was on the other side, where he'd left it. Shengo must have seen the sudden shadow in his eyes. "No matter," he said, and the old man paced back over the log as if he had no weight at all.

Tahr leaned against the rock, laughing quietly to himself. This was his valley, his bridge. He had conquered it. And without help—well, without holding anybody's hand, at least. As Shengo started back with the bag, Tahr gazed out at the hillside, where they'd struggled through the bushes, forging a track, like explorers, where nobody else had been . . .

And then the face looked out.

It was only a second, but right in the thick of the dark rhododendron leaves the branches parted, and a face, a human face, peered out.

"Look!" Tahr jumped up, pointing at the place where the leaves had closed again. It was so loud, so sudden, that even the old monk, with all his years of practicing one-pointedness, could not help but look. And that was when his foot went out from underneath him. As he went one way, so the log jerked away to the other, and for a moment the log and the man were slowly twisting shapes against white water. Then Tahr was kneeling at the edge, and there was only the noise and white foam, cold spray on his face, and like awful machinery the waterfall crashed on.

4

Paris on Location

Paris was going to be a movie director. That was the life plan, as of today. She slumped back in the canvas chair, and her fair hair flopped over her eyes. She flicked it away. She was fed up with it. If there'd been a good pair of scissors handy, she'd have chopped it there and then. There were lots of things she'd like to change right now. This place—this camp-site—for a start. And the waiting. If this was a movie, she thought, she'd clap her hands now and say, "Cameras . . . Action," and something would start to roll. Sheesh, they had the scenery in place—all the Himalayan forest Uncle Franklin's friends in high places could fix. But nothing was *happening*. There was a general clatter of expedition business going on among the tents, but nobody seemed to be thinking about *her.* And Paris was bored.

She could be a movie director if she wanted. Most girls her age wanted to be movie stars; not her. She was going to be the one who called the shots. The one who said "Action." Sure, there was the problem of finance, but her pop would probably stump up the odd million just to keep her out of his hair, and he'd write it off against expenses. The main thing was *contacts.* Uncle Franklin would know people in the business, of course, When she'd mentioned the plan to him, on the way to the airport, he hadn't answered straightaway. Pop would just have said, "Sure, sure," without meaning it. Franklin was different. He'd stopped, and looked at her a moment. "A one-person brat pack," he'd said, with his brief, dry smile. They'd hardly talked—not really *talked*—since then.

On the edge of the clearing, one leaf let go of its twig and slowly fell.

What did Franklin think he was doing, Paris wondered, bringing them here at this time of year? There'd been rubbish movies on the long flight, so she'd read the trekkers' guide from end to end. It was full of the glories of the place in spring—huge rhododendron blossoms, Technicolor butterflies, and all the other stuff that wasn't there now, in October. It was getting cool, too, and they'd pitched camp out of the sun. Very carefully out of the sun, out of sight. So much for the famous views of snow-capped peaks—a glimpse, maybe, between these stupid trees, which weren't very different from the trees in any of the places she'd called home.

Still, Paris was here. That was what mattered. All these years, she'd picked up hints, from things he said, about these "expeditions." Other people in the family smirked. "Franklin's *Boy's Own* adventures," Pop said. *Fine,* thought Paris. *I'll be one of the boys.* She'd started dropping hints to Franklin, and he hadn't said no. "In time," he'd said, "in time."

And here she was. She was a member of a very special club indeed—just how special, she was starting to understand.

She'd had a glimpse of the quiet phone calls to friends of a friend in this foreign ministry or that. In this language or that. Uncle Franklin could *fix* anything. So there'd been someone there to meet them on touchdown and to ghost them past the customs queue, on to where their sealed baggage would be waiting for them in the chartered jeep, untouched by prying hands. There'd been the police chief at the bottom of the valley, who had been expecting them, like a man who had his orders: point them on their way and then forget. And there was the local guide, Shikarri. He'd stepped out of the shadows in the final village, where the road ran out, like a man who'd been waiting, watching for them. He'd had no expression on his thin, sharp hunter's face, but when his eyes rested on her for a moment, Paris flinched. In the background was the team of porters, small silent men who sat in the shade and didn't mix with the villagers. They weren't local—Shikarri had brought them, and they waited for his orders. Five minutes later, they were unloading the jeeps, keeping their heads down, braced against the great unwieldy packs. They didn't look as if they were doing it for the fun of it, thought Paris, any more than the mules they piled high with the strange-shaped baggage.

Then again, the members of the expedition didn't look like people on vacation, either. They'd arrived in the lounge of the Ashok Hotel, New Delhi, one by one: Donald from London, Renaud from Paris, Harriet by chartered plane out of somewhere unspeakable in central Africa, Gavin by local flight from the Karakoram . . . and none of them talked about their flights at all. They were people on business, and they knew why they were there. Not for relaxing in the five-star comforts of the Ashok, that was clear. They had greeted each other with nods and Paris with a shrewd look, weighing her up, before they spoke. They didn't look so much like old friends as conspirators. They'd raised a glass—hard liquor or fine wine, depending on their style—in a silent toast. They'd clinked; then they were on their way.

Even now they weren't wasting much time on sightseeing, though as the trek got under way, they kept coming over rises to horizons crisp and sharp with snow peaks, a gift for the wide-angle lens. Shikarri kept the porters moving with his whip-crack tongue, and beside him, on a leash of thick, black plaited hair, came the dog. This was nobody's pet. It was a great gray brindled mastiff—bull-like shoulders, a wide head that hung with the weight of its square muzzle—and it would not be led or touched by anybody but its master.

"What—what's it called?" Paris had said to Shikarri, just to break the silence.

"Do khyi."

Franklin had come up beside them. "Not so much a name," he'd said, "as what it *is*. It means 'the dog who is chained.'"

Paris hadn't asked why. Franklin had caught her look and smiled. "I wouldn't want to meet it, not without Shikarri—would you?"

They had trekked on in silence, hours and hours, until Shikarri called a halt. It was nowhere in particular that Paris could see, but the guide had been definite. Here, he'd said, we make a base camp. Now most of the porters had been paid off and gone, all but a few, the ones Shikarri had picked for their loyalty and silence. They camped a little way off and sat quiet, waiting to be sent for, passing whole days playing vague, unfathomable games of chance.

There were a lot of men about, thought Paris. A *Boy's Own* adventure? There was Harriet, of course, but she hardly seemed like a woman. Harriet kept pace with Gavin on the whisky and with Donald on the slim cigars. Paris kind of admired that, yes, but Harriet, with that famous war-worn face, was kind of scary, too.

Paris found herself scanning the opposite sex—you know, the way you do. Not that she was crazy over them, like most of her classmates were. Creamy-faced kids from boy bands left her cold. When she let her mind wander, she remembered the black guy she'd seen break dancing once in the subway. He was lean—no muscle man—but graceful, all alive, and deep in his dance. She wanted him to look up when she dropped some money in his hat, but afterward she was kind of pleased he hadn't. No fake grin and "Thank you, ma'am." . . . He just went on with his dance.

Boys of her age bored her, and she wasn't sorry that there weren't any here. Still, let's be honest, she'd expected something from the expedition. From what she'd heard, it was Gavin who might just be promising, but when she'd seen him at the airport, she'd revised her plans. He was the commando type—beefy, leathery-tanned, and crop-headed—and he wasn't going to like her, she knew at a glance. He didn't see the use of her, and he'd said as much to Franklin, in that rough, dry Scottish way. Then he'd held out his hand. Paris flinched.

There were the stump ends of his three long fingers, missing at the tips. He'd seen her staring, and he pushed the hand toward her—*Go on, shake it*—with a private smile.

After that there was Donald. No thanks. And there was Renaud, whom she'd scarcely seen. There were the porters, of course. Sometimes they worked naked to the waist, man-handling the tent poles upright. The question of *fancying* didn't arise. She was taller than most of them, for one thing. But they were very much *there*. It was a bit unsettling.

Meanwhile, Shikarri was everywhere. Talking to Franklin, getting his instructions. Pointing to distances, poring over maps with Gavin. And when the first of the rifles came out of its packing, he was there to weigh it in his hands, squint down the sights, and nod approval. Shikarri looked straight through Paris, and she didn't feel inclined to find out more. She'd seen the way he cut through obstacles like fallen branches on the trail, with one hack of the glinting *kukri*—half knife, half machete—he wore at his belt.

Most of the day the mastiff sat tethered. Now and then it would leap up, straining at something it had heard or smelt, and the weight of it shuddered its stake. Then its mantrap jaws would open and rake at the air . . . but no sound came out. "Debarked," Franklin had said, casually, and Paris tried not to think what that meant. Shikarri was a hunter, he said, of a rather special kind, and in his profession stealth was of the essence. By night, Shikarri would pace out the edge of the camp, and the dog would be loose. Paris would hear it scuffling, panting, just outside her tent.

———

On the other hand, things could be worse. She could have been at school. Uncle Franklin had fixed that, too. This was going to be a real education, being part of Franklin's world.

Other kids had cool uncles. Paris knew that. But hers wasn't just cool—he was life on ice. Everything that was gross about her parents—the personalized license plates on Pop's limo, or Mom's drama-queen scenes and fads and silly causes—all of that was so *not* Franklin. He was Franklin, always—never Frank. Not like her pop, who'd gone from Woodrow to Woody by the time he was six weeks old. Uncle Franklin had that white hair he'd had since his thirties—stylish, startling with his unlined face. Pop was into hair dye and, recently, hairpieces.

No, her uncle was the real thing. Paris wanted to be the real thing, too.

And amazingly—lucky or what— he was the one with time for Paris. He'd liked her, from the start. Or maybe "like" wasn't quite the word for it. "Recognized," maybe . . . She knew how he'd watch her sometimes, coolly—in the same way that Shikarri held the rifle, with the same little nod at the end. He didn't try to buy her things, the way Pop did, or try to be all-pals-together, like Pop's latest little wife. He didn't tell her what she thought, as Mom did on their visits. No, Uncle Franklin would just be around—take her out to some Japanese restaurant he'd discovered, where there was so much bowing and scraping, so much business with the slivers of raw fish and white radish, that she didn't have to talk at all. So when Uncle Franklin told Pop that she needed a change of air and a bit of a challenge, her heart leaped inside . . . and when

Pop looked vague and said, "Sure, sure, why not?" Paris could have punched the air. But didn't. Uncle Franklin never punched the air, even when he got what he wanted. And getting what he wanted was the thing he usually did.

Paris heard the footsteps coming up behind her, but she didn't turn straightaway. There was only one person, really, it could be. Not Franklin, who'd have come with firm steps, quickly, and not Gavin, who made a point of moving like a panther even when he was only going for a pee. Not Harriet, who went everywhere as if she was pushing her way to the front of a crowd. And the thought of Shikarri coming up behind her made her shudder. No, this had to be Donald, shuffling slightly, as if he'd just got out of bed.

He stood at her shoulder for a moment, waiting to be noticed. "It's awfully . . . *green,* is it not?" he said, after a while.

Paris couldn't help smiling. He sounded as fed up with this place as she was. She considered, briefly, making friends . . . then turned round and remembered why it didn't seem a good idea. Donald might have been built to be the opposite of Paris. Where she was lean and rangy (people took her for a tennis player), he was short and smooth. Not fat but well fed on a daily, professional basis: Donald was a gourmet, not just as a hobby, but as a job. There was a buttery look to his skin, and he sort of *slithered* in the way he moved and spoke. He smiled too much. And most important, he was middle-aged—thirty-something, he said, *early* thirty-something, but he could have been saying that for years and years. What he was doing on a trek like this, Paris couldn't imagine.

Donald had brought his own French chef with him. Geez, just how decadent was that?

"Seen any more of the helicopter chappies?" Donald said.

Paris shook her head. She'd heard it that morning—a distant throb of rotors—and she'd scrambled up the slope till she saw through the trees. It was just a glimpse, and far down-valley: an olive green helicopter, heading away. It was the nearest thing to something happening there'd been, but it hadn't come near, and even if it had, their camp was tucked into a deep cleft almost overhung by trees. That was a little bit exciting. Franklin had made it clear that they'd chosen the spot for cover. "A sensible precaution," he'd said, enigmatically.

"Were they looking for us?" said Paris.

"Oh, I think that's unlikely," said Donald.

Paris looked at him again. Her question had been meant to be a joke.

"Some local fracas," he went on. "Revolting peasants—you know, that kind of thing. None of our business."

"So it's nothing to do with the guns?" said Paris slyly.

Donald laughed. "My dear, someone should tell you the difference between a weapon and a hunting rifle. Just in case you're in a real combat situation one day. Hmm . . . ," he said. "I rather assumed you were a trainee great white hunter yourself." Another pause. Paris guessed he was wondering: *Then what exactly is she doing here?*

"Me? No, I'm gonna make the movie of it."

He narrowed his eyes for a moment. "Oh, I see," he said. "Very droll." The two of them gazed into the tangle of forest again. Then Donald shrugged. "The things one does for one's art," he said and turned away. "If you fancy a proper coffee at some point," he said, "Renaud is getting his kitchen set up. Not before time." And he ambled away.

Then there was quietness, made of breaths of wind and forest whispers. There were loops of birdsong and the whirr of insects ticking over, but they all seemed slowed down, as if nature had started cooling and settling for the year. Paris let herself sink into it. A tiny sound-jacuzzi. She wasn't sleepy, but this place could put you in a kind of trance.

Then there was a crack and a rustle. On the edge of the clearing, branches parted, and out came a boy.

Whether he had seen her, or knew what was happening, Paris could not tell. He stepped out of the trees and straightaway he stumbled, as if he'd been leaning on them for support. He swayed. He was some kind of local, a kid, by the looks of it— bare to the waist and dragging what was left of a cloak behind him like a comfort blanket. Kids she'd seen in the villages they'd passed on the way had been snotty and grimy, but this one was different—streaked with mud and scratches, bruised and grazed. He lifted his head and looked round blankly, and his face was hardly like a child's at all, because he had no hair. Then there was a pad and a thump, as the great gray mastiff hit him, and the boy went down.

In hindsight, Paris thought, the guide must have been watching—watching her, and her and Donald—all this time. Next moment, Shikarri had covered the ground from the tents to the edge of the glade, and was dragging the dog off, thrashing at it till it cowered. Then he had the boy by the scruff of the neck, hauling him upright, peering close, then spitting questions in one language, then another. Whatever the words were that the boy managed to stutter out, they weren't what he wanted to hear. Shikarri was yanking him around, to steer him back toward the forest. Not just pushing him away. No, he was marching him out of the clearing, out of sight of Paris and. . . .

Shikarri's hand had dropped toward the *kukri* at his belt. "No!" Paris shouted. "Bring him here. He needs help." For a moment, the guide turned and glared at her—the first time he had really looked at her all week. "He's hurt. I'll shout for Uncle Franklin. He'll—"

"All right, all right." Franklin was there behind her and, in the way he had, immediately in command. He said something to the guide, a few words in his language. The man's grip loosened on the boy, who crumpled to the ground again.

"Well," Uncle Franklin said to Paris, without smiling. "What have we got here?"

"Don't let him hurt him," Paris started.

"Bring him inside," Franklin said. "We'll sort this out in private." He looked at Paris. "And you," he said, as she'd hoped he would. "Looks like you'd better come, too."

5

The Other Side of Somewhere

Paris was starting to wish this whole thing hadn't happened. If she'd just been looking the other way when the kid appeared out of the forest . . . well, she need never have known. Now the four of them sat in Franklin's tent—her, her uncle, the guide, and the boy—and the silence was tense.

Shikarri's voice was like metal on stone. It was *his* job, he said, keeping the campsite secure. He would do what was needed. But the girl had interfered. He didn't look at Paris or the boy.

Uncle Franklin was still, his features like an Easter Island statue. Now he nodded slowly and said a few words in the guide's own language. Paris glanced at the boy, but he didn't look as if he understood.

It was hard to tell, though. Washed and tidied up a bit, with his robe pulled round him, the boy sat cross-legged, motion-less. With a bit of bread and drink inside him, he looked less like a little old wild man and more like . . . well, just a kid. And yet . . . a monk. She'd seen Buddhist monks in pictures, and he looked exactly like that, only smaller, as if they made them in different sizes. The boy's flat yellowish pale face gave no signs that she could understand.

No, Shikarri's language wasn't what the boy spoke. When he opened his mouth at last, what came out was English—quaint, and in an accent so odd she didn't recognize it at first. Still, the kid wasn't dumb. He didn't seem keen to talk, but he'd have to talk plenty before Shikarri would be satisfied.

"Excuse me . . . so sorry," he said, suddenly, staring at the groundsheet. "Shengo . . . he is dead. It is because of me."

Franklin and Shikarri stared at him. It wasn't an answer to a question they had asked.

"Shengo?" said Paris. "Who's this *Shengo?*"

"My master," he said simply.

Paris stared. "Your master?" she said. "People don't have *masters* these days!"

In reply, the boy held up the hem of his robe.

"They treat their elders with respect," said Franklin dryly, with a look at Paris. Shikarri, though, had gone dangerously silent.

"So just send him back," said Paris, "you know, to his monastery or whatever. They'll look after him."

"There is no monastery, nowhere near here," Shikarri cut in. "This boy will not explain himself. Where is he going? This is a restricted area—everyone knows that. He can give no reason to be here." The guide paused, holding back his final card. "And how come he speaks English, if he is not a spy?"

"You speak English," Paris said. "That doesn't make you a spy."

"I work for people like you. Who does this one work for? Tell me that."

As the words passed to and fro, the boy's eyes fixed on the dog, tied up but straining, as if it had his scent now and would not forget. If that kid's a spy, thought Paris, he's a heck of a good actor, too.

"So what do we do with him?" said Franklin.

The guide didn't reply. He'd said all he needed to.

"Oh, geez," Paris burst out. Even the young monk looked up, surprised. "Just let him go. Forget him, okay? Just forget this ever happened. What's the problem?"

"Actually, there *is* a problem," said Franklin slowly. He rested his hands together, making a steeple of his index fingers, the way he did when he was thinking. "The problem, as Shikarri keeps pointing out, is this: It is quite important that no silly stories get around about our expedition—about us being in the valley—which, as Shikarri says, is out of bounds."

"But the police chief . . ."

Franklin gave a pained look, as if Paris was being young and silly, and she winced. "Several important people have . . . obliged us," he said. "But officially we are not here. If we're stupid and draw attention to ourselves, some friends of friends of mine are going to be embarrassed. And very annoyed. Besides, there's a war on here. A little one, but still . . ."

Shikarri said something, a few curt words in the language Paris was not meant to understand. Franklin thought a moment, nodding.

"Bluntly," he said to Paris, "we can't let him go. Half the villagers round here are rebels. The other half are government informers. Or maybe both. It is a ticklish situation. If your little friend goes round blurting out about our expedition . . ."

"Blurting out what?" said Paris. "The kid's in shock. He hardly knows where he is!" But even as she spoke, she had a feeling that it wasn't true. The kid was in shock, yes. But not stupid. Even with those drooping eyelids that half veiled his eyes, he was taking it all in, she could tell. But what did she know? She couldn't even guess how old he was, this boy the size of her pesky little stepbrother back home, with an old man's face on him. Maybe she really didn't know what was going on here at all.

"Okay," she said, "let's let him stay. He can be a porter or something."

Shikarri gave a snort of laughter. Paris thought of the porters, little wiry men, backs bowed from years of humping richer people's luggage. Whatever this kid was, he would not be one of them. "Okay, okay," she said. She wasn't going to back down, though the logic of the argument was getting horribly clear. He couldn't stay. He couldn't be allowed to go.

"I need him," she said suddenly. "I don't know a thing about this place. And nobody else is going to tell me, are they? Well?" Uncle Franklin hadn't overruled her yet. She pressed on. "You told the school this was going to be *educational*, didn't you?"

Franklin was smiling slightly. He liked her spirit, Paris knew, because he'd told her often, over the years. If she played her cards right, she was going to get her way.

"Besides," she said slyly, "I might find out something useful. Like: What he's *really* doing here. How much he knows. He might be useful."

"What you're saying," said Franklin, "is: Give him to you."

"Well . . . yeah. No one else seems to want him." Paris felt Shikarri twitching with annoyance. But this was a game between her and her uncle. And Uncle Franklin was the boss round here.

"Very well," said Franklin. "Let me know when you get bored." Only then did she look at the young monk, who had sat quite still through all this, his eyes lowered but taking it in. *Geez,* thought Paris, *what am I going to do with him now?* But she would sort that out later. For now, she felt sort of tingling and pleased all over, as if she'd just had a good sauna. She didn't quite know how it had happened, but she'd got her way.

Paris sat back, leaned against a tree, and watched him from a distance. He was sitting very still.

Tahr . . . It was some kind of name. She'd told him hers . . . and waited for the usual moment when people always asked, "Why Paris?" But it didn't come. "You know, Paris, France, not Texas," she said, and he looked at her in that blank way—not stupid, just taking things in. "Come on," she'd said, "let's fix you up a tent." No way was she having him in hers, thank you. There were little bivouac tents among the supplies, and she reckoned one of them wouldn't be missed. It was just about big enough for a backpack, but he'd thanked her anyway. Then he'd asked if he could sit by himself for a while.

He must have known she was watching. Well, she had to,

didn't she? What if he ran back off into the forest, after all the fuss there'd been? No one was going to get a chance to say "I told you so."

And what was he doing? Okay, meditation, she knew about that. Pop's latest, Marsha, went to classes in it, but it never looked like this. For one thing, he didn't make a song and dance about it. He just sat. It looked pretty smart to be able to fold your legs like that and sit up straight, but he must have been doing it since he could toddle, like they all did out here. And he didn't put on a "Look at me—I'm meditating" face for it. He just perched on a flat rock and . . . sat.

Where is he? thought Paris. What was going on inside that round shaved head of his? Was he saying prayers or mantras, was he seeing golden Buddhas, was he humming a song from a Bollywood movie to himself and laughing at her all the time? No, she guessed he wouldn't be thinking about her at all. Even though she'd saved his life. He hadn't asked her about her family, or Uncle Franklin, or what she was doing here, why she wasn't at school. If he was some kind of a spy, he was playing it cool; he hadn't asked a thing about the expedition. No, he just sat there and half-closed his eyes and went . . . where? To the other side of somewhere. You could get annoyed with someone who did that.

Then she noticed. His shoulders were shaking, very slightly. She got to her feet and tiptoed over to him. He didn't look up. There were little tight creases round the corners of his eyes, and after a moment something glinted and then dripped. He was crying, very softly. So he was a real kid after all.

"It's all right," said Paris, sitting down beside him. "It's all right . . . all right." She touched his shoulder, and he leaned toward her, suddenly sobbing. What should she do now? If he'd had some hair she could have stroked it, but that shaved head seemed . . . too bare. Emotional scenes were pretty normal in her family. Every day that she stayed with Mom she'd witness one or two. But this was different. No words, and not much sound, just something welling up quietly as water from someplace deep down.

What do I know? Paris thought for the second time that day. Her dog, Dembo, a big floppy pooch of a thing, had died when she was seven, and she'd cried till Pop took her to the pet shop. It gave her a bad feeling now to think that she'd stopped crying then.

"This . . . Shengo," she said awkwardly. "Tell me about him."

Bit by bit, as Tahr got back his breath, the words came out. A few, at least. Paris got a weird feeling that there wasn't much to say. Who was Shengo? An old man. Very old. A kind of monk. What did he do? Not much, by the sound of it. Sat. Chanted. Dug potatoes. Fed the goats.

There was a pause.

"And you?" said Paris. "What about *you?*"

Tahr looked at her as if he didn't understand the question.

"Your family. You must have a mom and pop. . . ."

He shook his head, simply—a matter of fact. Then the creases came around his eyes again, though the sadness did not overflow.

"I—I'm sorry," said Paris, as it eased. "I'm doing this all wrong, aren't I? Please, you mustn't feel so bad."

Tahr was looking in front of him, into the forest. "I call out to him," he said. "Just when he is concentrating. He always tells me never, never speak when he is meditating, and I. . . . And I know that it is wrong to be sorry. Often my master tells me so."

"It's okay to be sorry," said Paris.

"No. He starts already on a new life."

"You really believe that? You mean, getting reborn as—I don't know—a slug or something?"

"No!" The boy looked at her, shocked. "He was a good man." It was the first time their eyes had really met, up close, and his straight look made her catch her breath. He wasn't shy, he wasn't cheeky; he wasn't any of the things a kid would be back home. He just . . . *was.*

"Sorry. Sorry again. I didn't mean . . . Oh, I'm out of my depth." Paris was flustered. "I'm just being dumb."

"No," Tahr said. "Excuse me, please. . . . You are kind."

What? Paris stopped and stared. Had anybody, ever, called her *kind* before? She was smart, she knew that—smart enough that any kind of school got boring in a week or two. Some people thought that made her special. And Marsha kept telling her she could be pretty if she put her mind to it. Paris took one look at Marsha, up and down, and thought, *No, thank you.* Oh, yes, and she was going to make movies, that or something, and be a household name one day. But *kind . . . ?*

This kid just didn't know her. He had better find out now.

"Don't count on it," she said, taking her arm off his shoulder. "And you can cut out the 'Please excuse me' stuff."

"So sorry. Beg your—"

"Shut up! Look, if I get bored with you, you're out, okay?"

6

Gods and Titans

The world had gone slippery under Tahr's feet. When he looked, he seemed to be on a broad path through a field of flowers, but when he closed his eyes, he knew that was illusion. *Samsara*. He felt how it really was—greasy, precipitous, like balancing on a slimy, wobbling plank. There was a crashing of water, as hard as an avalanche, somewhere very near. *Don't move. Don't breathe.* The muscles of his legs were aching with the strain. One careless move and he'd be plunging over, lost.

Like Shengo.

Shengo! As Tahr called the name, his feet went out from under him. He fell. The field, the path, the world went rushing past him and he couldn't breathe, and he thrashed and he moaned as he struggled awake.

There was a strange green light around him: morning, through the thin cloth of the tent. He couldn't get used to it, though he'd been here for several nights now. The sleeping bag, that strange light fabric that felt nothing like a blanket, would always wind itself around him, and the tent was hardly bigger than a bag itself. Tahr woke sweating and hot, but worse than that was the emptiness rising up inside him. He could call, but Shengo wouldn't answer, ever. His old friend was gone.

If I hadn't shouted, Tahr thought, *he'd be here now. Or rather, we would both be somewhere else.* But how could he have helped it? It had been such a shock, that face among the leaves. Now, in the cool green light of early morning, that felt like a dream. It must have been a monkey, surely: one of the shy dark-faced langurs that loved the deep forest. But he knew it was no monkey face. It had seen him; it had met his eyes, the way a person would.

As Shengo had fallen, the face had vanished, too. In the end-less minutes afterward, Tahr had yelled and shouted—"Help, help!"—through the crashing of the waterfall. No one had answered. Tahr had crept to the lip of the drop, the very edge, peering over, fighting the vertigo as the rush of water swept his gaze away. Then he had crawled back into the forest, from boulder to slippery boulder, hanging on to roots and creepers, trying to fight his way back to the water's edge. Sometimes he had managed it—down at the base of the fall, beside another swirling pool, where fallen branches caught and tangled . . . but there'd been no sign of Shengo. Tahr had peered into the frothy water, waded out until the current dragged him and he'd had to clutch at boulders to stop it snatching him, too. He called to the forest, called to anybody who might hear him, and if the helicopter had come over just then, he'd have stood on a rock and waved and shouted. But there was no helicopter. No one came. And the forest had closed in round him, swallowing his cries.

What would Shengo have said, here in the green, cold morning? *What you feel is . . . just a feeling. Sit. Back straight. Palms up and open. Let the Wheel of Life turn. Let it go.*

Let it go? How could he let *Shengo* go?

The Wheel of Life . . . It came back now, what Shengo had said when they'd talked in the snows. "I met people who were gods and titans," he'd said. Was that a warning? Did the old man know what was to come? That Tahr would stumble on down, losing the banks of the river, as the muddy crumbling slope gave way to sheer drops or the undergrowth muscled in, forcing him aside? That he'd scramble and slither and clutch his way among boulders, into dead-end gullies, losing all sense of direction until hunger made him faint and he gorged on berries and was sick? That he would raise his head to catch the faint smell of campfire smoke and cooking on the wind, and plunge into the forest, trying to track it like an animal? That he would wander, lost, not sure which way the river was among the steep side valleys with their rushing streams, then stumble at last into a clearing, into the arms of. . . . Who the people were, Tahr hardly cared, these people who weren't quite like people—too tall and too pale and too loud when they talked—people who brought a village carried on the backs of servants, and more things piled in just one tent than there had ever been in Tahr and Shengo's hut? Weren't they like the gods in the picture—lucky, rich, and blessed?

Gods and titans . . . Maybe it was he who'd died, not Shengo . . . and the Wheel had turned, and here he was among the gods.

If that was so, Tahr must be blessed himself. He didn't feel it. No, he felt the way he'd felt in the dream—as if the ground was not quite steady underfoot and that somewhere, though he couldn't see it, was an awful drop.

But there was the girl. She had a kind heart, though she didn't want to show it. She didn't seem to want to be a girl, either, in those baggy shorts and a shirt with pockets, like a man. She was as tall as most men he'd known, for one thing, and sprawled in that chair of hers with one leg dangling over the side, so that Tahr felt uneasy and had to look the other way. No woman Tahr had ever met talked with a voice so loud and sure, and no girl ever argued with her uncle like that, looking him straight in the eye.

Maybe they did things differently among the gods?

The thing he mustn't do, he knew, was *bore* her. That was a word in English Shengo hadn't taught him, but he got the sense of it. She needed him to tell her stories, and he hoped he had enough to tell. It made her smile to hear his little English, and it pleased her to teach him some more every day. He was learning quickly. He needed to. When he got the voice right, she would clap and say, "Good! You're a smart one!"

Other times, she ignored him, flopping down with her little music box, sticking its wires in her ears. Then she would nod her head and tap her fingers. When she'd seen him staring at her, she had called him over and stuck the wires in his ears, and laughed, not very kindly, when music had exploded in his head. Another time, she'd seen Shikarri looking at them, coldly, from a distance, and she'd put her arm around Tahr's shoulder, leading him away. Shikarri, the man with the *kukri* . . . That one wasn't a god, Tahr knew. He'd met men like that in the villages, and dogs, too—trained to kill wolves and strangers, answering to no one but their owner. When Tahr met men or dogs like that, he kept away.

"Come with me," said Paris. "I'm going to see what's going on down there."

As Tahr stepped out into the clearing, he stiffened and began to shake his head. Beyond the early-morning sounds of the campsite, in the stillness of the valley, he could hear another sound. It wasn't close, but the trees and the slopes confused directions, and he couldn't guess where the helicopter might be.

"Come on—Franklin isn't looking." Paris towed him by the hand. "You scared? Don't worry, we'll stay under cover, promise." There was another sound, too, which came through clearer as they scrambled higher up the slope—a high, thin crackling, like twigs breaking.

"That's gunfire," Paris said. "That isn't just a patrol— they've found somebody. Hey, look!" Through a parting in the trees she pointed to the sky, where a column of dark smoke was starting to thin and drift away. Paris monkeyed up the lower branches of a tree to get a better view, but whatever it was was hidden by dense forest farther down the valley. There was nothing to see—no leaping flames—and Paris made a little sound of disappointment. That would have been a great shot for the movie. . . . As she watched, the helicopter banked and slipped away, and the valley was quiet again. When she climbed down, Tahr was doubled over, struggling for breath.

"What's up?" she said. It couldn't be the smoke. It was miles away. "Hey, you haven't got asthma, have you? Have you got an inhaler?" Tahr tried to look up, but another fit of wheezing took him. Paris looked round, as if someone might run up and help. Then she squatted beside him and laid an arm across his shoulder. "It's okay," she crooned. "Okay . . . Take it easy. Breathe . . . just breathe. . . ."

It was several minutes before Tahr looked up, his face blotchy with the effort. "Thank you," he said. "That is just as Shengo says. *Said,*" he corrected, and for a while the forest was very quiet and still.

When Paris came out of the forest, the first thing she saw was Uncle Franklin. Waiting. He had that Easter Island look again—a look she practiced sometimes in the mirror. Now, it was scary. Franklin didn't speak, just looked at her. He went on not speaking till she squirmed and burst out: "*So?* I just wanted to take a look around."

"Take . . . a look . . . around." He spoke each word as if it had a sour taste. "This is not a package holiday," he said.

"I know, I know." As Tahr came out behind her, he froze. He felt the anger in the air. He waited for the man to strike her, but instead Franklin's lips curled in a kind of smile.

"Do you?" he said. "I am starting to wonder. I don't want to find that I've been wrong about you." Paris winced. "Remember, this is not an ordinary expedition. No one here is ordinary. Look at Gavin . . . Harriet . . . even poor Donald and Renaud. You know what they are. Well? So stop acting like an ordinary Californian adolescent on vacation."

Paris stared at her feet. "Well, maybe that's what I am," she said sulkily. "Maybe you made a mistake."

"I don't think so. I don't make many mistakes. Especially

not about you." His voice softened, slightly. "We're members of the same species, don't forget."

That was the phrase that said it all. That was more than being family, and more than being friends. They were *the same species*—something rare and proud, maybe endangered, but fierce, too, and they recognized each other at a glance.

When had Paris first known that? Maybe at the poolside, years ago. It was a family party, and a swarm of little stepkids and half-brats were splashing and screaming, kicking each other off the huge inflatable alligator in the swimming pool. It was green, with a big grin and inflatable teeth they could ram each other's heads between. "Go on, get in there, Paris!" Pop yelled, and she shrank back in the shadows, hoping her baggy black T-shirt might just make her disappear, as in a fairytale. Then she realized Uncle Franklin was sitting in the corner, a glass in his hand.

He raised it—something frosted with the cold—ironically. "Cruelty to alligators," he said.

"Cruelty to people," she said. "Cruelty to people who aren't gross and stupid."

"Mmm . . ." He looked at her, one eyebrow raised, as if he was really thinking about it. "Most people would say *that's* normal. Well adjusted." He tipped his glass toward the shrieking poolside. *"Homo sapiens!"*

"Count me out," said Paris. "Can I be something else?"

"I think you might be. Welcome to a slightly different species."

Paris looked at him and grinned. "Are we rare?"

"Extremely. The one thing on our side is this: The others, mostly, don't know we exist."

It always made her smile, that memory. But when she looked up now, her uncle wasn't looking at her. He'd turned to face Tahr.

In his years with Shengo, Tahr had learned to be slightly invisible. When people came for consultations with the master, he could melt into stillness, and they would forget that he was there. There was a village proverb, too: *When the gods begin to argue, the wise man is dumb.* But now he felt Franklin's sharp gaze on him. "What did you see in the valley?" Franklin said.

Tahr shook his head. "Fighting, I think. Burning. Too far to see."

"Nothing new, then." Franklin said, like a joke to himself. "Isn't that what we do—we humans? The strong and the weak . . . The Wheel of Suffering—isn't that what the Lord Gautama taught?"

Tahr stared, and he felt his chest tightening. With Franklin's eyes full on him, he could feel why the others obeyed this man. He was powerful—a leader, strong and clever—and maybe wise, in some way. He spoke the name of the Buddha with ease, like a friend. But if that was so, why did Tahr feel the slippery feeling, the dangerous edge, that he'd felt in his dream?

"What do you think of my niece here?" Franklin said, not waiting for an answer. "Isn't she a fine girl?" Tahr looked down, embarrassed. Suddenly, all these people felt too big, too close up—and the bare skin of the girl's legs, arms, and shoulders, in particular. It looked burnt in the sun, and if she walked around uncovered, it would burn worse. For some reason the thought made his own skin smart a little, too.

Franklin laughed. "You don't have to answer that. You think she's a spoiled kid. I can see it in your eyes." Franklin took a step closer. Without looking, Tahr could feel his presence— like a cliff overhanging a track, and if you don't move quietly, you might dislodge a stone. "Maybe you think that about us all. You're right—spoiled kids. But some of us are going to grow up, if we dare."

With that, he turned on his heel, leaving Tahr and Paris staring as he strode away. Franklin looked back. "Oh, and Paris, get some proper kit on. We're going hunting at last."

"Hunting?" Tahr caught the thrill in her voice. "What for?"

"We'll have to see," called Franklin. "The scouts are coming back with some interesting sightings. Tell your friend there that he can come, too." Franklin held them both in his gaze, then gave that cool laugh. "No, don't worry. Shikarri wanted me to make him come. Shikarri's not a Buddhist, you see, and doesn't have much time for nonviolence. 'Put him face to face with a bear,' he said, 'with a gun in his hand, and let's see what he does.' Never mind," he said to Tahr. "We'll spare you that, for now."

Tahr watched the hunting party as it left the camp. They looked like a little army, though in different uniforms. Special light trekking fabrics for the tall white people, this and that for the porters, one to each of the hunters, who came with the bags and the guns. When the action began, though, the rifles would be in the white people's hands.

Shikarri led the way, with the dog tugging and snuffling but eerily silent. Even Franklin kept his distance. Then came

Gavin. . . . He was the tall man, very fit and weatherbeaten, with hair cropped almost as short as Tahr's new-grown fine stubble. He'd spoken to Tahr once—barely spoken but looked at him, summed him up in one glance, before he went on arguing with Harriet, the stocky woman who drank strong drink from a bottle and had a voice like a man's. Tahr had not taken his eyes from Gavin's hand, which was missing the end joints of three fingers.

"Gavin's not his real name, of course," Paris whispered in Tahr's ear. "Nobody's is. You heard what Franklin said. These aren't any old trekkers. These are big fish—I mean, real celebs." Seeing the blank look on Tahr's face, she leaned closer and whispered a name. "Oh, come on," she said, "you must have heard of *her*. She's been everywhere." She was losing patience. "Don't tell me you don't have a TV."

"Paris," Franklin called back, and she hurried after the party, pushing her way past the porters to the front.

For a moment, Tahr was on his own. That was a relief. Oddly, it seemed he was trusted—gradually more and more each day. If he'd wanted, he could have run off easily by now, though there was always the feeling that they might be testing him—giving him the chance just to see what he would do. They seemed to play games with each other like that, too, games Tahr didn't start to understand. Gavin and Harriet were always vying with each other. Donald always scolding his cook Renaud and Renaud scolding the porters, and Franklin always *testing* Paris, as if he was training her for something, though what the test was, it was hard to see.

Yes, Tahr could try to escape. He could run into the forest

now, but why? There was nowhere he could run to, in this valley full of strangers, of strangers and dangers. Even if he could retrace his steps, if he could find a way across the murderous ravine, if he could find the track back up the mountain, and not get lost in the snows, and remember the way back down to their little hut . . . it would be empty. What would he do there, without Shengo? "Let the goats go," the old man had said. Now Tahr thought back, a hundred small things told him: Shengo had known that they were never coming home.

Does it matter to anyone, Tahr thought, *if I live or die?*

It seemed to matter, for some reason, to the girl. She was sad, he could see that. She never spoke about her mother or her father. And she wanted her uncle to love her, most of all. Now and then Franklin would talk to her, when he felt like it, and she would drop what she was doing, and she'd forget about Tahr. He would be waiting when she came back later. So it seemed that she trusted him. That was good, wasn't it? Tahr wasn't sure, but he felt glad about it all the same.

There was a clatter from the tents, and angry voices. Donald pushed through the canvas flap of the big kitchen tent. Right behind him, gesturing with a long thin carving knife in hand, came the chef. "Tell me," Renaud shouted, in an English Tahr found puzzling, "tell me how I *work* in such conditions. Eh?" For a European, he was short, but very broad across the shoulders, like village wrestlers. A thicket of black chest hair poked from the neck of his vest. "How *prepare?*" he shouted after Donald. "How . . . when no one tells me *what?* This is not supportable."

Donald turned to him, unruffled in his linen suit. "Adapt,

dear boy. That's the art of it." Then he caught sight of Tahr watching. "Don't look so alarmed," he said. "It's just his way. These celebrity chefs. He's just missing the camera crews."

When the boy's puzzled expression did not change, Donald came over and bent toward him. "What do you people eat around here, mainly?" Donald said.

"Often . . . potatoes," Tahr said cautiously. "And rice. Beans . . ."

"No, I mean for special. You know, for a celebration?"

Tahr tried to find words for *momo*. In his mind, he saw those little dumplings, bobbing in a good broth, and suddenly he was sad and lonely. Nothing he'd eaten with these people felt right or like home.

"Not much in the meat line, I suppose," Donald interrupted. "Don't you Buddhists give yourselves a treat from time to time? Pity . . . There are *so many* possibilities." His voice trailed off, dreamily, and he smiled to himself. "Let's see what our big brave hunters bring back, shall we? I'm told it might be rather special."

As Donald sidled away, it struck Tahr that it was the first time anybody here had asked him anything about his life. No one—no one except the girl—had mentioned Shengo, though they knew the story from his first day there. Now Donald was asking for recipes. Then again, all Tahr had ever heard him talk about was food. With a pang, Tahr thought: *I wish I could tell Shengo. I believe I've met a Hungry Ghost.*

7

The Ultimate Diners Club

H ave you used one of these before?" said Gavin. He was losing patience, and not making an effort to conceal it. Paris fumbled with the rifle, trying to get it to feel right against her shoulder.

She wasn't happy. It was a lighter, slimmer gun than the ones she'd seen the men with; it looked like a toy, a girl's toy. "Why haven't I got one of the big ones?" she said.

"You want a fractured collarbone?" Gavin threw a look in Franklin's direction. "Och, she's got no experience," he said, letting his accent harden. There was always a hint of sourness in it; this was undisguised scorn now. "We haven't got the time."

"Get off her back." That was Harriet. She squared up to Gavin, face to face. It was sort of fascinating. Paris had seen that face of hers on TV, looking *outdoor,* looking tough, but they must have makeup artists with the cameras, even in a war zone. It was a shock to be close up and see how weathered that face was. In Mom and Pop's world, no woman let herself look like that until she was really, horribly *old.*

Harriet wasn't old. She was off-camera, and she didn't give a damn.

She gave her own rifle a deft professional squint down the sights. "Get off her back," she said to Gavin. "If she was a boy . . ."

He snorted. They'd had this sort of argument before. "You know what I'm saying," he said, still to Franklin.

I know what you're saying, Paris thought. *You're saying, "What's the spoiled brat doing here?" You're thinking, "Is she really his niece? What kind of dirty old man is he?" But you don't dare say it out loud, not to Franklin's face.*

She looked at the two men—Gavin, the hard man, famous climber, former SAS, they said; Franklin, shorter, slighter, quieter . . . and undeniably the boss. There *was* something special, Paris thought, about her uncle. He was an extraordinary man. And besides, she knew what kind of dirty old man he was. Not the kind that she need worry about. That was cool by her. Once, at school, she'd handed in a composition titled "My Gay Uncle," just so she could enjoy the expression on her teacher's face.

"Paris is coming with us," said Franklin. "She'll take to it. You'll see."

Harriet bent down beside her. "Small bore for the small game," she said. "If you want to bag a buffalo, well . . ." She nodded in the direction of the nearest bearer's pack, where a bigger, blacker weapon lay with its barrel just in sight. "Use that on a pigeon, you'll get feathers and mincemeat."

"Pigeon?" Paris said. "We're hunting *pigeons*?"

"Target practice. You boys," Harriet said over her shoulder, "leave us girls for a bit of woman talk, will you? Now . . ." She eased the rifle closer into Paris's grip. "It's got to feel like it's *part* of you. . . . There. If that creep bugs you, you just let me know."

Paris glanced at her sideways. Harriet was looking where the gun was pointing, not at her. That hard-edged voice, that war-zone way of speaking, never softened, and there were lines of weariness etched deep around her eyes. It was hard to imagine anybody being friends with Harriet. *She's just doing this now to spite Gavin,* thought Paris. And the "us girls" thing did not appeal to her at all.

"There," said Harriet. "Speckled pigeon. Got it?"

"Where?" Momentarily there had been a movement in the branches, some thirty meters away. Now everything was still. "It's gone."

"You *are* new to this game, aren't you?" said Harriet. "You ever killed anything?" She waited. Paris felt herself blushing. "No," said Harriet, "I thought not. Well, we'd better put that right, before Gavin finds out." She looked at Paris. "Or don't you want to?"

"'Course I do," said Paris. "Where's this pigeon?"

Harriet leaned closer, squinting along the other side of the barrel—two warm faces either side of cold steel—as she eased the sights up. "Got them now? They keep very still. A silly instinct. Sitting ducks."

It was true. Now that she had the range, Paris saw five or six of them, lined up along a branch—plump purplish bodies, little gray heads. Cute but stupid looking—like the girls she knew back home, or in the many schools around the globe she'd spent a term in. Suddenly, all the week's frustrations settled to a nice, tight focus, with a pigeon in the crosshairs, asking for it. Paris squeezed the trigger.

The recoil cracked against her shoulder, but she hardly noticed. The birds vanished—several of them beating wildly to and fro. One small dull weight fell through the branches. Paris had a feeling it was not the one she'd aimed for. Still . . .

"Well, well." Harriet sounded as surprised as she was. "First blood. How did that feel?"

"Good," said Paris. "It felt good."

The sun had crossed the valley before the party turned for home. Now they walked single file like prehistoric hunters coming back to the tribe, behind two porters with their prey strung on a pole.

Paris was stiff all over. Shikarri and his scouts had led them into deeper forest, steeper valleys, picking their way through undergrowth with never a hint of a trail. "Go quiet!" he'd snapped at them all. In this terrain the slightest hurry meant a crack or a rustle, and the game would have scattered for a mile around. It was painful progress, moving cat-foot, stepping over every twig, and when once Paris spoke—"Look!" and pointed to a dried-out snakeskin on a rock—everybody turned and stared at her, not it: *Shh.* Sometimes they'd stopped, as Shikarri bent down to some slight mark in the mud, and the others had gathered round, nodding wisely. The more this had happened, the slower they went, and finally came to a halt in a small glade, where they'd shared the dullest trekker's lunchpack Paris could imagine.

But they'd been still, and gradually the forest came alive around them. First it had been bird cries—the shriek of a jay, a magpie's chatter—then the flit of small birds in the branches. Once there'd been a rustle at ground level, deep in the undergrowth, which made Paris think about the snakeskin. Were they poisonous? If so, *how* poisonous? Why had no one told her things like that? But she couldn't ask now. They were under vows of silence, and the others' faces looked as solemn as people in church. The dog quivered slightly at each sound. If it moved, Shikarri gave it a cruel whack. It never bit back but cringed and went still.

No, hunting hadn't been what Paris had imagined. But for the presence of the guns—mysterious, dangerous killing tools, not toys—it could have been as dull as a day at the camp. And Paris had started to ache with the strain of it— simply squatting on a fallen tree branch, keeping still.

Then the action had happened, and it was over and done so quickly Paris scarcely saw.

The scouts had been alert first, one of them bending to whisper to Shikarri—just a word, which was passed on, to Franklin, Gavin, Harriet. . . . Not Paris. And everyone had glanced toward the bearers, who had begun to hand them each a rifle, when it happened. Paris had been staring into the undergrowth, roughly the way the others seemed to be looking, when the leaves overhead started shivering, as if it had come on to rain. She'd looked up to catch a glimpse of one, no, two, no, a whole troop of dark slender monkeys, moving with a steady flowing motion through the upper branches. There'd been a click as someone cocked a rifle, and then there was panic—monkeys scattering, chattering, throwing them-selves in huge leaps across gaps from tree to tree. For a moment, as Paris looked up, the space against the sky had been full of improbable, leaping, long-tailed silhouettes.

Then *crack* . . . and one of them seemed to hesitate in flight. It hit the tree awkwardly, sidelong, as its companions slipped into the leaves and flowed away. Gavin and Harriet were crack-ing off their third and fourth shots after them, but it was too late. Then there was a slither and a thump, and something hit the ground not ten meters away from Paris. It was still crying and trying to drag itself off when the dog was on it. With a curt impatient shake, it snapped its neck.

That was what swung on the pole now as they marched in triumph back to camp. They'd tied it by its hands and feet, with its long tail dangling to the ground. Paris didn't want to look too closely, and yet . . . and yet she did, just to prove that she could. She could look at the little dark face, dangling backward, and at the ragged red black rip in the fur at its shoulder. It had a narrow ribcage, like a very skinny child.

The rest of the day, after the monkeys, had been a bit of an anticlimax. This wasn't all they'd come for, evidently. The sun had slipped down behind the mountain ridge before there'd been another alert. This time it was Franklin who went first. One word to his bearer, and he had a shotgun in his hand. Then he and Shikarri were slipping deftly down a bank toward the sound of water. The others held back, and there was a long hush, in which the stream seemed to grow louder . . . then the double-barreled shot.

The two had come back grinning, with something dead in a

bag. Whatever it was, thought Paris, it was nothing like as impressive as the monkey—and when she'd gestured to the bag her uncle gave an "Aha, that would be telling" sort of wink. He looked triumphant, and they started home, sending one of the scouts in advance with the good news.

"Friends," said Franklin. The church-like silence was over. "Friends, a celebration is in order. The Ultimate Diners Club will meet tonight."

The campsite had become another world. The porters, just the trusted few, were dragging trunks from the supply tent, and out of them came the most expensive dinner service, Paris guessed, this jungle glade had ever seen. Meals so far had been functional, but now the folding table came out, and the linen tablecloth, and, yes, the silver candlesticks.

Donald was in his element at last. In dinner jacket and a bow tie as exotic as a tropical butterfly, he was the proprietor of an exclusive restaurant that was materializing from the shadows. He was everywhere, issuing orders, supervising cut glass and a whole array of subtle cutlery—many kinds of knives with blades of silver and ivory handles. *Ivory: Isn't that banned now?* Paris thought. Her mom, who was into good causes, would have had a fit. That thought gave her a little private thrill.

Meanwhile, the kitchen tent was being transformed, as Renaud's equipment came out for the first time—copper saucepans glinting in the light of a hurricane lamp, chopping blocks as big as tables, and, of course, his professional knives. He had his own team of fetchers and carriers, handpicked by

Shikarri. They might not understand his English, but Renaud at work was theater—no, more like opera—and they got his drift, all right. Paris might have seen Tahr among them, if she'd thought to look.

She lounged in the door of her tent, watching it all happen. *Crazy,* she thought. *But not dull.* Just then Donald swept by.

"Aren't you going to change for dinner?" he said. "Little black number or something, as befits the occasion?"

"I don't do dressing up for dinner," she said. Secretly, she'd slipped into her suitcase a silk top Uncle Franklin had admired once, but she wasn't going to tell him that. Across the way, she saw Harriet emerging from her tent, power-dressed in the smartest safari suit Paris had seen.

"Is this it?" Paris said. "We come all this way to eat a monkey?"

Donald gave her a pained look. "*Eat* is a crude way of putting it," he said. "Renaud is in there pipetting the *jus de viande* from the aforesaid animal for his very own *civet de singe*—with Italian wild mushrooms, French shallots, and several bottles of the kind of Burgundy collectors kill each other for at auctions. When we get to savor this, I hope you don't intend to simply *eat.* . . ."

Paris knew this kind of talk. He put it on to make her feel like a kid. "Does he do burgers?" she said. Donald was just about to blast her with another speech when he spotted the glint in her eye. He was so easy to wind up, was Donald. It was hardly fair.

"Pretty specialized stuff, this, isn't it?" said Paris. "It isn't legal, back home, is it?"

"That," said Donald, "is rather the point. We live in a world of dull people eating dull cows, pigs, and sheep."

"I've had alligator," Paris said.

"Wild? Served by the man who killed it? I think not. It will have come from a cage, on a farm. Huh. Farm an alligator, and it might as well be a chicken with teeth."

Paris left it at that. Donald was the greatest food bore in the world, and rather a famous one. But just remember: She was here, and that was what mattered—one of Uncle Franklin's private circle. If that meant eating monkey, that was fine by her.

Above them, the sky glowed pinkish orange for a while, as the last of the light caught snow peaks that were not in sight from here. Then the darkness came fast, and in the clearing where the table was laid it was like swags of black velvet drawn around the edges of the candlelight. There was a thin moon in the black above them, but it felt as close as the ceiling of a very private room indeed. Everybody—everyone who mattered on this expedition—took a seat.

At the edge of the circle of light, the darker faces flitted to and fro. For a moment, Paris caught sight of Tahr. He'd stopped in the middle of some errand, gazing in for a moment with no expression she could fathom. Paris looked away. Coming back from the hunt, her first urge had been to tell him all about it. But he was bound to have some kind of Buddhist feelings about it, wasn't he? *I can't handle that right now,* she'd told herself. Besides, her place was here at the table, and his wasn't. That's what it came down to in the end.

The show began. Renaud swept in, in full chef's uniform,

and presented each of the guests with a minuscule dish of a pigeon terrine. Her pigeon. It was only a mouthful, but as the first glass of wine was poured, Franklin raised it to Paris, and she glowed inside. Then came the main course: thin slivers of the dark meat in an even darker sauce, which teased her palate with its rich tang. *Tell yourself it's venison or something,* Paris thought, as the memory bobbed up in her mind of that wide-eyed, dangling monkey's face.

Donald raised his glass deliberately. "To our dear cousin, the common langur," he said. Paris raised her glass, but it seemed to be trembling slightly. All the others drank, and one by one, she felt, they turned to look at her. She took a sip, quickly, but Donald had noticed the slight hesitation. "I'm told we share ninety percent of our DNA with that pigeon," he said.

"What Donald doesn't mention," Franklin put in dryly, "is that we share thirty percent of our DNA with a banana." Everyone laughed—but quite why, or at whom, Paris couldn't be sure.

"That was a lucky monkey," Gavin said casually, glancing at Paris, daring her to ask him why. "In a perfect world," he went on when she didn't, "it would have been *man han chun shi.* Remember that time in Kung Shi province . . . ?"

Harriet laid a hand on Paris's shoulder. "This is for your benefit," she said. "He wants to gross you out—you know, the way little boys like to make girls squeal? He wants you to say: 'What's *man han chun shi?*'"

Paris swallowed hard. She wasn't going to be a squealing little girl for anyone. "So what's this man han . . . whatever?"

71

"Monkey brains," said Donald. "I think that's all you need know."

"No, it isn't." Paris willed herself to keep her eyes on Gavin, who was leaning back with a satisfied smirk on his face. "Tell me."

"They have a special table, with a hole in it, just the size of—"

"Leave it, Gavin," said Harriet. "You're more of a kid than she is."

"We're having a conversation, aren't we, Paris?" Gavin smiled. "The thing is, brains have to be eaten absolutely, *absolutely* fresh—"

"Enough!" said Donald sharply. "Children, children . . ."

It might have been the wine, but for a moment the ground seemed to rock beneath Paris's feet. With the coolest voice she could muster, she said, "Really. Let's see what this one tastes like, then."

To tell the truth, the slice of meat stuck in her mouth. Her teeth wouldn't do what she told them to and bite it, though her mouth flooded with saliva at the rich taste of the sauce. Then Franklin spoke, gently.

"Good girl," he said. "You see, my niece is *one tough cookie.*" The way he said the words, he might have learned them from a phrase book. Still, Paris's heart gave a skip of pride. She swallowed, and the meat went down. And the spotlight moved away from her, as if she'd passed the test.

"To Gavin." Donald raised his glass. "The great white hunter!"

Almost modestly, Gavin bowed his head.

"It doesn't compare with last year," said Harriet. "That was an adventure."

"Ah, the *fugu*," people sighed.

"Is this another gross-out?" Paris said.

"Not at all. Very civilized," said Donald. "This wonderful little establishment in the Ginza district of Tokyo specializes in a species of blowfish. The most delicate meat in the world. In certain of its organs, it secretes a poison that's a thousand times as strong as cyanide. Acts like nerve gas. No antidote. Hundreds of people a year die. Eating it is like . . . Russian roulette. Now, there"—he looked at Gavin—"*there's* an extreme sport for you." Paris was getting a feeling she knew well from many playgrounds, when kids start boasting to each other: *Mine's bigger than yours*. These people did it as an art form.

"I think Franklin has a surprise for us," said Gavin. There was an expectant pause as plates were cleared and more wine poured. Then in came Renaud with two dishes held aloft, each beneath a silver cover. He laid them in front of the guests and whipped back the lids.

The two cooked carcasses looked rather scrawny. The odd thing was the way the two heads had been preserved. A couple of ducks! Paris almost laughed. But she didn't. There was a solemn feeling in the air.

"Now . . . ," said Franklin, savoring the moment. "Has anyone guessed? No? If I were to say *Rhodonessa caryophyllacea?*"

Donald's face lit up. "Not . . . the pink-headed duck? Which is known to be extinct."

"*Believed* to be extinct," said Franklin. "Last definitively

73

sighted in 1935. But I have friends in the bird-watching world. There were rumors. I've invested quite a lot of money in tracking down these little beauties."

"So they're not extinct at all," said Paris.

Franklin laughed, quite gently, and the laughter rippled round the table, as the guests grasped the joke, one by one.

"Oh, but they are," said Franklin. "Our toast! To the unknown sailors who made a meal of the very last dodo. Poor stupid birds. Poor sailors, too—too stupid, I'll bet, to appreciate the situation. But we can. My friends, to the Ultimate Diners!" Paris touched a drop to her lips. It felt like cold fire, not like wine. "Now eat," said Franklin, with a glance at her. "And make sure you savor every last morsel. Because there'll never be another like it. Literally. Isn't that . . . *exquisite?*"

8

Lights Out

Fetching and carrying wasn't a hardship. It was what Tahr had done for Shengo—and most days Shengo fetched and carried, too, though as the old man grew older, and the boy had just grown, well, wasn't it natural for him to do more? The thought of Shengo was still with him, in a different way now from the first days—half a comfort, half a burden on his mind. But tonight there was no time for thinking.

Renaud had spotted him quickly among Shikarri's other trusted servants because he had some kind of English, and from then on he got all the tasks that needed instructions— ones where the gestures alone would not do. So Tahr stayed back in the kitchen tent, packing the precious plates and glasses back in their velvet-lined cases as soon as they were washed and dried. He had never seen anything so delicate, and made to be so pointlessly fragile—plates like crusts of snow and glasses like thin ice. Renaud made quite sure that he knew what would happen to him if there was the slightest crack or break. "Irreplaceable!" said Renaud. "Do you understand me? Cannot be replaced. Unlike you." Meanwhile, the other servants watched him with a cool suspicion. Why should he, this upstart from who knows where, get the soft jobs? They spoke to each other, seldom and under their breath, in the language of another valley, and they never spoke to him.

Outside, across the clearing, the voices of the dinner guests were loud and clear. Sometimes one would make a speech, and sometimes they all talked at once. Now and then they laughed together in a way that made Tahr feel uneasy. Dry monk that he had been, Shengo would sometimes hoot with laughter at some stray thought or something they saw together, and Tahr knew how people in the villages would drink and laugh and sing. But this was different. It was a bit like naughty children keeping a joke to themselves, something that would make their parents angry if they knew.

Tahr didn't mind being given jobs to do. Days in the camp were strange—unpredictable and formless. These people did things when they felt like it, with no routine, no ritual, no observances that he could see. Sometimes Tahr tried to sit and meditate, but he kept losing the words of chants he had known since he could speak. There were things in the air, as unsettling as the smells of strange cooking, that made his mouth water and his stomach knot up at the same time. Sometimes he felt as if he'd just woken from one of those dreams you can't remember—you just know it felt good, but it shouldn't have. "Calm your mind, let it go," would be Shengo's advice. But Shengo wasn't here, and Tahr's mind would not be calm. Or else, just when it began to settle, the girl would burst in without asking, looking as if he should be glad to see her, and say, "Hey, come with me!"

It was late when he picked his way back to his tent. It was dark, too, only starlight, and he was careful of the guy ropes, in case he tripped and woke one of the big people, who seemed to be asleep by now.

All except her. The girl was sitting cross-legged at the entrance of her tent, and at first he thought she was meditating in some untrained, restless way. Then she saw him, and he saw her eyes were wide, her breathing rapid, like someone who's had a bad dream.

"Hey, what's the matter with you?" she hissed as he made for his tent. "Aren't you speaking to me now?" She patted the ground beside her: *Sit down.* He sat. She didn't smile.

"I know what you're thinking," she said. "Running away like that. You think I'm some kind of monster, don't you? Just because I ate that stuff."

"I—I was not thinking," Tahr said.

"Yes, you were. You're thinking all the time. I've seen you. Watching and thinking. Thinking you know better. Just because you people eat—I don't know, lentils and brown rice—it doesn't mean you're oh-so-perfect."

Brown rice? Tahr frowned. Why was she angry about rice, or about its color? But then, she was drunk. He could smell it, that and the meat smell, on her breath.

"You were listening, weren't you?" she said suddenly. "I saw you eavesdropping out there at the table. And you understand, don't you?"

"I beg your pardon?"

"Oh, come off it. All this "beg your pardon" stuff. . . . You speak pretty good English. How come?"

"My master taught me."

"Why?"

"Why?" Tahr frowned and thought a moment. "I think . . . he was happy when he was younger. He spoke English then. Up in the mountains there is no one else to speak it with him. But I am not trying to *listen* to you, like Shikarri thinks."

"Well, maybe you should be. If you'd heard Uncle Franklin talking, then you'd understand."

"What is . . . 'eaves drop'?" Tahr said.

"I would've thought like you, I guess," she went on, as if she had not heard him. "Until tonight. I was like that as a kid. Like my mom. She was always doing Save the Whale or Save the Panda—all that bleeding-heart routine." The girl leaned forward, as tense as a spring. "It was all crap. Uncle Franklin showed me that. People like Mom going on about saving the indigenous people—with a house full of Mexican servants. Designer clothes made by kids in the Philippines. Hah! That sounds like some old bore from Greenpeace, doesn't it? That's not what Uncle Franklin's saying." She gazed out into the dark, her eyes wide, as if there was a big screen out there.

"No," she continued in a hushed voice. "*It's okay.* That's what he's saying. People kill things. *Homo sapiens* is a killer species. And your peace stuff and your Buddha and your eating lentils—it won't change a thing." She looked at him fiercely. "The great thing about Franklin," she said, "him and his friends, is: They've stopped pretending. Look at Harriet. She's seen *everything*—war, murder, people starving. She's been in places where people are so hungry they'll eat dogs, rats, spiders. . . . We'll do anything, you see? The thing that most people—ordinary people—don't dare think is: 'It's okay! We don't have to apologize for being what we are.'"

There was a long pause. Among the still stars overhead there was one moving, maybe an airplane, unthinkably high. "Well?" Paris said. "Say something."

"I think . . . I do not understand all of your words." said Tahr.

The girl's eyes suddenly blazed. "Oh, what's the use of talking to you?" she said in a fierce whisper. "You don't know anything. You've never heard of anybody. You've just sat in your hut for years and years, not thinking. You're a waste of space." She paused, breathing quickly. "Well, aren't you? Now you're sponging off us. Expecting us to look after you. Expecting *me* to! I've got other things to think about."

Breathe, Tahr was thinking. *Breathe and stay calm.* It had scared him, once, in the village, when Shengo had been called to drive the evil spirits from a man who had gone crazy. They'd seen the man before, many times, and he'd waved to them, calm and smiling . . . and now there he was, shouting and lashing out at phantoms. The man had screamed at Shengo, bunching his fist to hit him, when the old monk came and sat by him and started chanting. Slowly he had calmed down . . . calmed down and finally put his head in his hands and started sobbing like a child. How terrible if this strong tall girl, a princess of her people, had gone mad like that. Tahr wished he remembered the words.

"Great peace . . . ," he murmured. "Great peace. Great compassion . . ."

"What?" the girl said, and Tahr realized that, for the first time since he'd been here, he had spoken his own language. She stared at him as if it were he, not she, who had gone crazy. Around them all the world was dark and still, and Tahr felt sad and empty.

"I think . . . I think it is better if I leave," he said.

"Don't be stupid. They won't let you. Especially now that you know about the hunting."

"Still, I think I will try. Because of Shengo." He looked for a hint of understanding in her eyes, but there was nothing. "The thought of him is with me," he said. "I think that I failed him."

"Oh, come on," said Paris. "It wasn't your fault. We've been through this."

"No. I did not search until I found him. I was not strong enough." In his mind, Tahr saw the steep slippery banks, the broken tree trunks, tangled creepers, clinging undergrowth, thorn bushes. . . . He remembered the slips and scrapes and stings. He saw the sudden rockfalls where the water undercut the bank and swirled in foaming pools. "He should be covered with earth," he said. "There are words that should be said. I know a few of them. . . ."

"Listen," Paris said. "You can't go. Really can't. They'll kill you. And . . ." She seemed to struggle with the words. "And I'll miss you, too."

Tahr looked at her, puzzled again. Maybe those few words he'd said had been enough and the crazy fit was passing?

"You won't try running away, will you?" she said.

He could hardly see her in the dark, but she felt very big and very close up, very strange. There was something wonderful about her—she was brave—but it couldn't be right, the way she sprawled about in her immodest clothes, as if she didn't care about herself at all. And yet she talked about herself all the time.

Danger, the thought came, as clear as a voice in Tahr's mind. *Whether I run away or stay, I am in danger.*

"Promise?" said Paris, leaning forward in the dark to touch his shoulder. And she would not let him go back to his tent until he had agreed.

He wasn't asleep, he was sure of it later. He was on that nice border between sleep and waking when you feel calm all over and the thoughts in your head just start slipping away. Then suddenly the forest parted. No, it was as if he knew that the forest was only a thought, an illusion—a wonderfully detailed picture painted on a sheet of cloth . . .

. . . which ripped. The face stared out. Stared straight at him.

Tahr cried out, and in the same breath tried to stifle the cry, because it was his shout—not the face in the leaves, but him—that had killed Shengo at the waterfall.

The face he saw now was the same face, but much clearer in his mind than before. It looked straight at him with its deep-set eyes in shadow, underneath a heavy forehead that gave it a worried, sad expression. *No, it isn't fierce,* he thought. It had just been so sudden—that was why he cried out.

Why had it come back to him now? As if it wanted something from him. But what? And what or whose face could it be?

It wasn't a monkey, he was sure of that. When the hunters had brought the langur back, they'd dropped it on the kitchen table, just like that, with Tahr standing there. He'd flinched, but when he looked at its little round face, turned up toward him, he saw that it was only a dead body, and the poor little sentient spirit in it was already far away. And it wasn't the face he had seen.

Not a monkey, then. And not a man, or a woman or a child, either. It was something else. A demon, come to cause the accident and do them harm? No, Tahr had seen pictures of demons on the Wheel of Life, and they had gaping jaws, goggling eyes, and tusks for teeth. He could not imagine a demon looking sad and worried. Then it came to him.

A Mountain Spirit. *Yeh-teh* . . . What had Shengo said about them, up there in the Snows? "They won't be up here this late in the year. They feel the cold like us." Where could they be, then, but down in the valleys, eating the fresh autumn berries, in a place like this?

The flap of Tahr's tent parted, and he jumped again.

"Hey," Paris whispered. "What's up? You were making a Godawful noise. Hey, kid. . . ." Her voice suddenly softened, as a little light from outside touched his face. This wasn't some creepy little monk from the back of the beyond but anybody's little brother, on his own among strangers and scared by a bad dream.

"Okay," she said. "That's it, easy. . . ." She ruffled his soft fuzz of hair, then put an arm around him, and he didn't pull away.

"It's okay, okay," she found herself repeating, just the way her mom had when Paris was little, when she woke up crying in the night. "Okay . . . No scary monsters here, right?"

"It was not a monster," Tahr said. "It was *yeh-teh.*"

"It was just a dream."

"Not a dream. I saw it, by the waterfall, when Shengo died."

Now she looked at him, holding him at arm's length in the darkness. "Hey, you mean it, don't you?"

So he told her, as well as he could.

When he finished, Paris let her breath out, very slowly. "Let's get this straight," she said. "This is the yeti, right? The abominable snowman? That's what we call it. You say *Mountain Spirit*. We've heard all about it, right on the other side of the world. We've even got something like it—they call it Bigfoot."

"You, too? You have seen a Mountain Spirit?"

"Not me, no! I wouldn't want to. Huge things, long arms, hair all over. Pretty scary."

"Shengo said they were sentient beings, like us. He smiled when he spoke about them."

"Shengo saw one, too? I mean, before the day he. . . . Sorry."

"Not one," said Tahr. "A family. Two and a little one."

"Well, hey, what about that?" There was a sound in her voice Tahr had not heard before. "A little yeti," she said. "With its family. Well, how about that?"

She kept her arm around Tahr till his breathing became slow and deep. "I'm sorry I was mean," she whispered. "I guess I get kind of scared, like you."

Tahr was making a little-child-snoring sound, like a purring. Paris laid him gently down and let him sleep.

9

Mornings After

What now? thought Paris, flinching from the sunlight. It couldn't be that late in the morning, could it? But it was, and the sun fell right into the clearing from high in the sky. Her head hurt. There wasn't much sign of the others. All signs of the night before, down to the folding banquet table, had been tidied away, and the things that had happened—or she thought had happened—had the jumbled feeling of a dream.

She was halfway to the kitchen tent before she heard low voices. There was Franklin, and Gavin, Harriet, Donald—looking almost as crumpled and listless as she felt. Even Franklin didn't have his usual crisp look. Anticlimax hung round like a gray mist everywhere.

"What now?" said Paris aloud.

"The very question we were just debating," Donald said. "I mean, after last night's triumph . . ."

"Well, we can't just pack up and go home." That was Harriet. "Just because we happened on Franklin's star turn on our first day out." She looked at Paris. "Oh, fix yourself a coffee, girl. You look like a ghost."

Reaching for the kettle, Paris stubbed her foot on something. Something heavy, soft . . . It groaned.

"Ignore him," Donald said. There, flat on his back beneath the trestle table, Renaud lay, his mouth wide open. Several empty bottles lay around him. "Morning after a great performance," Donald said. "One must allow for the artistic temperament."

"I don't know about any of you," Gavin cut in, "but I need a bit of action. There's more interesting game than monkeys round here—with due respect to your wee ducks." That was aimed at Franklin. Paris waited for the cool riposte, but Franklin seemed hardly to notice it, or if he noticed, not to care. "Black bear, maybe? Or red panda—there's a local specialty."

"Count me in," said Harriet, yawning. "I didn't come here to pick flowers. Ready for a bit more sport?" she said to Paris.

"I meant *serious* shooting," Gavin said. Harriet opened her mouth for the usual argument, but Franklin spoke first.

"Sorry to put a damper on it," he said, "but we should be careful. Shikarri's scouts report some military business down the valley." He glanced over to the corner of the tent, and there sat the guide. He'd been so still that Paris had not seen him there. "They're flushing out villages," Franklin said.

So that's what they'd seen, thought Paris—the column of smoke that rose and faded as the helicopter tracked off. "But that's miles away, isn't it?" she said.

"Not far enough," said Franklin. "They're only driving the rebels deeper into the jungle. Sometime the army is going to follow them—search and destroy."

"They'll have their work cut out," said Gavin. "Terrain like this, it's as bad as Vietnam."

"Even so. But the government wants the valley cleared. I think the word is 'pacified.'" Franklin sighed. For the first time this trip, Paris saw a shadow of that black mood of his that she understood so well. Not black yet, just muddy gray. "It wouldn't be a good idea to go firing off guns in the forest. Wouldn't you agree?"

Gavin had been on his feet all along, but now he'd started pacing, like a caged tiger in a zoo. "So what do you suggest? A game of Trivial Pursuit?"

"Apparently," said Donald, "there's a local dish they make from leeches. Place is full of them, in the rainy season." For a second even Gavin paused, then scowled. He wasn't in a mood for teasing.

"There's no reason why we shouldn't reconnoiter," said Harriet, ignoring Donald. "Get the lay of the land. No dog, no weaponry, no pursuit—just observation."

"I suppose that's something," Gavin said. Paris looked round at the grownups. Grownups! They were tense and scratchy, like a bunch of little kids kept indoors when it rained.

"Two things, though." Gavin went on. "One: We agree what we're after. I'm not going for a bloody ramble."

"Panda," said Harriet. Franklin made a weary gesture: *If you must. . . .* As he got to his feet, he glanced at Paris. "Better get kitted up."

"Two," said Gavin. "The kid doesn't come. She slowed us down enough last time."

Paris looked at Franklin. Now he had to put Mr. SAS hard man Gavin in his place. This wasn't just about Paris. Franklin wasn't undisputed boss round here—that's what Gavin was saying. But she saw at a glance that she'd be disappointed. Franklin was bored with all this, and one look at Gavin told her Gavin knew this, too. "Agreed, then," Gavin said.

"Wait!" Paris put in quickly. "I've got a better idea."

That was enough to stop them in their tracks. "Better than your panda," she said. Now they were looking at her, all of them, and for the first time that day she felt a pulse of adrenaline in her veins. There was something Paris knew about this place that Gavin didn't know. None of them did.

"You want to see a yeti?" she said, as coolly as she could. Gavin made a "Give me patience" sort of sound. Paris ignored him. Harriet was listening, and so was Donald. And at last there was a little quirk of interest in her uncle's eye. "Can't get rarer than that," she said, "can you?"

"That's just a story," said Harriet. "What books have you been reading?"

"There's been a sighting," said Paris. Franklin glanced toward Shikarri. To Paris's relief, the guide did not say "Nonsense!" He gave a noncommittal shrug: It may be so.

"Well," said Donald. "Now, that *would* be original. You wouldn't care to tell us where this information comes from?"

"I might." Paris waited. "So I'm coming, am I?" No one spoke up. "Right, I'm coming. And Tahr's coming, too."

She felt bad about Tahr. She hadn't done anything wrong, she told herself, in mentioning the *yeh-teh*. Everyone knew that old story, didn't they? And it probably wasn't even true. It was just that . . . well, that time in the middle of last night, when he'd woken crying from his dream. . . . That felt like a different world—a world in which people trusted each other—and she'd wanted it to stay that way.

Paris believed in white lies. They worked. After all, how often had one of her parents told her something later, when the divorce or whatever was over, and said: "We just didn't want to upset you at the time"? So there was nothing *wrong* in telling Tahr that the expedition was going to check out the upper valley . . . and *he*'d been there, so, hey, what about it, he could help them, couldn't he? Still, she crossed her fingers mentally behind her back. She kept them crossed, as he hesitated. *Don't say no.* . . . She played her trump card: Maybe, she said, maybe they could find some trace of Shengo. That was what he really wanted, wasn't it?

Before they set out, there was another bad moment, when Shikarri appeared by their tents. He had already cornered Tahr when she came out and found them.

"I must ask this boy some questions," the guide said. "Excuse us, miss."

"That's okay," Paris said. "I'll stay." That would bug him, she knew. But he wouldn't dare cross her. Uncle Franklin wouldn't stand for it.

"He must tell me all he knows," Shikarri said. "And I am warning him: If this is any kind of trick—"

"That's crazy," Paris butted in. "I mean, look at him. He's only a kid."

"Your uncle gives me a job," the guide said stonily. "To keep you safe. You know there are people in this valley who would be very happy to have Americans and English in their hands."

Paris looked at him. He meant it. And her mind scanned back through news reports. Nasty stories. Kidnappings, hostages . . . "You mean—for ransom? Money?"

"If you are fortunate," said Shikarri, darkly. "Others only want you dead." He waited for the words to sink in. "You know this boy?" he said. "You know anything about him? You are happy to trust him . . . with your life?"

It was only a second that she hesitated. Just long enough to flash back to the two of them, him folding into her arms like a frightened child. She looked the guide straight in the eye. "Yes."

"Very well." There was no more that he could say. "So he must tell me all about the way . . . the places . . . and this creature."

Paris looked in Tahr's eyes, and she saw the moment when he got it. She had told about the Mountain Spirits. She'd told secrets whispered in the night. His features hardly changed, but in his eyes there was a tiny glint of pain.

"We will look for your master," she said. "Truly. That was why I . . ." She trailed off. The boy didn't speak, but she couldn't stand that look in his eyes. She turned away.

Behind her the guide stepped very close to Tahr and said in a quick, low voice, "Not my idea, this foolish journey. But it amuses these people. You just have to know: If this is a trick, you die first, before any other. Get me?"

Tahr nodded. Whatever else he didn't understand about these people, this he understood: This man meant what he said.

The sound of the waterfall grew so slowly that Tahr scarcely heard it. It was more as if he felt it, as a dull pain in his head. It wasn't easy to retrace the way he'd come, that bad day. Then, he had been stumbling, crying, in a panic, and the trees had seemed to swirl around him. Now it was guesswork that guided him, and here and there a boulder or a particular fallen tree he thought he might recognize . . . that, and the slowly growing pressure of that sound in his mind.

They were close now, moving slowly. The hillside was steep, so steep that in places the earth and rock had slipped away. In this warm, damp, secret crease of the forest, things grew fast, and undergrowth and tangle swarmed into the spaces, hiding dangerous drops. Shikarri went first, prodding each bush, testing each foothold, as they went. Without his dog, he seemed edgier, more cautious. They were getting close. One of his men was sent ahead and came back saying that the coast seemed clear. Even so, Shikarri held back, whispering with Franklin. Then he called to Tahr and pushed him forward.

"He goes first," the guide said to Franklin. "If I am a bandit, and I make an ambush, here is where I do it." He leaned his head close to Tahr's. "Remember what I say," he whispered. "Any trouble, you die first. Okay?"

Tahr edged out. On his left, dripping stone went straight up, almost overhanging, almost hidden by brilliant green mosses and plants that plumped up on the cool spray in the air. There was a shifting cloud of it rising from the black cleft on his right. He didn't need to look. Those crashing wheels of water were printed—with the sight of Shengo falling—on his mind. And the noise blotted everything out: birdsong, sounds of the forest, the others' voices, even his own thoughts. He could feel Shikarri's gaze like a rifle sight trained on his back.

He was out on the ledge now, exposed and alone.

The place was just as he remembered it.

Nothing had changed.

Nothing.

Tahr gasped as he realized what he was looking at. The log, dewy with spray, was still there. It was as if none of it had happened—all this week had been a dream, one of the kind when you wake from what seemed like days of it and find that a minute has passed. If he waited a moment, then Shengo would be there, coming across the log to join him. . . .

"Why do you stand like that?" Shikarri had come up, unheard, right behind him. "This is not the place you said?"

"Yes—yes, it is. But . . ." Tahr stared. "The log. It was gone. I saw it go. . . ."

Gavin was with them. Squeezing past, he bent down by the end of the log, touched it . . . peered closer . . . felt the ground around it. "That's never a week old," he said. "Twenty-four hours, I'd say, max."

It's a bridge, thought Tahr. Someone had laid it there on purpose, and now they'd put one there again.

"Interesting." Franklin was beside them. "Did you see any sign of a trail?"

"Not the way we've come," said Gavin. "Can't see any sign of one across there, either. I'd expect a boot print, at the very least."

"What—what if it wasn't a person?" Paris said.

"Well, it wasn't a monkey." Gavin sneered. "That's for sure."

"Tahr," she said. "Where was this . . . face when you saw it?" He pointed into the thick leaf cover opposite. The air was very still around them. Nothing stirred.

Gavin seemed not to be listening. He was bending closer now, examining the trunk, picking at it with his fingernail. Then he let out a low breath: "Well . . .

"That's not just broken," he said. "That tree didn't just fall. Look, it's been hacked at. Some kind of crude tool, must be." It was clear—the short blunt gashes at right angles to the splitting of the grain. "Chips of stone," he said, almost to himself. "If I didn't know better, I'd say that was done with a stone ax."

Franklin looked at Shikarri. "The people in this valley . . . ," he said. "Are there any primitive tribes—you know, Stone Age—living in the jungle?"

The guide shook his head, and for a moment everyone was silent, as if a thought had dropped over the edge of the cliff and was still falling, terribly slowly, the way Shengo fell.

"Some kind of ape, then?" Harriet had pushed onto the ledge beside them. "Chimpanzees use tools, don't they—you know, sticks into ants' nests, things like that?" She paused. "But there aren't any great apes in the subcontinent, are there?"

Franklin was shaking his head. Tahr looked round the faces of the others. They seemed to have forgotten him, even Shikarri. "Just suppose . . . ," Franklin was saying. "Just suppose . . . it uses tools, just like a prehistoric human." He looked round, and his face had that look of crisp purpose again. "I want to meet this creature," he said.

Paris stared at him. Yes, he'd said "meet." Not "track" or "hunt" or "catch." Meet, as you'd meet a person.

All around—as if they'd stumbled on a secret—the great *husssh* of the falls went on and on.

10

Bloody Eden

It was treacherous ground. It could fall away under your feet the moment your attention wandered, and if you slipped, there was no telling how far you might fall. "Stay in pairs," said Gavin. "Fan out, but try and keep visual contact. Any sightings, one of you alerts me, pronto. Any trouble, two blasts on your whistle. Quick ones, like this." He mimed it, not making the sound. "Got that?"

Everybody nodded. Back at camp, it was Franklin's expedition, but out here in the woods, in action, everyone knew Gavin was the man. "Operational command," he'd have called it. That was what he was here for, after all.

"If there's *big* trouble," he said, "leave it to Shikarri and me." Paris glanced at the butt of the handgun holstered snugly at his belt. No guns, that's what they'd agreed, but no one felt like disagreeing now. "From here on, maintain silence. Move as slowly as you need to. We've got all day."

He meant it. In the hours that followed, Paris thought back to yesterday's careful tracking. It seemed like fast-forward compared to this. Every footfall, every handhold, was a problem to be looked at, weighed up, tested with a touch. . . . Every now and then a twig cracked anyway, and Paris was glad when it was Harriet's fault or Franklin's—though it usually wasn't—and not hers. Not far off, there was Shikarri, moving smoothly as smoke. He could have slashed straight ahead with his *kukri* and walked through bushes it took half an hour to circumnavigate, but the orders were: Silence. And besides, the guide was paired with Tahr, who looked pale and clumsy, and was painfully slow.

Poor kid, I got him into this, thought Paris. *I didn't mean to, honestly. The stuff about the* yeh-teh *just came out.* What was he feeling right now, on the inside of that blank face? Was he mad at her? Or did he understand? Did he forgive her, in his odd, calm, quiet way?

They were tracking the river—that was the best way to think of it. You could hear it somewhere near, sometimes muttering, sometimes roaring, sometimes scarily quiet as it cut down deep among the rocks. It hid—it had an instinct for it, heading for impassable places, deepest thickets, that dangerous edge. . . . Time and again, they would reach it for a moment and perch by the edge of a small pool, only to see it swerve, duck, and drop away somewhere they couldn't follow, and they'd have to detour back into the forest, following the sound of it downhill, downhill.

It took hours. This was pointless. Paris was stiff and aching from yesterday's expedition, and she wished that she'd never mentioned Tahr's dumb story. She'd rather be kicking her heels back at camp than this. *Ouch!* Every time she let her mind wander, she missed her footing. She slipped, clipped her elbow on a rock, and swore aloud.

She glanced round, waiting for the usual dirty looks from

the others. But all of them were looking somewhere else. Without a sound, something had happened, and everyone was moving to the same spot. Harriet nodded that way—*Come on.* And they went to see.

Gavin and Shikarri were bent down, conferring. Nodding. Looking up for Franklin. As he came over, they pointed to the bush beside them. It had been stripped neatly of its purplish berries down one side. *So?* thought Paris. Birds or monkeys— everything ate berries, didn't it? But Shikarri was pointing down by their feet. As everyone clustered in, Paris saw it. In a patch of scuffed mud, there was one mark that was clear and unmistakable. A footprint, as long as Gavin's size-13 combat boot, and broad, and bare.

Shikarri poked the mud beside it with his finger. Soft, it gave to his touch. He looked at Franklin.

"How long?" Franklin broke the silence.

"One hour, maybe. Not more."

Suddenly, the forest round them felt alive, and watching: very still.

After all the slowness of the stalking, Paris could hardly believe the first glimpse when it came. There were no more tracks to help them, so they went on, slowly downhill, as before, and the sun moved down behind the mountain and there was a hint of evening in the air. If anything, the slope was getting steeper. After a while, the sound of water changed to a steadier, deeper sort of roar. They weren't even close to the edge when Paris gave herself a leg up on a tree stump, and through a gap in the trees she caught a flash of turquoise blue.

Harriet turned around to see her waving. Climbing up beside her, she saw it, too. Way down, there was light on water—peaceful water, clear enough to see the stony bottom rippling, and a shadowy green of the reflected trees. It was like a strip torn from some tourist brochure, pictures of that one unspoiled spot . . . which would never be like that when you got there because, well, you and the others were all there. To Paris now, it looked like perfect rest after a sweaty, bruising day. On the far side, a gray, smooth rock sloped down into the water, and on it. . . .

What *was* on it? Something red brown—crouching, maybe? An animal, must be . . . but not moving? Was it asleep? Or dead? How big was it, how far away? Hard to judge from this angle. Harriet was waving toward Gavin. When he came over, he squinted hard through his binoculars, and frowned, then handed them to Harriet. She handed them to Paris.

It was something, all right. Red brown fur, rucked up at odd angles. But Paris couldn't make out head or legs or tail. It made no sense to Gavin, either, because he didn't speak at first. No terse commands.

"Okay, then," he said quietly, after a while. "Let's investigate."

There was a hush round the pool, and there was birdsong, and the steady chant of water—peaceful as a perfect summer evening, but still bright as day. It had taken them half an hour to pick their way down the hillside, turning back time and again from what looked like a way down that led to the edge of a drop, or into hopeless thickets. They didn't get another clear sight of the pool until the slope suddenly eased and they knew that they were nearly there. Paris saw light through the trees just ahead of her, and she parted the heavy leaves with care.

They were right by the side of the pool. After the clammy moistness of the woods, the air felt clear. The light was bright but with a pearly sheen on all the colors, as a fine spray drifted downwind from the falls. Upstream, the water had come in one gush, as hard as tensed muscle, but here it scattered into channels, each finding its own way down, through cracks, from ledge to ledge, and half a dozen small falls hung like beaded curtains, rippling and folding as they fell.

A haven. Sanctuary, thought Paris, surprised to find these old-fashioned words in her mind. It felt like a place where any animal or creature—*sentient being,* wasn't that what Tahr said?—might come to drink at dusk. Paris wished she could just kneel beside it, and dip her whole face in that pool.

The flat stone they'd seen from above was right there, close. And the thing on the stone? It wasn't a creature, or not anymore. It was fur, all right . . . but human hands had shaped it, trimmed it around the edges. It was something *made,* she thought—maybe a cape; and look, there was a clasp at the neck, so that must be a hood. The way it lay there made her think of her own jeans, tossed aside for the night, so Mom or Pop could come in and say, "What's this mess here?" in the morning.

Clothes, thought Paris. *It wears clothes.* And she felt her skin prickling all over. Whatever it was, this creature, it had been *here.*

A gust of wind rose, and the leaves swayed around her. In

the air she caught a slight, familiar smell. Smoke. Cooking. Paris looked upwind. There, tucked under the overhang, between two curtains of falls at the head of the pool, there was a flickering in the shadows. A fire. A trickle of smoke. And there was something moving, crouching at the fireside for a moment, with its back to her. No, two shapes—one large, one small—crouching there together.

"Well, look at this," breathed Harriet, at her shoulder. "Bloody Garden of Eden . . ."

Then everything happened at once.

It was some time afterward that Paris managed to splice the different bits of the film together in her head. It might have been Harriet's voice that made the creatures look up, if they had phenomenal hearing, or it might just be that instinct that makes you sense when someone in a crowd is staring at your back. Whichever, one of them, the larger one, was turning, getting to its feet, and Paris would have got a clear sight of its face then—if it hadn't been for Tahr.

He'd gone mad. That was what it looked like, in that moment, because there he was leaping out of cover, shouting, splashing knee-deep through the pool. "Get back, get back!" people were calling at him, but he didn't seem to hear them, way out in the open, splashing on.

Then Paris looked where he was heading, and that picture hit her like a camera flash. Harriet must have looked right at that moment, too, because she said, out loud, "My God, they've killed somebody." And here came Gavin, crashing through the bush behind them.

It was under the falls, but nearer this bank, almost as near to

Paris as to the figures by their campfire, and a little higher up: a ledge, hollowed out into almost a cave. On the ledge there was a body, laid out full length and somehow very clearly *dead*. And bloody. There was red splashed everywhere, livid and gory—on the hands, the feet, and where the face should be.

But Tahr . . . He was splashing toward it, hands out, shouting. "Shengo!" he cried. "Shengo!" as the creature by the fireside saw him. For the first time Paris saw how big it was—broad-shouldered, hunched, and looming—and it leaped toward him, going rock to rock in horribly agile bounds, more animal than human. In the same instant, Gavin pushed past, thrusting Paris to one side. He plunged into the water and yelled once, just the way SAS men do in hostage dramas, without pausing for a moment, as he brought the pistol up to aim. And fire.

Crack. Echoes . . . and the short ping of a ricochet. The creature crouched, stopped, but the strangeness of its movement had fooled even Gavin's professional eye. He fired again, and this time it jerked sideways, with a yelp of pain. Shikarri was out in the open now, and the two men forged toward the thing, but it was on its feet—on all fours—and leaped through the falling water, disappearing, as the gun cracked, and the echoes cracked, again.

The smaller one had vanished from the fireside—ducked behind the falling water, too. And Tahr? As if he hadn't noticed any of it, he was forging on. He was out on the shore, and scrambling up the rocks, slipping, scrambling again. Then he was up there on the ledge, beside the body. *Oh, my God,* thought Paris, *what's he going to see there?* "Tahr!" she called, and started after him.

"Get back!" Gavin shouted, but she wasn't listening. *Oh, my God,* she thought, *what is Tahr looking at?* What had those things been cooking? That smell . . . What did human meat smell like? *I don't want to see this,* Paris thought. *I really, really don't.* But it didn't stop her splashing on, and scrambling up the rock.

There he was, on the ledge as she got there. He was kneeling by the body. Yes, it was an old man, she could see that—with a monk's robe folded round him. She couldn't stop herself looking for the ghastly bit. But no . . . The limbs were there: both arms, neatly folded on his chest. Both bare feet poking out beneath the robe. If it weren't for the blood.

Paris hadn't seen much blood, except the odd cut finger and the gore you get in horror movies. Still . . .

Is that blood? she thought. *Is blood that red?*

No, she thought, *no, it isn't.* It was more like red mud—ocher mud made redder, maybe, with the red of berries. And it wasn't splashed about the way she'd thought. Someone had painted it—smeared it carefully across the old high forehead, smoothing out the wrinkles. Someone had painted like a mask across the sunken eyes and mouth, as if to seal them closed. Someone had traced a spiral pattern on the back of each gnarled hand, then led five lines down the thumb and fingers, and the same on each foot. What did it mean?

As Paris knelt beside Tahr, she felt him shaking. She held her breath a little, because there was a smell, a sweet-sour scary smell that had to be decay. But he was crying quiet, gentle tears.

"It's okay," she said, automatically.

"Yes, very okay," he whispered. "They laid earth on him. With ceremony. Look."

She looked again. It wasn't easy. From close up, this really was a dead man, with the skin not quite like live skin and all his hollow places caving inward. You could start to guess the skeleton he'd be. And yet . . . Tahr was right. Someone had done something here *with ceremony.*

"I think he will have gone on," Tahr said. "Good, good. On his way by now."

There was another shot, very loud beneath the overhang, and Gavin scaled the ledge, a little farther over. He looked round. "You see them?" he said. "They were up here some-where?" Tahr was motionless, and Paris shook her head.

"This way." Gavin turned at Shikarri's call behind him. "I see where they climb."

As Gavin slipped off the ledge and followed, Paris found herself up on her feet, jumping down, splashing after him. "Don't shoot!" she yelled. "They're harmless."

"There!" Shikarri shouted, and everyone turned, Paris among them. Up in a crack in the rock face, where a side stream came in splashes, there were two figures, struggling against it like salmon swimming upstream. The larger one was higher, going strongly but clumsily, wounded somewhere, Paris guessed. "Please. Please don't shoot!" she yelled again.

That might have stayed Gavin's hand for a second, but it wasn't quite enough. At the top of the cleft the larger creature turned, shaking itself free of the water, then leaned down to help the small one, pulling it up through a flurry of spray. The pistol cracked again, and the larger figure jerked back, losing its grip, and the other one fell, struggling, buffeted by water, striking the ledge hard, then rolling with a dull splash into the pool.

"Take it," said Franklin, sharply. He was in command again. "Take it alive. I want to see this."

Above them, the other creature hung in silhouette, then reeled back and away, with a wild cry of grief and pain.

Shikarri and Gavin were dragging the thing from the water—like a wet sack, struggling a little, with a bubbling, whimpering sound. A young one, Paris realized, with a shudder. Gavin gripped its two arms from behind in a fierce lock, as Shikarri took hold of its hair and yanked its head up.

"Well," said Franklin in a low voice. "What in the world have we got here?"

11

It

"Forgive me for stating the obvious," Donald said cautiously, pacing round the tent, "but we could be sitting on a gold mine here."

The meeting was as private as anything could be under canvas—in Uncle Franklin's inner sanctum—just him, Donald, Harriet, Gavin . . . and no one had raised an objection to Paris's being there, too. One dim battery light cast a glow like a candle, and it made the tent seem small and the forest night seem very close outside. Shikarri had been posted to make sure no one came near eavesdropping, but still. . . . No one seemed keen to speak first, or say anything the dark outside might overhear.

Paris looked round, to see who would react to Donald's gambit.

Not Uncle Franklin, that was for sure. Why should he? There didn't seem to be anything in the world he couldn't buy already, or make sure he got by subtler means. He did not speak but looked a little pained, thought Paris, as though Donald disappointed him.

"Okay," said Harriet slowly. "Let's say—let's just say this thing *is* what we think it is. We've got the one and only yeti in captivity. Isn't that a bit like stealing the *Mona Lisa?* I mean, you can't do anything with it, can you?"

"Correction," said Donald. "I know of collectors who'd mortgage their souls to have the *Mona Lisa* . . . just for their own private vault. There are always individuals with the means and"—he glanced aside at Franklin—"discriminating tastes."

"You mean, you're going to *sell* her?" Paris said.

"We're not going to donate her to London Zoo, if that's what you're suggesting," said Donald.

But Gavin broke in with a little snort of scorn. "'Her!' Listen to that. Aren't we getting a wee bit *personal?*"

"Paris is right." That was Harriet. "That's the problem, isn't it? Is our little trophy an it or a she?"

"Well," said Donald, "clearly a female of the species, but—"

"But what species?" said Harriet.

"What is this?" Gavin was starting to lose patience. "You want a scientific name for it? Or do you want it to be named after you? Could be embarrassing, explaining how we came to find it."

Harriet pressed on. "What if it's *Homo sapiens?*" she said.

"Are you saying she isn't a yeti?" Paris said.

"I'm not saying that," said Harriet. "Look, if someone had told me we were coming here to hunt a yeti, I'd have been expecting great ape, I'd have been expecting something like orangutan. Maybe I'd have been wrong. I mean, what are the features? Posture: Upright. Skin: Largely hairless. Face? Now,

that's interesting. What does it make you think of: Low sloping forehead, heavy eyebrow ridge, strong jaw, slightly snout-
like? She's wearing *clothes,* for God's sake."

"Like a caveman," Paris said. "Sorry—woman."

"Close," said Harriet. "You know the word 'Neanderthal'?"

"Yeah, sure," said Paris, vaguely. "They died out, didn't they?"

"Our sweet ancestors finished them off. As we do. And not
long ago, either: thirty thousand years—that's *yesterday* in
earth terms. Or—or what if they didn't. Not quite . . ." She
looked at Franklin, and the others did the same. He'd sat quietly through the whole debate, aloof, as if none of this talk
struck him as the least bit interesting. Now, though, he made
that steeple of his fingers and nodded in his thinking way.

"Ingenious . . . ," he said. "They were alive and well in the
Ice Age. And if some retreated with the glaciers, back into the
mountains . . ."

"Och, this is academic," Gavin said.

"Oh, I think not. If Harriet is right, our little find is human.
Homo neanderthalensis . . . Certainly a *she.* If not, then an
animal: *it.* And I think that makes an *interesting* difference,
don't you?"

"Oh, come on." Gavin's voice was getting louder. "You
mean, if it's human, we lay out the red carpet. Fly it to the
United Nations. *Take me to your leader.* Is that what you
mean?"

He stopped abruptly, and the silence of the night felt big
around them. Somewhere nearby there was a strange, low,
mournful cry. Then Franklin smiled a small and secret smile,
one that Paris had sometimes glimpsed but never found the
key to.

There were things he knew, her uncle, that no one else did. "Let sleeping dogs lie, Frank." That was what her pop had said when Franklin had started inquiring where the family's wealth came from. Their father had been dead since before the brothers were the age Paris was now, so what difference could it make? But Franklin couldn't help but want to *know*. That was what Paris saw when she looked at her uncle: someone who wasn't afraid to ask the questions, and wasn't afraid of what he'd find. He could have been a scientist . . . an investigative reporter . . . a detective. But he had questions, even bigger questions, about science, and the media, and the law. There was no knowing where it would end.

Yes, her uncle was an extraordinary man, not like anybody else she knew. It gave her a thrill, that thought, a thrill that was a little like a shiver.

"Oh, by no means," he said. "There are *so* many possibilities. What has happened to your imaginations, all of you?"

The crying rose into the night above the camp. It lasted a moment, but it spread out across the clearing, it entered the forest and vanished there, as something stopped it at its source. Tahr sat upright, listening. The sound had not been loud—more a moan than a shout, and not at all like someone weeping, shedding tears. Tahr had heard a person cry like that once—a villager crushed by a felled tree. The man had lain there like a broken insect, past all hope or comfort, and the sound he made was scarcely human. Tahr had not slept for nights, just as he could not sleep now.

He sat upright, at the entrance of his tent, and looked toward the supply tent where they kept the creature. One of

Shikarri's men was on guard outside it. Nearby, Tahr guessed, there would be more. What had they done to the creature to make it cry out like that? And to make it stop so suddenly? He listened, but the crying did not come again.

Farther off, from Franklin's tent, he could hear the rise and fall of the white people's voices—loud when they were arguing, almost as loud when they thought they were making secret whisperings. Tahr understood the tone but not the words.

It was his fault the creature was here.

The thoughts of the day came back, and back. The sight of the poor thing struggling—stunned and in shock, but still a sturdy, broad-boned creature—in the arms of Gavin and Shikarri. It had moaned then, till they'd gagged it with a bandage, and still it gasped and made a whimpering deep inside its chest. At last, he was glad, it had given in and let itself be jerked along between them, on its own feet. At least they did not string it, like the monkey, on a pole.

And it wasn't just a *creature*. Should he say "Mountain Spirit"? It seemed too muscular, too flesh-and-blood to be a "spirit." Looking at it, Tahr was saddened—disappointed, even. Was this all the *yeh-teh* were, after all? It was dirty and hurt. It smelled. And it was something like a person. She— they'd all seen, in the struggle, that it was a female, though not yet a grown one—she wore a tunic made of roughly woven wool, blue gray, like the wild sheep of the mountains. And the cape . . . Only Tahr had thought to wade over and pick up the red brown object from beside the pool. It was hers, it must be, judging from the size. He had taken it for her, following just behind as they dragged her away.

He had to follow, because it was his fault. In the confusion, he could have run off, easily. But he had made this happen, and somehow, somehow, he must try to put it right. Who had told Paris about the *yeh-teh?* He ought to have known she had no secrets from her uncle, that strange man who had the power to get inside her mind, and others', too. Who had led the hunters to the waterfall but him, Tahr? And then—worst of all—who had startled the *yeh-teh* by running like a wild beast out into the open, shouting?

Tahr clutched the rough fur cape, with its clasp and its hood. Maybe she needed it—she was only a child, this *yeh-teh,* though she was twice as broad and powerful as he. He must try to get it to her, though he'd been warned already to stay well away.

He wanted to tell her two things, somehow. One: That he was sorry, oh, so sorry. Two: That he was grateful, more than words could say. Because they'd taken care of Shengo.

Back at the pool, Tahr had wondered, briefly, whether he should stay with Shengo. But Shengo was gone, well on his way through the *bardos* to whatever his next life would be. Only his body was left, and that was crumbling. Tahr remembered the night the old monk had told him about the people of the land beyond the mountains, and their sky burials. With no wood to make a pyre, no earth to dig a grave, the people laid their dead out in a high place for the birds to clear away. Tahr had shuddered, but the old man had been smiling, mildly, so Tahr guessed he wouldn't mind what would be happening to his body by the pool.

And the *yeh-teh* had cared for him—laid him out, with ceremony, then watched over him, keeping the wild beasts away. When Tahr had rushed out of the forest, he must have seemed like a wild beast himself, and the older *yeh-teh* had leaped up not to attack, as Gavin had thought, but to protect the dead man.

And then Gavin had pulled out his gun.

What can I do? Tahr prayed, to all the good souls and good spirits, all the incarnations of the Buddha that might hear him in this night. *Tell me what I can do.* He let one hand stray behind him, to feel the familiar touch of the other thing he had brought back from the pool, besides the fur cape. Shengo's water bottle, with the inscription "H.M. Property."

"Hey, you, little monk boy, over here . . ."

The words were English, but the accent strange. Tahr looked up.

It was Renaud. With a day's stubble and his long hair everywhere, the chef looked like a man who'd spent a day sleeping under a table. *Still sick from last night's drinking,* Tahr thought. But that wasn't all.

"Tell me. . . . You know about these creatures—these *abominables.*" Renaud crouched down beside him, coming closer on his hands and knees. His breath smelled sour and bad. "Nobody tells me *nothing,*" he said bitterly. "But just now I hear Shikarri and his people talking—in their jibber-jabber speak, of course, but I know what I hear. Those men are *frightened.* They are asking of Shikarri, "Please, please," something. But he says, "No, no." So at last I ask him, and he tells me."

The man's crumpled face came closer. "'Only superstition,' he says. But I see the fear in his eyes, too. Think: The creature has family. A whole tribe, maybe. One of them we injure, but not kill. It is alive . . . out there." His glance flickered round the dark edge of the clearing. "And we take away their young—their baby. What does Franklin think they're going to do?"

The cook gave a panicky little laugh, which had nothing to do with anything funny. "What does Franklin think we do when they *come for it*—the big ones? What good are his guns? What if they come by night? That's what Shikarri's men are saying. Let the thing go, they're saying, Let's get out of here. And Shikarri says all this to Franklin, and you know what Monsieur Franklin does? He laughs! As if all this was a fine game! I tell you, we are here in the forest with madmen." Tahr saw that the man's hands were quivering. "You tell me—how is your Buddha going to save us now, eh, eh?"

At first, Tahr had been frightened, but as the words spilled out, he thought: *This is a man with a bad dream, just like me the other night.* So Tahr sat calm and breathed, and gradually the chef fell quiet.

"Why did she cry out just now?" Tahr said.

"Oh, they try to feed her. They take off the gag for a moment and . . . you hear. All the forest hears it. All the *others* . . . If they did not know already, they know now." Suddenly, Renaud took Tahr by the wrists. "Help me. I beg you. If we run off now, you guide me. Take me to a town, a bus, a railway station—anywhere away from here."

"I can't," said Tahr.

"Name your price. I have money."

"I don't know the way. I don't know any ways round here. I am sorry."

There was a pause. The man's eyes flickered round, as though he might just make a dash for it anyway.

"But," Tahr said, "maybe I can help a little. If I could make the *yeh-teh* peaceful. Stop her from crying. Maybe make her eat?"

Renaud looked at him, as if astonished. Then he nodded slowly. "Yes, maybe. If anybody, maybe you can."

"Will you ask Shikarri?" Tahr said. "I think he does not like me."

"Okay. Okay." As Renaud went to scuttle off, he glanced back. "How can you sit there?" he said. "*They* could be out there . . . right now."

Tahr closed his eyes. *Please,* he thought, *let him say yes. And if there are* yeh-teh *out there in the shadows, give me a chance to speak to her before they come.*

"There is another possibility," said Franklin. The conference under canvas, in his inner sanctum, was still under way. Gavin, Donald, Harriet, and Paris waited.

"She could simply be an idiot," he said. "You are familiar with the old stories about *enfants sauvages*—wild children brought up in the forest by the wolves. When studied, they always turn out to be defectives of some kind—deformed or stupid, so their parents threw them out."

"Uh . . . this one had a parent, didn't she?" said Harriet.

"True," Franklin conceded. "Or they could be a family of inbred retards. It happens in mountain communities."

"So?"

"So we must be careful. If she turns out to be an idiot, that makes us a little stupid, does it not?" Franklin's face had an icy charm about it. "And I *never* let that happen. Whatever we decide to do will be so much more interesting if she is really what we think she is. We must . . . investigate her more closely. But first, let us have a good night's sleep."

"Pardon me for asking," Donald shuffled, "but—but does Shikarri have security well in hand?"

"Of course. Why do you ask?"

"Just that I gather there's a bit of restlessness among the natives. Porters getting worried that there might be . . . *more* of the blighters out there."

"Oh, Donald," Franklin raised an eyebrow. "I'm surprised at you. A man who does not blench at eating *fugu!*" He treated Donald to his coolest smile. "I'd say that the odds on being eaten by a yeti are a little—just a little—less than that."

12

A Cave of Eyes

The supply tent had become a prison. Tahr slipped in. The flap fell shut behind him—shut and lashed in place.

One of Shikarri's men stood outside with a gun. Another sat inside, keeping watch. In the dim light, Tahr recoiled. It stank like an animal's pen.

She was tethered to the tent pole like a bear tied to a stake. Tahr saw the trodden circle on the earth where she'd paced till she'd sunk exhausted. She was slumped now, back against the pole. Still, she heard him enter and struggled up unsteadily, turning her head to where her ears told her somebody must be. One strip of bandage was a blindfold, and another gagged her, dirty-damp with the food they'd tried to force into her mouth, or maybe with her own blood as she tried to bite it free.

There was not much of her face to see. Long hair fell forward, not quite hiding the heavy forehead and the broad nose.

And the smell . . .

Tahr's stomach heaved, not so much with disgust—in the world of Shengo's hut there'd been no shame in needing to go to the lavatory, it was simply what a body did—but with anger at the men who'd tied her there. The shame was theirs, not hers. In some way it seemed to be his, too—staring at her like this. But he couldn't help it. When Shengo had talked about the *yeh-teh,* Tahr used to imagine something noble—quiet lords of the mountains, living where nobody could, tougher than people and more free. But this poor thing in front of him? She looked more wretched than the poorest villagers he'd ever seen. Maybe Franklin was right when he said that she might be an outcast, turned out in the woods because she was stupid and deformed.

She was watching him, too—or rather, listening. She was so still and alert that for a silly moment Tahr was afraid that he'd spoken his thoughts out loud, and he felt ashamed again. No, she didn't seem stupid. And ugly? She was different, that's all: about Tahr's height, but sturdier—strong bowed legs, broad shoulders, and the kind of stoop that looked as if at any second she might duck and run, or spring. She would be quick as a cat, and just as unpredictable, if she were free.

The guard spoke, and Tahr turned. The man looked tense, uneasy, like someone acting on orders that he didn't understand or like. He would be cruel because of it, Tahr guessed. Tahr did not know his language, but the meaning was clear: Keep back, the thing is dangerous. Looking again, Tahr saw that they had lashed her arms tight to her sides. Where she had struggled, he saw livid chafe marks on her skin. He stood a moment, swaying with the rush of feelings. ("Let your mind clear," Shengo would have said. "They are only feelings. Let them go.") No, there were too many feelings for him to swallow them all. They stuck like something solid in his throat.

The guard was watching him hard. Tahr made a humble gesture, then he pointed to the floor: *Can I sit?* The guard nodded, and leaned back to keep a good eye on them both—the monk-boy who they said had walked in out of nowhere . . . and this creature, who was either something fabulous or else not worth the bother at all. At the man's belt hung the *kukri,* and his hand strayed to it every now and then.

Tahr settled himself on the floor cross-legged, as close to the circle of scuffed earth as common sense said it was safe to be. If they'd treated the *yeh-teh* like a frightened animal, she might lash out like one. And even a kick from those legs could do harm.

Around the tent, the baggage that had filled it had been pushed aside—piled high against the tent sides like an inner wall. Even if the *yeh-teh* broke loose, she couldn't fight her way through that—or not before the guard had shouted. If he shouted, then Shikarri would loose the gray dog and be ready with the gun.

Whatever I do now, Tahr thought, *I mustn't make anyone panic—not her, not the guard, not me.* It was up to him, with all his seething feelings and the sickness in his stomach, to be the one calm thing in here.

As if just thinking that had made some difference, he saw the *yeh-teh* relax a little. She let her weight rest back against the pole, and in a while she slid back to a wary sitting crouch.

"Who—who are you?" Tahr said in his own tongue, then in English. No reaction, either way. For a moment, he wondered if she might be deaf. He shifted his weight, and she tensed: she'd heard him, heard him very well.

"I'm sorry," he said, though he knew she would not understand him, and reached out his hand. "No!" snapped the guard's voice, unmistakable in any language, and the *yeh-teh* flinched, too, pressing her face against her shoulder, as if she expected to be hit.

She is afraid, thought Tahr. *What can I do to calm her?* He began to chant.

Many times he had watched old Shengo soothe a panicked animal—a goat that had worked itself onto an impossible ledge or a horse that had bolted in the village. What all the words were, Tahr never quite caught, and what he chanted now was a hotchpotch, any right-sounding phrase that he found in his mind. Not for the first time Tahr thought: *Why, oh, why didn't you teach me everything, Shengo, while there was time?* He was almost a man—surely he'd been old enough to learn? And not for the first time he found himself wondering whether the old man really had known all the chants and rituals. Maybe he had forgotten some of them with age. . . . But then, he'd been a soldier, hadn't he? Had he ever been a proper monk, in a monastery? What if—what if Shengo had been making it up all the time?

It was a terrible, disrespectful thought, but for a moment Tahr could have sworn he heard the old man's wicked chuckle in his mind. *Maybe I was making it up!* he was saying, like a child found out in a good joke, happy to be found out so that they could share it now. *So you can make it up, too.*

Tahr almost laughed—and lost the rhythm of the chanting. So what if the old man had never been a real monk? If he was just a man who'd been a soldier and had seen too much?

Maybe that was enough? It seemed enough for the villagers in the valleys, and enough for the goats and the peace of their small *gompa*. And enough for young Tahr, too. *Yes,* thought Tahr, *I always knew it, really.* Perhaps Shengo had been telling him it gently, planting clues Tahr would unpick when he was old enough to know.

Thank you, old friend, Tahr thought, and feeling stronger now, he reached back in his mind to find some words and phrases and began to chant again.

Out in the dark the forest world went on. The usual unquiet stillness of night. Insect noises. The rush of a little night thing in the undergrowth. The hush of water carried closer, then farther away, by a shift in the breeze.

On the slope behind the campsite, boulders crouched as usual among the trees, and trees crouched among boulders. A parting of leaves, or a movement of moonlight, picked out shadows from a sudden angle—there, then gone.

In her tent, Paris slipped into sleep, but not deeply. She lay bobbing just beneath the surface of a queasy dream.

When you chanted right, it was a form of meditation, and a wave of warmth came up inside you, making you feel light and sharp, not sleepy. Tahr felt it now, the first time it had worked for him since he'd been at the campsite. How could he feel calm here, in the smell and squalor of this jail-tent? Well, Paris wasn't here, for one thing. There was something about her that always made his mind feel scattered, like her own. But now, somehow, he found that he could meditate.

Don't stare, Tahr thought. The *yeh-teh* felt it, and it scared her. He kept his eyes down, lids at half-mast, in the way of meditation. Still, now and then he was sure that the *yeh-teh* had raised her drooping head and somehow—there was no other way to put it, though she was blindfold—*looked* at him.

Don't stop chanting. When the words ran dry, it came down to the kind of mumble Shengo used to make sometimes. That was enough. Behind him, Tahr could hear the guard's breath settling to a steady rhythm. *Sleeping,* Tahr thought, *but not deep. One sudden noise, he'll be awake—awake, alarmed, and angry, with the* kukri *in his hand.*

Don't stop chanting. Great love, great compassion . . . The jewel in the heart of the lotus. *Om . . . Mane . . . Padme . . . Hum . . .*

Then Tahr knew that the *yeh-teh* was watching him, somehow. She had raised her face in his direction and now, as he looked, she started to edge her body carefully toward him. Tahr did not flinch or back away. She crept out to the end of the rope that held her, and stopped, an arm's reach away. The smell of her, so close, was not as bad as he had thought it would be. She was just a person, dirty, hurt, and in a sweat from fear.

If I could just loosen those ropes, he thought. *If I could grab for the guard's knife, could I set her free?* Then he thought of the hand on that knife, and the hand on the gun just outside, and besides, did he know what *she* would do? She might panic, try to break out, or even attack him. If he just loosened the gag . . . But she would cry out, make that terrible call for help again, and that would be the end of everything.

119

Very slowly, making no sudden movement to alarm her, Tahr reached under his robe and took out the present he'd brought her. The cape, from the rock by the pool. He held it out, not pausing in the chanting, and brushed it over the back of her poor bound hand.

None of the worst things happened. She did not struggle, or panic, or rattle the pole, or lash out with her feet. She hardly moved, but for a moment her whole body tensed . . . and then relaxed toward him. Even with his eyes closed he'd have heard the slight change in her breathing. *It's all right,* Tahr thought. It was a comfort. She shuffled a little, straining to be closer, and he slid the fur down a little, till she hooked a little finger round it. Without words, every inch of her was asking, *Let me have it*—and asking it gently, saying, *Please.* He let the cape go.

She did not turn away. Instead, she craned her neck a little, pushing her face toward him, asking . . . asking what? Very gingerly, Tahr stretched out his hand and touched her hair. He felt the warmth beneath his fingers, and she did not draw back. Then the strange face turned a little, nudging round until Tahr's fingers touched the filthy gag. Was that it? But she moved again, drawing his fingers to the blindfold. *Yes,* her tiny movement said. *Yes, that.*

Don't stop chanting. Om . . . Mane . . . Padme . . . Stay calm. If he could hold that stillness, no harm could come to them.

But it was hard. Tahr's fingers slipped along the edge of the bandage, easing it. He felt the bony ridge of her brow, and worked the blindfold up, up, inch by inch, and as the edge slipped up and over it, he looked the *yeh-teh* in the eye.

She saw him. Now was when she could go wild—recognizing him as the one who'd charged out at the waterfall, just as the shooting started. Now she might lunge at him in anger, or turn her back and never look at him again.

She did neither. She did not even show surprise. She nodded slowly, keeping her deep eyes on him, as if to say, *I knew, all along.* . . .

Tahr lowered his head a little, and his hand, which had removed her blindfold, stayed raised like a greeting in the air. When he looked up, she was watching. He could hardly see her eyes, they were so deep-set. Tahr thought of the place beneath the waterfall where they'd laid Shengo, in the *yeh-tehs'* secret cave beside the pool. As in that cave, there was a fire burning in the darkness of those eyes . . .

. . . and the memory shifted, as thoughts do when you're falling asleep. In his mind, Tahr saw a thin boy running, splashing through the water, shouting like a wild thing—running at the sacred still place where the old man's body lay. That boy was going to do it some harm. The moment was lit up by a flash of feeling. Anger. Fear.

All of that, in an instant. Then Tahr was back inside himself, shielding his eyes as if he'd looked at lightning. He'd lost the thread of the chant, but the guard had not stirred. The boy he'd been seeing was *him*. But it wasn't his memory. . . . He had seen himself from the outside, from the other side of the pool. And the fear and the anger—they weren't his, but *hers*.

Almost afraid to breathe, he lowered his hands and looked again. She was still watching, but he'd lost his meditation calm; his heart was thumping. What had happened?

Calm, stay calm. It was like the moment when you've climbed too high and mustn't let yourself know it or you'll be afraid. What he'd seen in her eyes had been only a flicker, and he'd lost it, but under the gag she made the faintest sound— quite soft, almost musical, a kind of hum. The tone didn't change, but wasn't there a rhythm in it, like the rhythm of his chant? Now she bent her head toward him slowly, like a greeting, and he was certain: Whatever had happened to him then . . . *she knew.*

Stay calm, he thought. *Don't be afraid. Don't look away.* Once he had asked Shengo what meditation was. "Just listening," the old man said. "Listening to silence." In her silence, she had spoken. If he could be quiet, maybe she would speak again.

She wasn't sitting like a prisoner now, but upright, leaning forward and alert, like someone waiting for news. *Go on,* her whole body was saying. It was his turn . . . but how, when even a word might wake up the guard. Without thinking, Tahr stretched out his hand to touch the back of hers, as he looked in her eyes.

He was my friend. Tahr fought the urge to speak out loud. Instead, he thought it, conjuring an image of old Shengo at his most benign and twinkling. He felt it, and she saw the feeling somehow, maybe in his face or in the little gesture of his arms.

My friend . . . In spite of himself, Tahr saw the moment when he'd seen the old man lose his footing and fall, fall, fall, as if he'd be falling forever. And beyond him, the face in the leaves.

Tahr had known, at the pool, that the face had been a *yeh-teh*. Now he knew for certain that it had been hers. *You!* he thought, and for a flicker saw a scene through parted leaves—himself, on a rocky ledge opposite, pointing and calling, and yes, Shengo falling, from the angle that she would have seen.

It was her thought, and with it came a feeling. It was a feeling Tahr knew oh, so well. He'd known it ever since he was little, but in this last week it had been with him again and again. *My fault. My fault.*

She was sorry for what happened, too.

And I'm sorry. Tahr bowed his head. In his mind was a picture of the *yeh-teh* bound and frog-marched through the forest, and the older *yeh-teh* reeling back in pain. He looked up at the young one now, with a slow helpless shake of his head. *What can I do? I'm sorry.*

Then the strangest thing happened, there in the menagerie-prison of the supply tent, in the middle of the night. As if the choppy pool of all those feelings suddenly went still, he looked deep in her eyes and saw *No blame. No blame.*

13

What's Unspoken

"The trouble with Franklin," Paris's father always said, "is that he has never *arrived.*" An odd thing for him, of all people, to say: every few years she'd be uprooted, parked in some International School in London, Oslo, Rio de Janeiro, as Pop took charge of some newly bought-up subsidiary. But she knew what he meant. Pop was settled and proud of it, with a house near Cape Cod that he'd retire to one day, and each little wife he'd married had been more American than the last. He'd done what his and Franklin's father had never managed, though the Herr Professor had been smart enough to leave his sons their impeccably unforeign names and a small family fortune in the bank. He—Woody, Paris's pop—had *arrived.* But Franklin . . . ?

Franklin was different. It was as if some shadow of his father's history came with him, and he couldn't let it be. While Woody had invested and made money, Franklin had studied: psychology, philosophy, strange languages. He had studied and traveled, knowing more and more and saying less and less about it. Just by being there, he made everyone else seem sort of local, small-scale, stuck in the mud.

An unsettling man, Franklin. He was always *passing through.*

As Paris got older, she got to visit him more, in his surprising places—almost-seedy neighborhoods in foreign cities that hid an apartment he would furnish with unshowy style and taste. Somewhere near would be a café where he and the intellectuals (or that's what they sounded like, in languages Paris wished she understood) would meet and argue through the night.

Pop dragged her round the world, and Paris sulked and made him suffer. But she'd follow Uncle Franklin anywhere.

And now they were here. In the light of early morning, she felt wretched, after wretched sleep. Everybody she saw around her looked the same. Only Franklin was cool and in command and ready. It was scarcely human. *Franklin's different from the rest of us,* she thought, and it hurt her to think it, because she had always hoped to be a Franklin kind of person, too. Being one of the club, along with Harriet, Gavin, Donald— that made her feel she'd arrived. Maybe that was her mistake. Last night she'd looked at Franklin's face and seen him looking at the others, slightly disappointed in them as if, no, they really hadn't got the point at all.

"Franklin?" her mom had said once, with a shudder. "That man's scary." *Great!* thought Paris. Mom was scared of all the interesting people . . . and Paris was practicing to be one of them. This morning, though, she wasn't quite so sure.

He came out, striding in the direction of the supply tent, with Harriet behind him, looking grim. "Ah, Paris," said Franklin. "Come and help us."

"What, now?" she said automatically, and heard her voice

sound like a kid's. "Sorry," she said. "I mean: Sure." She tagged after them. "Help with what?"

"Information," he said. "Time we got some from this *guest* of ours."

There was something in the way he said it that made even Harriet wince. "She won't talk. You saw her yesterday. She'll just scream."

"Oh, come on, Harriet," he said patiently. "You know—you of all people—there are always ways to—"

"I mean, maybe she *can't* talk. Neanderthal brains—I mean, the skulls they've found—they're not the same as ours. Smaller in the place where we do speech."

"So they *are* stupid?" Paris put in.

"No, no. Their brains were as big as ours, apparently. Bigger. But . . . a different shape." She paused, with a look toward the supply tent. "Feels strange, doesn't it, to say *were?*"

"We'll see," said Franklin. As they came to the tent he nodded to Shikarri, who lifted the flap and stepped aside. Paris ducked in, squinting at the darkness . . . and recoiled, stumbling back outside.

The smell, for one thing. She hadn't known it would be like that. "Sorry," she said. "Oh, geez, I'm feeling sick."

Uncle Franklin scarcely looked back at her. He sighed. "You'd better run along, then." She'd failed the test, before it even started. She had disappointed him again. Now his voice said a word from the tent, and Shikarri went in, too. The flap shut. Paris told herself she needed coffee, and moved away quickly. Whatever happened in that tent, she didn't want to hear.

———

"I think her kind does not speak."

Tahr spoke, stiffly, being formal. Paris was relieved to find that he would talk to her at all.

"Harriet said something like that," she said. "Something about the shapes of their brains. How did you know?"

"Last night I sat with her."

"You *what?* They let you?" She thought of her glimpse of the supply tent. "Feels kind of bad in there, doesn't it?"

He sat by his tiny tent, with his half-grown hair all fuzzy and that private look on his face—looking younger, somehow, than when he was shaven-headed. Then again, how old was twelve in this part of the world? Weren't they already working in the fields, like grownups? Once, without thinking, she'd asked him what grade he was in, and he'd just stared. No, there was a lot she didn't know about him. And he wasn't helping her. If she didn't speak, he wouldn't either, and that would be that.

"Look, I'm sorry," she said. "There, I've said it. I'm really sorry." He looked up, as if mildly surprised. "I'm sorry I let it slip," said Paris. "I mean, I'm sorry I told them. If I'd known . . . Look, I feel lousy about it, you can see that, can't you?" She felt her voice rising. *Keep it down.* She didn't want Donald or someone coming over, messing up her chance to talk to Tahr alone.

"Well, can't you?" she said, and he nodded simply. "Good," said Paris. "This is really hard for me. It was so important, coming here with Uncle Franklin. He's kind of like my hero. . . . You know the word 'hero'? Like, the way you felt about Shengo . . ."

"He is your master," Tahr said.

"No! No." Paris was flustered. She plucked at a guy rope restlessly, making it twang. "If you knew my mom and pop, you'd understand. I mean, everything about them, it's so . . . tacky. Both of them, in different ways. And they're always nagging me, and. . . . Oh, crap." She gave up on it. "You know how families are."

There was a silence.

"Oh, heck, that was dumb of me," said Paris. "You don't, do you? There I go, messing up again."

Tahr gave a quick, quite unexpected smile. "No blame," he said. "No blame." Another silence. "I think that if you spend some time with her . . ."

"Me? What can I do?" Paris stopped in midbreath. From over in the supply tent, there was an unmistakable brief cry. Paris pulled closer to Tahr. "I don't like this any more than you do," she said. "Just because I'm here with Franklin, don't think—don't think I'm like him."

"I think you are kind," the boy said. "If you sit a little with her—quietly—then you understand."

"Understand what?"

But Tahr had looked up. There, across the campsite, Franklin strode toward them. He looked straight at Tahr.

"They tell me you know how to handle the creature," he said.

Tahr lowered his head. It was true. The guard had woken, last night, to the odd sight of the monk-boy and the *yeh-teh* sitting face to face, and the *yeh-teh* was calm. After a while, Tahr had cautiously gestured to him: "Drink? She's thirsty." The guard made a gesture of the creature knocking a drink from his hand, but Tahr shook his head. "Me," he gestured.

"Let me." And very warily, hand still near his knife, the guard had eased the bandage round her mouth, just enough for Tahr to lift his water bottle—Shengo's water bottle—to her lips.

"Good. Make sure she's fed," said Franklin briskly. "Get food from Renaud—whatever you think the things eat. I don't want her to die on me."

"What are you going to do with her?" said Paris.

"Too early to say. I want her alive . . . and conscious. It's very provoking not to know what's going on inside that unusual skull." He had that flash of pure cool interest in his eyes. "Imagine if we'd had an in-depth interview with the last dinosaur. Get inside its thick skull—hear just what it feels like to be on the edge of extinction, just about to go. Or even the stupid dodo. How exquisite . . . Our pink-headed ducks didn't offer any famous last word, sadly. But *this* one . . ."

"She's not the last, though, is she?" Paris said.

"Well, that is the question, isn't it? How many of them are there? Young Tahr here is local. If he's got some inside information . . ."

Tahr kept his eyes on the ground. Once, as they talked, Paris had used the words "white lie," and he'd asked her to explain them—how being dishonest could be not a bad thing, after all. Suddenly, he understood.

"I think there are many," he said. "My master always says: Beware of *yeh-teh*. They live in tribes and are strong."

"Hmm," Franklin said to himself. "So we double the guard." Tahr did not look up until he heard his footsteps going. He didn't know much about Franklin, but he knew he was hungry for rare things, and the rarest of all, the *last* of anything, was what he looked for most. If he thought that the *yeh-teh* weren't so rare . . .

"There's something you're not saying," Paris said. "You know something, don't you? Don't hold out on me."

Tahr shook his head. He didn't want to lie to her. But though she meant well, still her uncle's will was stronger than her own. How could he trust her to know what he'd seen last night, while the guard slept and the night was at its darkest?

It might be that he had fallen asleep and just dreamed that he was staring into that dark cave of the *yeh-teh*'s eyes. But the images did not fade, like most dreams, with daylight.

Looking into a pool . . . a still pool . . . seeing only one reflection. The feeling had been emptiness, then panic. *Turning to look for her . . . for mother . . . not there . . .* He'd heard—he'd felt—the mother's cry of pain and fear. *Dark forest all round . . . staring, listening to catch her nearness.* No, he'd felt in a panic, there's no nearness. Just a memory of mother: *Holding me tight . . . her arm around me beside the still, gone, older brother, the last of the others. And her eyes on me, saying, Precious, my only-one now . . .*

The flap fell shut behind them, and they were in the supply tent. Shikarri had nodded them through, warily, though the dog had pulled its lips back in a voiceless snarl. *Saying what his master means,* thought Paris. They were one thing, that man and his dog. No wonder Shikarri didn't have a name for it. The dog was part of him, simple as that. Now all that mattered was that they were here on Franklin's orders—maybe Paris was trying to make up for her failure of nerve earlier, her uncle thought. Inside the tent, she held back.

"I don't know what to do," she said.

"Just sit," said Tahr. "Here. Beside me . . ."

The *yeh-teh* scarcely raised her head. They had left off her blindfold, but the gag was still in place. She slumped against the tent pole, sullen and exhausted. At first she would not look at Tahr directly.

"We must be still," he said to Paris. "Try to be calm. I chant a little."

It was several minutes before the *yeh-teh* met his eyes . . . and it came like a slap in the face. *Fear . . . Hurt . . . Betrayal* . . . But he made an effort not to look away. He held up the flask. Yes, she was thirsty. Then, very slowly, he reached for Paris's hand, raised it, and put the bottle in it. "You give her," he said. He felt her skin flinch, but she did not argue. "I loosen the cloth round her mouth. Now, calmly, calmly, slowly, slow . . ."

As the gag came off, Paris flinched again. The skin around the lips was chafed and bleeding . . . and that face . . . "Ugly" was not the word for it. If this was . . . a person, you would say *deformed*—with that bony overhang of forehead, the big flattened nose, the heavy jaw, the long teeth bared a little now. . . . Hadn't Franklin said she might be just some kind of retard? People like that always made her feel bad.

"Look at her eyes," said Tahr.

And that was when she knew, for certain, that this was *someone*—a whole person in there, looking out at her. She would have said the eyes were black but for the slightest glow of amber in them. They were like a tunnel back into a place, a *world,* too far away to see.

"You are both frightened," Tahr said softly. "Give her drink." He reached out to guide Paris's hand, keeping it steady and slow, to the other one's lips. She drank, just a sip at first, and then with all her thirst. When she had finished, Tahr reached into the bag beside him and brought out the best Renaud had been able to offer—what was left on the bone from a haunch of some small deer. It wasn't exciting fare, by the expedition's standards, but the *yeh-teh* had been cooking something like it at the waterfall. And it was right. As Tahr held it close to her lips, she lunged at it and sank her teeth in, so he almost flinched. But he kept it there as she relaxed and closed her eyes, lost in the pleasure of it, simply eating. When that was done, they settled back, all three of them.

Then the *yeh-teh* was looking at Paris, making a small crooning sound. "Oh, geez, what does it mean?" said Paris. "Tahr, help me, what am I meant to do?"

"Tell her you are her friend."

"Me . . ." Paris faltered. "Me . . . friend . . ." The sound was so jerky and wooden that the *yeh-teh* pulled away.

"No," said Tahr. "*Be* her friend," and gently he guided her hand to touch the *yeh-teh*'s. There was just enough play for the fingers so that, when Paris's touched hers, they locked. Paris stiffened, surprised by the strength. But she didn't let go. She looked into the creature's eyes again. That amber glow seemed stronger.

"Friend." Paris said it again. This time her voice felt warm and true.

That was it. Nothing spooky. Tahr hadn't told her what to expect, but there'd been hints. He seemed to have had some kind of . . . experience. Something kind of paranormal, maybe. But it didn't work for her. Maybe she'd misunderstood. She and the *yeh-teh* just kept contact for a while, and then it was too long—Paris felt embarrassed, and she loosened her fingers carefully, gave an awkward smile, and turned away.

Shikarri let them out. They passed Donald and Renaud, and across the clearing Franklin raised a hand in passing, though he didn't stop and speak.

Paris let out a gasp. When Tahr turned, she was motionless and pale.

"What is it?"

"I don't know. A horrible feeling. Uncle Franklin . . . I thought . . ." Paris's voice fell to a whisper. "I don't know what I thought. He just waved. But he scared me, scared me really bad. Geez," she said suddenly. "Is that how he scares *her?* What's happening, Tahr?"

Tahr's smooth forehead creased. "I do not understand. But you must not talk of this. Not to your uncle."

Paris shook her head.

"You must swear to me," he said. "I want to trust you."

"Trust me," said Paris. "Please."

Tahr took a deep breath. Words weren't enough, not for a risk like this. He gazed as deep into her eyes as he had into the *yeh-teh*'s. "Will you help?" he said.

"Of course," she mouthed. If she was lying, Tahr knew, her gaze would have flickered then. But it held firm.

"Will you help me to help *her?*" Tahr saw the brief shock in her eyes. Fear. It made her pupils widen for a moment, then she steadied.

"Yes. I will." And he believed what her eyes said when she whispered, "Tell me how."

14

Into the Dark

The little monk sat calm and upright, in his meditation posture . . . with a meat knife up his sleeve.

It had been easy to steal. He was surprised by this, just as he'd been surprised to hear himself telling a lie to Franklin—telling it again when Franklin dragged him in front of all the others, saying, "Tell us everything you know." Yes, he'd repeated the story, and more. Yes, they were fierce, he'd said, the *yeh-teh*. People in the mountains went in fear of them. For all their great size and strength, they moved through dense undergrowth silently and very fast. They might come after nightfall, since their eyes were good for seeing in the dark.

Why had he not felt bad, spinning these falsehoods? And—even more puzzling—how could they not *know?* If these were "people who were gods and titans," as Shengo had said, how could such powerful beings not see the truth inside him, as easily—as easily as it seemed the *yeh-teh* did?

But they didn't. They were blinded by their own ideas, the way Paris was, often. Whatever you said to her, she would answer by speaking about herself. One moment they would be talking together, then it was as if he'd lost her in the thickets of *herself.* It left him puzzled, and it left him sad. But he must not think about that now. Now his mind must be clear.

The cook Renaud had been blinded by his fear, most conveniently, when Tahr had paid a call on him in his tent with more tales of the *yeh-teh,* just to make the man a little more afraid. It had been easy to spot where Renaud hid his case of knives, and Tahr had come back later for the sharpest one in the box.

Only Shikarri looked at Tahr with shrewder eyes. But his men were afraid, too. Maybe he even saw Tahr's game, and was content for him to play it? Who could tell who was hiding what from whom among these people? Tahr had seen the tall man, Gavin, and the Hungry Ghost one, Donald, whispering together, and he'd guessed that it must be about the *yeh-teh.* All the white people's arguments these days were.

All Tahr knew for sure was that none of their schemes would do *her* any good. And time was getting shorter. He must act.

And that was why he now sat in the supply tent, as calm and poised as Shengo could have wished . . . feeling the blade of the hidden knife against his skin.

He sat face to face with the *yeh-teh.* They had cleaned her up a little—as much as a bucket of cold water could do—and sluiced the ground around her. The blindfold stayed off, and they'd let him ease a little food past her lips. Apart from that, the gag stayed on, because the camp was twitchy. Everyone was listening in the night.

As Tahr had hoped, they were alone. With Franklin's doubling of the guard, all available men were facing outward, toward the hostile night around them. The one at the door of the tent looked in from time to time, but what he saw was dull and caused him no concern. Everyone who could handle a gun had been issued one—even Paris. When she'd insisted to her uncle that she take a turn on watch, Franklin had nodded. *Good girl,* he must have been thinking. *She's coming along.*

Tahr faced the *yeh-teh*. With his gestures, with his mind, he was trying to tell her about the knife. "Not to hurt you," he wanted to say, but it was hard to get across the idea of a not-thing. Simpler, he touched the rope that tied her, and then cautiously mimed "knife." She was very still now, watching. He mimed "knife" again, then touched his sleeve. *I have it. Here.*

And Tahr was waiting for the moment. He was listening to the distance, with his mind as clear and sharp as he had ever managed in his years of meditation. He thought of Shengo, who used to sit without flicking an eyelid—in a trance, the villagers would say—and then turn to Tahr and say: "One of the goats is in trouble." High and tiny on the hillside, it had cried, and he had heard it.

Tahr and the *yeh-teh,* waiting for the moment . . . He wanted to tell her what the moment would be like, so that it would not scare her, but it was hard when he did not know himself. Mostly, he just thought: *Calm . . . and ready.*

And they waited. Waited.

Now.

———

There was a shot. Then voices, someone shouting, urgent questions, warning, and the sound of running feet. It was a noise to make people drop what they were doing, run and see. Maybe only Tahr, of all the people on the campsite, didn't. This was the moment he'd been waiting for.

He hadn't asked much of Paris—nothing that would implicate her later. She just had to take her turn on watch, as Uncle Franklin would have wanted . . . and make sure she was somewhere on the other edge of the camp, as far away from the supply tent as possible . . . and wait till well past midnight, when a mixture of boredom, drowsiness, and nerves on edge had a chance to set in. And then this.

She had set up a good little panic, just the way a jittery teenager might. "There!" she'd be yelling. "I saw one, down there, in the bushes!" Gavin would be forging over, telling her to keep her voice down, but she'd be slightly hysterical—"No, there, look—another one!" And the odds were that somebody else would think they saw a shadow move, and let off a round at it . . . and they had. By now everyone would be turning, straining their ears and eyes in that direction.

There would be minutes, only, before Franklin or Gavin took charge, and said, "Stay at your posts!" or "False alarm" . . . But if the *yeh-teh* did not panic, minutes might just be enough.

Tahr got to his feet, moving as quickly and calmly as he could. Without taking his eyes from hers, he stepped around her, to the tent pole, and with two, three quick hacks of the knife, he cut the rope. And now was the moment when anything could happen.

Startled, the *yeh-teh* was up on her feet, reeling backward as the rope that had held her gave way. She blundered into the piled-up bags and boxes, sending the little night lamp spinning on its side. She backed into the shadows it cast now and dropped to a quivering crouch.

What she saw as she looked up at Tahr, he couldn't tell. A bandit—the wild boy who'd charged at the waterfall, but this time with a knife? No wonder she backed off, cowering. But she must not. She was free, but she wouldn't get far if both her hands stayed tied. Tahr tried to mime "cutting" . . . "careful" . . . , but light glinted on the blade. The *yeh-teh* gave a little snarl of fear.

Outside, the false alarm couldn't possibly last much longer.

The *yeh-teh* wouldn't let him near her. But whatever the risk, she had to understand *right now*. Taking one step forward, Tahr leaned down and laid the knife between them. Then he stepped back, miming "both my hands tied," miming "cutting rope with knife."

She stared at him, uncertain, and he couldn't see or feel what was happening in her eyes. He spread both his hands, palms upward. "No harm," the gesture said, "defenseless."

She leaped for the knife. Tahr closed his eyes. Maybe all the dumb show about friendship had been cunning. Maybe she was just a wild thing, doing what she must. If she was going to kill him, it would happen now.

And nothing happened—not to him, at least. When he opened his eyes, she was squatting on the groundsheet, with the knife gripped in her long prehensile toes. She peered closely at her wrists, then quickly, deftly, sliced her bonds away. Tahr scarcely had time to marvel at the skill of it before she was up, the cut rope falling round her. For one moment, she simply stretched her stiff arms, long strong fingers flexing; then she gave a shudder like a wet dog and spun to face the door.

"No!" Tahr signed urgently. "Not that way." He mimed the stance of a guard with a weapon. "That way!" he tried, pointing to the opposite wall of the tent. He ran over, tugging at the piles of bags and boxes. For a second, she watched, uncertain; then she was beside him, yanking out heavy sacks like plucking flowers, tossing them aside.

Outside, the panic was subsiding. Any moment, everyone would be spreading back out to their own posts, covering all exits. "There!" Tahr pointed at the rough seam where tent wall and groundsheet met. It had been lashed together, more to keep small creatures out than large ones in, but it would be easier than trying to slash straight through taut canvas. "There!" he mimed the cutting, and the *yeh-teh* frowned a moment, weighing it up. Then, with that unnerving speed of hers, she was leaping and slashing, and as the seam parted, she threw her weight against it, flattening herself like a cat and squeezing through.

It must have been the noise of the baggage being thrown aside that alerted the guard at the door. He must have peered in just long enough to get the picture, just as Tahr had lain down flat and was struggling to get through the gap that the sturdier *yeh-teh* had pushed through with ease. And so Tahr was just wriggling out into the open as the guard came running round the outside of the tent, shouting for help as he came, with his bare *kukri* in his hand.

And the *yeh-teh?* Gone, as if she'd dissolved into the night air. . . . All that existed in the world was Tahr, on the ground, wriggling as helpless as a worm out of its hole . . . and the man looming over him, and the *kukri*. For a second the guard hesitated. Then he lunged at Tahr.

The *yeh-teh* hit him, out of nowhere. Whether she'd been crouched in the shadows nearby, or whether she'd already reached the shelter of the forest, then turned back, crossing the ground in long leaps faster than his eye could see, Tahr never knew. But there was a crunch above him as two bodies met in midair, and a clash as both the *kukri* and the knife went spinning out of their hands. The man fell backward, winded, and lay still.

That was lucky for him. The *yeh-teh* crouched above him for a moment, watching for a movement. Her fingers flexed, ready for the coup de grâce that cracks a wild deer's neck.

Then there were voices shouting, flashlights flickered, and she wheeled to Tahr. For the first time, he felt the strength of those big hands as she yanked him to his feet and dragged him, stumbling, over the last stretch of clearing and into the trees.

There was a ringing shudder in the air, and a shot thumped into the tree trunk just above Tahr's head. The *yeh-teh* did not slow. She was ducking and wriggling through the blackness of the bushes, yanking Tahr behind her, scratched and battered, as he tried to find his feet. He was slowing her down—without him, she could have melted through the undergrowth, very much as he'd told Franklin that the *yeh-teh* could. With him in tow, she was a slow and clumsy target. But she wouldn't let go.

Then, even in the dark, he felt the rocks loom up in their way. They were cornered. In all his plotting, he hadn't thought beyond this: If they could make it out of the tent . . . if they could get clear of the campsite . . . what then? He hadn't stopped to think out the lie of the land—the fact that Shikarri, like an experienced guide, had picked a site so sheltered, tucked well in its cleft, that prying helicopters could fly overhead and miss them. Yes, the ground rose steep and rocky on two sides at least, and now they'd run into a trap—with the rock wall in front of them and the voices catching up behind. There was Shikarri's cry, that sharp *Hup-ho!* that he made to the dog, meaning, "Go, fetch, bring it down." . . . The dog! It would be coming, faster than a *yeh-teh* through the forest, with its teeth bared in that awful silent snarl.

But Tahr had forgotten what he'd seen by the pool that first evening. The *yeh-teh* had arms as strong as legs, feet as agile as hands. The moment she touched rock, it was like an otter touching water: in its element at last. She was climbing, effortlessly, fast . . . but didn't let him go. Releasing his wrist, she caught up a fold of his robe, so his hands would be free, and hoisted him a little—not so hard as to make him lose his balance, but helping him, guiding him up. He gained a little height, a little more. . . . All he could do was trust her—trust her, trust his hands to find the holds he couldn't see. Below, he heard the mastiff break through the undergrowth, scrabbling and dancing at the rock face. There was no way except up. Tahr climbed.

Tahr: mountain sheep. That was Shengo's name for him, back in the days when he scrambled for the joy of it, on the rocks above their hut. Had Shengo known, even then, that his *tahr* would have to scramble one day for his life?

Tahr could feel they were high now, and a starry sky leaned in above the upper branches of the trees. Looking down, he saw the flashlight beams picking out the rock face. Any moment now, the lights would come flickering upward and catch them exposed.

And then the strong hand hauled him up and over. They were on a ledge, a crack that opened inward, just wide enough to wedge their bodies in. With backs to one wall, hands and feet against the other, they could squirm up . . . as the flashlight beams skittered past them, fixing on nothing, then panning away to search another outcrop. The *yeh-teh* saw this, too, because her big hand rested on Tahr's shoulder, and he felt the feeling surge between them. *Thankfulness . . . Relief . . .* They had made it. They were free.

But it was too soon to relax, and for a while now the climb was terrifying. As the numbness of fight-and-flight left him, Tahr began to take in where he was. How high was he, how far the drop below? It was worse not to know, with the darkness, and for a second he thought his head was going to start spinning with vertigo. But there was Shengo's voice, very small in the back of his brain, saying: *See? I told you: It is only thinking that makes us afraid.* And as Tahr smiled, the fear ebbed, and he edged on up behind the *yeh-teh*, till the crack opened out and they could slip right through, between two blocks of outcrop, and crawl out on hands and knees on solid ground again.

They didn't stop, not while the dog might be near, but

stumbled on and felt their way, deeper in, higher up, till not the faintest sound or flicker reached them through the forest night. After a while, a small moon came up over the ridge, and Tahr saw they were in thinner forest, with tall slender pines among the oaks. They moved faster.

The *yeh-teh* did not slow or look back, except to check that he was there, until they reached a small stream. To Tahr it felt chill, but she shuddered and splashed like a dog. Then she crouched down and, gathering handfuls of water, washed herself all over, dipping and squeezing the rough wool of her clothing. On her face was pure pleasure, as the filth and the shame of her captivity were sluiced away.

Hours later, they found a cleft between two boulders and squeezed inside it, ripping a blanket of thick moss from the stone and wadding it around them, glad of each other's warmth as the sweat cooled on their skin and exhaustion set in. The whole night wrapped itself around them, and the thought swept over Tahr: The last time he'd slept in the open, it was with an old wise man, his master. Now it was with a being that wasn't quite human or quite animal—or maybe she was both.

And so the Wheel turns, he thought, wondering, as he tipped into sleep.

15

Survivors

The light touched the top of the mist first—nearly pink, like ripe apricots. It spread down through the cloud that lay among the higher forests, so first the air was milky, then the colors came. The world began to appear, like a photograph developing: the bare trunk of a fir tree, broken stumps of lower branches, then the mass of twigs and green. The birdsong started. Overhead, the cloud became too bright to look at. Suddenly, there was pure sky, and huge distances. The forest fell deep into shadow beneath them, and above . . . a jagged rim of apricot-orange-pink, like a flame. The sun had touched the peaks, with their icefalls and rockfalls and undisturbed snow.

In his dream Tahr was thirsty, stumbling through the woods with the panting of the voiceless mastiff somewhere near. He must find water—not just for himself. He had to fill old Shengo's water bottle for him. He felt at his waist, and then he cried out, because it was gone. What was the good of water, if he'd lost the special flask, the "H.M. Property"?

He opened his eyes. Where was he? There were rocks

around him, a cushion of moss for his cheek. Aching limbs. Grit and dampness, and beside him was . . . a space. Where was Shengo? *No, no,* he reminded himself: *Not Shengo.* It came back: last night, the climbing, the chase. Tahr shuddered. The dog was no dream. And the *yeh-teh*? He looked beside him. The *yeh-teh* was gone.

Oh . . . , he thought, but it was sadness, not surprise. Why should she stay, now that she was free? She was back in the place that must be home to her. She had thanked him, in her way, by coming back to save him, with the dog's teeth at their heels. He thought of her back in the supply tent, tethered like that mastiff, treated worse than it was, and he was glad of what he'd done. Maybe he'd even undone the harm he'd caused already, or some of it. At least he wouldn't be forced to be her keeper, gaining her trust just to betray her to . . . whatever Franklin planned to do. That was terrible *karma* he'd escaped from. But the main thing was: She was free.

He was free, too, but it wasn't the same. This wasn't his home. Even the campsite, with its strange talk and its queasy smells, was out of reach now. Surely he couldn't be *missing* it? The thought of Shikarri's face, and the dog, was enough to cure that. But still . . . For days Tahr's waking hours had been filled with Paris—Paris talking, Paris interrupting, Paris being . . . Paris. It felt sort of empty now that she wasn't here.

Tahr got to his feet just as the cloud around him parted and the mountains spread out their arms. They were the same he'd seen with Shengo, after all. They held the valleys, and everything in them. All the scared and hunted creatures . . . white people like gods who fed on strange things and were driven by strange hungers . . . the hunter and his dog who were like two faces of a single being . . . the smoke of burning villages, the faint sound of the helicopter with its insect menace . . . and him, one lost boy, the smallest thing of all. The mountains gathered all this in their arms, and held it for a moment, burning with their cold pink light. And then the sunlight shifted, and the peaks were simple white against blue sky. *Now you fend for yourselves,* the mountains seemed to say, and turned their faces away.

There was a long low note—almost like singing, but not birdsong—and Tahr spun round, looking up and down. Perched on a boulder uphill from him was the *yeh-teh*. Without thinking, he waved, then put his hands together in a solemn bow.

Did she smile? Hard to say, when the light was behind her, but she beckoned, in just the same way that any person would, pale-skinned or normal, child or grownup. *Hey, look, come and see!*

Now she was moving up the slope in front of him, almost like a game of chase. She was at home on steep slopes, built for scrambling, using hands and feet. It was standing upright on the level that was strange to her. If this was a game, she could lose him in minutes . . . but she stopped and waited. As he scrambled up toward her, he could see her head cocked, listening, and he heard the whisper drip of water. Soon they were crouching by a trickle flowing from a crack. She cupped her hands and, efficiently, drank. Then she filled them again and held them out toward him. As he bent toward them, she gave a flick and the cool water splashed his head, his face, his hair. "Hey!" Tahr cried, and she gave a gentle whoop of something not quite like a person's laughter. As he blinked, she splashed some on her own head, and blinked hugely, too. She was watching him, and as he got the joke and smiled, her own mouth widened in an easy grin. Then they both hunkered down and drank together.

Once the thirst of his dream had gone, Tahr looked up. On the stone between them, she was arranging little things—some roots, some groundnuts, and a clump of berries. "It's not much," her hands and face said. "But it's something," his said. "Thanks." The first rays of the sun warmed them as they ate.

What is she? Tahr thought, glancing at this creature dressed in rough wool like the poorest peasant girl. *What or who?* She was crouched in that half-sitting way she had. At the slightest alarm, he guessed, she could be up and running, before he had even found his feet.

What she was now, though, was *eating*. Every inch of her was doing it . . . not like the stiff, strange people at the camp. They couldn't eat a mouthful without talk—as if it was words they were eating, not the food itself. She ate more like an animal. But Shengo would have approved. "When you walk, walk. When you eat, eat," he used to say. Most of Shengo's lessons—meditation, sitting, breathing—had been about doing one thing at a time. "For animals, it's easy," the old man had said. "We have to *learn* to do it." Wherever she came on the Wheel of Life, the *yeh-teh* didn't need to be taught.

She felt him looking at her, smiled an instant, then went on. *How could this be so natural?* Tahr thought, as if people ate with Mountain Spirits every day. With his new companion, there was no wondering what she really meant—every look and gesture said it, clearer than words. She made Tahr think of a dance troupe he'd seen in the village, acting out stories with their hands, their feet, an angle of the man's head, a flash of the woman's dark eyes. . . .

The *yeh-teh*'s eyes . . . Tahr didn't want to look in them right now. He still couldn't say what it was that had passed between them in the supply tent. Had he really thought *her* thought and felt what *she* was feeling? Was that how they talked to each other, the *yeh-teh,* instead of speaking words out loud? He hoped not. It was too much, and it had left him shaken. Now, the *yeh-teh* seemed to feel the same, because their eyes made contact only fleetingly, in passing. For most of the time just a nod or a touch of the hand said everything they needed to.

What was she . . . and who? It seemed strange to him not to have a name for her, or tell her his. "Tahr," he said out loud when she looked up from the last few berries. "Me . . ." He pointed to himself. "Tahr."

She looked at him, head on one side, puzzled. He opened his mouth and bunched his fingers on his lips . . . then spread them out toward her, as if he was passing the sound over. "Tahr." His fingers came so close to her lips that he could feel her warm breath. "Tahr . . . ," he mouthed again, and drew them back to him.

Once a woman had brought a small boy to the hut, and while she was with Shengo, Tahr had tried to keep the child occupied—making faces, playing finger games. When he ran out of those, he tried to teach him to curl his tongue . . . and learned for the first time that some people simply *couldn't*. Oh, but the look on his face as he tried . . . That was how the *yeh-teh* looked now. She knew what he wanted, but she *couldn't*.

What if they didn't have names? The thought made Tahr's head spin. What *was* a "name," anyway? How come that sound—*t-ah-r*—was him?

Tahr leaned forward, taking her hands. "Tahr . . ." He tried to *see* the wild sheep he'd been named for, high up on the rocks, casually grazing on their ledges. It wasn't enough. He mimed it: "up in the rocks," he gestured . . . "climbing" . . . "four feet" . . . "horns like this" . . .

She grinned uneasily. Looked up, around them. Looked back puzzled when she saw no sheep. *No,* Tahr shook his head, thinking sheep again, and pointing to himself. She grinned, and shook her head. *Yes,* he nodded. Then the *yeh-teh* laughed, and clapped, and pointed at him.

So a name was a joke, was it? Okay, why not? Tahr grinned back, then pointed back to her.

The grin dropped from her face so suddenly that he wondered if he'd hurt her feelings. Did she think he was laughing at her? No, she was thinking. Her eyes narrowed, her brow creased; he'd lost her for a moment . . . then the small fire in the cave of her eyes was flickering again. Tahr saw something he couldn't make out—an abstract shape of white and gray— and as if she saw his trouble with it, she was miming, almost molding something out of air. Something to do with "high," with "climbing" . . . then a narrow place, something narrowing in . . . and something hiding deep down in it, something cold to touch . . .

Snow. He'd had the picture in his mind but hadn't grasped it. Now he knew what he'd seen. It was one of those small deep gullies you sometimes found in the rocks, so high up and so much in shadow that it could hide a tongue of last year's snow—gray, gritty, and pockmarked, dripping slightly round the edges. Only when you touched it did you realize that it was a tiny bit of winter—not just last year's but maybe years and years before—maybe all the winters, right back to the times when snows had covered half the world. *Geng-sun,* that was what Shengo called it. *Snow-surviving.*

And what had the white people said about the *yeh-teh*— that they might be a few, a very few, of an ancient tribe— survivors from the Age of Ice?

Geng-sun. Tahr couldn't quite hold the picture in his mind. It was the melting he saw—melting yet surviving, surviving yet steadily melting—and he wondered if that was how the whole world looked to Geng-sun: not so much *things* as things *happening.* No wonder names were a problem. *Geng-sun.* She might not need the word, but as he formed it in his mind, he saw the melting-surviving more clearly, he felt its toughness . . . and its sadness, too. He pointed to her and said the word aloud.

He thought that she might laugh, the way she'd laughed at his name. No . . . Instead, a wave of sadness rose up through her, through her gaze and into him. It was so big that Tahr thought he'd have to look away. Then Geng-sun stood up, beckoned, and was scrambling—climbing so fast it was more like running—up the rock outcrop above them.

Tahr climbed as fast as he could. What did she want to show

him? She was already up there, where a spire of rock poked out above the trees. She was looking away as he reached her, but the way she sat still had that sadness in it. Tahr came up behind her, keeping back from the drop that swayed at her feet each time the wind moved in the trees.

The slopes fell deep and steep beneath them, swallowing themselves in folds of green—swallowing, too, all traces of the humans in them. Tahr could see no hint of where the hunters' camp must be. For a moment, this creature beside him could have been any of the ancient Ice-Time people, surveying a world that still belonged to them.

But Geng-sun was not ancient. She was here and now, and though Tahr did not know how years were counted with her kind, he knew she was young, maybe as young as he.

He saw that she'd tied her hair back, parting it in three strands, clumsily, and plaiting it. It was coming undone at the ends. He thought of the women and girls he'd seen in the village, sitting with each other, chatting, or just sitting, while the mothers plaited their little girls' hair. Did *yeh-teh* mothers do that for their young? With that thought, he felt the sadness of that dream, if it had been a dream—her mother's eyes on her, thinking, *Precious . . . Only-one . . .*

Tahr reached out his hand and laid it gently on her shoulder, willing it to mean, *You're not alone.*

With a speed that surprised him, she caught his hand, pulling him forward, right to the edge of the drop. As she stretched out his arm, it pulled them close together, till he must be seeing just what she saw.

One way, she pointed. There, the valley opened out a little, getting broader, flatter, till it turned between two hillsides and was lost to sight. No far view of the plains beyond, but Tahr knew that was where it was going—out into the wide world. There was a tension in her hand, an urgency. "Look," it said, "closer." Gradually, his eyes picked out small signs—a clearing in the valley bottom, or a patch scorched brown, or a straight line where a broad trail or a road had been cut through. She glanced at him. "You," the look said. "Your kind." He found himself scanning up the valley for the slightest traces. How far up had people got? How near were the villages they'd seen burning, and where had the rebels gone to hide? How close had the helicopter come so far, and how much closer would it come? Every question was a little stab of fear.

His kind . . . Tahr saw it, for a moment, as she saw it—like a dark stain spreading up the valley, into the safe places. He saw it like some kind of blight, some disease. Where it touched even once, the world was not safe. Trees would fall, there would be poison in the water, and there would be other dangers, harms that happened out of nowhere, but they hit you, made you cry out, made you hurt and die. Tahr saw the *yehteh* mother falling, wounded, that night by the waterfall.

Where was she now? Was she alive? Shikarri had scoured the place that evening and reported back: a little blood, no creature. Yet she hadn't come, had she, to save her daughter? He felt how Geng-sun must have looked and listened, reaching out with all her senses, even ones he barely understood. She could not find her mother.

Now her eyes and his met, and he knew that her mother was in her mind, too. Releasing his hand, she pointed, sharp and urgent, up the valley. They must go. Must go and find her mother. Must go *now*.

Tahr couldn't help it. He couldn't control what she saw in his eyes. *No!* all his feelings shouted. Not that way. That way was the campsite, the silent gray dog, the people, the guns. Even the thought that Paris was among them was no comfort. It felt worse, because that was over. Snatched away. She had been something like a friend—though who could tell what "friend" meant to those people? She had wanted him there . . . maybe just as a plaything, he thought with a pang. But she had needed him, too, a little.

Before that thought could make him sadder, Tahr brushed it away. Geng-sun needed him more. Tahr wished he could have said thank you to Paris, but there was no way now, and that must be the end of it.

And now Geng-sun wanted them to go back that way! How could they go to the waterfall, back to the *yeh-tehs'* place, when the hunters knew about it? They might even be there, watching, waiting for them, now.

Yes, it showed in his eyes. She saw it. Angrily, she turned her head away. For the first time, Tahr knew what it felt like when that contact, eye to eye and heart to heart, was snapped off roughly, like frayed string. It hurt. He was stung, bereft, and lonely . . . as lonely as she.

She had lost her mother. At that thought, something twinged inside him, too. Any time Tahr had asked Shengo about his mother, the old man would say, "I don't know who she was. She must have loved you. She sent you to me."

Shyly, Tahr put out his hand and touched the *yeh-teh's*

shoulder. She did not turn, at first, till he shook her, very gently. She turned sharply. Then he nodded: "Yes."

She studied him: "Do you mean that?"

Yes. She smiled as he pointed: "That way . . . we'll go . . . you and I."

16

Idées Fixes

Paris was waiting for the storm to break. She'd behaved like a panicky, stupid brat—that's what they would be saying. They'd be saying Franklin should have never brought her. Gavin had said it already, with some force, in the middle of last night.

That was okay. It felt bad, but it was okay. She'd done the right thing for once in her life.

It was a pity that Tahr couldn't be there to tell her so. She would give a lot to hear him say it right now.

No one could blame her for anything definite, could they? (*Could* they?) Yes, she was the one who'd made friends with the monk-boy, she was the one who'd insisted they keep him—and now look what had happened. There had been a moment last night when she'd thought they were going to sit down and hold a postmortem there and then, with Shikarri's dog still panting in the background, its blood-lust up. But Franklin had been strangely cool. "Enough," he'd said. "Let's get some sleep. We'll talk it through in the morning."

That scared her worse than Gavin's sneering. Worse than

Shikarri's implacable "I told you so." (Hadn't he told them at the start that the boy was a spy?) This was like the classic school principal's trick: "I'll see you in my office . . . later." But it was worse, because this was Uncle Franklin. She had never seen him so icily controlled before.

If she could just tell Tahr all this, he'd help her. Every time she told him things about herself, they seemed to make more sense. In his odd way—the way he listened, and sometimes lit up in a little smile—he was good for her. But Tahr was somewhere out there in the forest, with the yeti. Or maybe not by now. The yeti was a wild thing and she'd probably run off back into the mountains, and Tahr was just a boy, after all. The thought of him abandoned in the forest, on his own, gave her a twinge inside. She wanted to comfort him, the way she'd done the other night.

Or to put it another way: She missed him.

There were voices in Franklin's tent, arguing. She had heard them first thing when she woke. She hadn't been invited. They would be arguing about her. Paris knew it. In her experience, people always did.

They couldn't prove anything, though. The false alarm last night . . . It wasn't just her. Other people had been shooting at the shadows, too. And it wasn't her fault about Tahr. Hadn't Uncle Franklin agreed—no, *ordered* him to take care of the yeti? Right—so she was in the clear, wasn't she?

It didn't feel like that. What was Uncle Franklin going to say?

Someone rattled the flap of her tent. But it was only Renaud. These days there was a hunted look about him—scuttling from tent to tent, always looking sideways at the forest, as if it was going to pounce. And wasn't it *his* knife Tahr had stolen? Right, then—he was implicated, too. Paris made a mental note to remind the others, if she needed to.

Renaud crouched at the entrance, glancing out from time to time. "I do not understand," he said in a hushed voice. "What does he *want?*"

"Who?"

"Your uncle—Monsieur Franklin. Pardon me for saying, but . . . he is a man obsessed. He has an *idée fixe*—one thing he wants that he cannot make himself let go of. But I do not know just *what.*"

"What do any of them want? They're all pretty weird."

"*I* know what *I* want." He talked fast, not looking at her. "Only this—to be a big name in my business. Make big money. Serve big people—special people, maybe special tastes. So simple. Really, I am just your normal guy." He gazed balefully out across the clearing. "That Gavin, now . . . he is not normal. Hates these mountains, all because they took his fingers. I tell you, if he could kill these mountains, he would. And that Harriet . . ."

"Gavin wants to kill her?"

"No. Or maybe yes. I mean, she too has just one *idée.* Hates people, all of *Homo sapiens.* She has seen too much of the bad. That is why she is soft on your caveman-creature. She says, 'Okay, let her go.'"

"'Let her go?' She *has* gone," Paris said. "Remember?"

"You tell that to your crazy uncle. He will not accept it. He swears he will fetch them back. . . . Whatever." Renaud glanced outside. "Look. You can tell him *now.*"

"Wait," Paris said, but the chef was gone already. There was Uncle Franklin, coming over with that quick, sure stride of his. She flinched. That dreamlike thought of him right after she had been with the *yeh-teh* . . . Maybe he had always scared her slightly, but it had felt like a thrill before, not a fear. Right now, Paris wasn't so sure.

Outside her tent, he stopped. He didn't squat down, like Renaud. He didn't speak. He waited.

"Hi . . . ," said Paris bravely. He didn't reply, until she started crawling out on hands and knees.

"I suppose," he said, as she came awkwardly to knee height, "I suppose you think that was a good scene for the movie, last night."

Paris flushed. She hadn't thought about the movie thing for days. It sounded childish now—the way it must have always done to Franklin.

"I suppose," he said again, "you wonder why I'm not angry."

"Aren't you?"

Uncle Franklin's coolness relaxed into an even cooler smile. "Oh, you'd know if I was, believe me! No, what happened last night was . . . was just what I had in mind, actually. If your little friend had not released the creature so . . . theatrically, I'd have sent her on her way myself in the morning."

"You?" Paris struggled to her feet. She sounded dumb, she knew it. She could see it in his face.

"I was almost disappointed that the monk-boy proved to be so wrong. About the avenging hordes of yeti, I mean. Though in hindsight, of course, he was lying." Franklin paused. "Having *one,* you see, is neither here nor there. It's knowing whether that one is the *last* one—that's what interests the *connoisseur*. . . . We let her go, she leads us to the other." He glanced at her wryly, relishing her startlement. "Shikarri is of one mind with me, even if the others aren't. Though it's less the creature that interests him than the boy. Shikarri's right, of course: He knows too much to be allowed to go."

"No . . ."

"You'll come, of course," Franklin went on, as if he hadn't heard her. "Oh, you will. Just to make sure there's no mis-understanding about your little error of judgment last night."

"Anyway," said Paris, "they could be anywhere by now."

"Oh, the dog will find them. Particularly as they've left us this." He held up the cape of red fur. "Really, it's almost as if she *wanted* me to find them."

"Uncle Franklin, I—I'm not sure—"

"Stop!" he cut in. "Not another word. This is only weakness. You'll be ashamed of it later." Franklin's hand came down and rested on her shoulder, like an honor being conferred. "Paris," he said, "we are friends. The same species, remember? But there's more than that. We're family."

"Family?" Paris looked at him. This didn't sound like Uncle Franklin.

"Not in the ordinary sense. You know that doesn't interest me. But there is something . . . something very basic. Every-body needs to have someone to pass things on to. The knowl-edge. The life's work . . ." He paused, still holding her at arm's length, as if to look her over one more time. "It has to be you. No"—she'd taken a breath—"you can try to deny it, but I've watched you. I know you better than you know yourself.

You've got what it takes to appreciate what's happening here—to see just how *exquisite* it might be. Think of how many other people—scientists, explorers, stupid peasants—this has been denied to. Almost as if . . ." There was a light in his eyes for a moment, as if he was looking at some vision just behind her. "Almost as if they were *saving* themselves, the last Neanderthals, for you and me."

The *yeh-teh* was trying to hunt. But, it dawned on Tahr slowly, she didn't know how to . . . or not on her own. After all, she was a young one, probably as young as he was, in her way. She kept looking round, as if *he* should know something about it, or maybe in a vain hope that her mother might appear. As each hunted thing got away, she looked more frustrated and downhearted, and he didn't know what to do for her.

She was doing well, considering. She could sense the slightest movement in the underbrush, and often she stopped dead, with her nose raised, combing through the airwaves for the slightest hint of game. Once she was on the trail, she could creep right up behind a shy small muntjac deer, skulking in the undergrowth, and it would never even twitch its ears till she was in spear-throwing distance. And that was where it all fell down. She had no spear, though she tried her best to find a long stick—tried even to split it and to wedge a sharp stone in the end. But it was no good. No, her people weren't animals—they had tools, they worked in groups, had *tactics*. . . . She had the instincts, but her kind weren't meant to get by on their own.

She spent half an hour, with excruciating patience, trying to make a slingshot from her yak-hair belt. It wasn't wide enough, and the stones she could find on these slopes weren't smooth enough to fly. She gave up with a throaty groan and threw the things down. Tahr reached out to touch her hand but didn't want to meet the bleakness in her eyes.

They were on their way downhill now, and neither of them felt easy about it. They had to give the hunters' camp a wide berth, and at first they'd done the natural thing and climbed—away from the valley bottom where he'd seen the human presence spreading like a stain. After a while, though, the ground grew steeper. Sheer slippery slabs of cliff began to block their way, and in the gaps between were screes, where the slightest wrong step sent stones clattering. The sound seemed to hang in the air above the valley, like a flag waved to Shikarri and the hunters. As they moved out into the open, Geng-sun kept scanning downhill. Tahr tried to tell her, as far as he could in gestures, about binoculars and guns with telescopic sights.

They turned back and headed down. This was weary business, picking their way back down the ground they'd spent two hours climbing, recognizing trees and glades they'd seen before. As they got near the place where they'd slept, Geng-sun was all on edge, stopping, listening. Once Tahr caught her eye in passing and he shuddered, with a glimpse of what she must be thinking: the gray brindled mastiff throwing itself at the cliff, drooling and scrabbling after them. Shikarri must have brought it to heel last night, but it had their scent in its nostrils. It would not forget.

There was no cutting back round the hillside that way. They would have to drop down to the valley bottom, then—Geng-sun mimed all this—follow the course of the river up, to where her mother might still be. With every step downhill, though, Geng-sun grew tenser, and Tahr felt it. They were both hungry, and she scratched up what roots and fruits and berries she could find until even Tahr could tell that any more would make him sick. Yet he was no less hungry. It was what the white people, at their complicated meals, called an *hors d'oeuvre*—a little bite to eat that makes you hungrier, ready for the feast to come. Only now there was no feast, and no chance of one, either.

"Come on," gestured Geng-sun, as if she had had an idea. She had given up hunting long since. Now she stopped and sniffed the air. She found a good climbing tree and vanished up it, into the topmost branches, and swayed there, taking in the view. When she came down, Tahr thought that a change had come over her. She moved with a low gait, sidelong and defensive. If she'd been one of his kind, he might even say guilty . . . skulking. But she was off on the trail of some plan now, pulling him behind her, stopping, ducking, peering again and again. When they came to a stream with a flat stretch of mud beside it, she stepped carefully around it, in the bushes, so as not to leave a print. All the time she was urging Tahr on with little scolding gestures: "Quiet . . . careful . . . you'll give us away . . ."

She must have sensed the clearing long before he did. All Tahr could do was try to keep up as she ducked from cover to cover, shade to shade, and at last they squeezed into a rhododendron thicket, parting the dark leaves, and he had his first clear view.

It was a village. Or it had been. There were the stone huts, built low, walling in a low enclosure where goats should run and scrawny chickens scratch, where a mule might be idling in its lean-to and a dog be tethered, yammering and leaping at its leash at a stray scent. . . . But there was no sound. The emptiness felt like something solid, like a statue, standing in the space between. Tahr could tell from the empty window that no hearth was burning in there, no children's faces would peep out, and no old man would be squatting at the door. At the edge of the village, forest plants were taking back a foothold. One more spring, one more monsoon, and they'd be swaggering across the clearing. Five years, and the village would be boulders in the forest that a traveler might chance upon.

Even so, it was a while before Geng-sun stepped into the open. First she sidled round the edges, ducking and peering, till there wasn't an angle that she hadn't seen. Then she ran to the shelter of a doorway, and the next one, and the next. "Follow," she signaled back to Tahr. By the time he caught up with her, she was coming out into the sunlight with some findings.

Dry rice in a bag. No good for now, without a pot to cook it—but Tahr looked at her anew. She had known where to look, the kind of places village people hid provisions. She had a handful of potatoes—wrinkled but not rotten. Best of all, there were some strips of salt meat, and the two of them wolfed them in the doorway, on their feet.

As the food reached his stomach, Tahr's whole body cried out thanks. And yet . . . He looked at Geng-sun, trying to take in this new knowledge. Up in the cloud forest she had been a wild thing. She seemed noble. Now . . . she was a thief. Had the Mountain Spirits, too, been brought to this—scavenging, learning how to skulk and snatch and run?

As if she saw the thought in his eyes, Geng-sun thrust the potatoes into Tahr's hands and turned away.

Then something took Tahr by the throat, and he dropped

the potatoes as it welled up in his chest and lungs. Revulsion. Fear. Somewhere near, very faint, was the smell—the smell of burning that came with the sound of helicopter, and the memory. . . . No, he did not want the memory.

But it was there—beneath the dust, behind the walls, washed through by weeks of monsoon rains—and it would never wash out, anymore than it would wash out of his mind from a village not unlike this, years and years ago.

As Tahr stumbled and gasped, he leaned into the doorway. Inside, unexpected, was a patch of light, coming down from a patch where the roof was torn back, charred around the edges. Yes, the smell of burning . . . On the ground beneath it was a pile of what might have been old sacks, bags of sticks, discarded clothes . . . like the remnants of a bonfire put out by the rain.

Not sacks, not sticks, not rags, but people. Old men and old women, children . . . Or they had been. Had they been herded in here, or were they bodies already, piled in, before the fire was begun?

Tahr turned and bolted, retching. The smell seemed to reach inside his chest, and he was tiny, almost too small for his legs to take him, but he was running as his mother pushed him out into the forest. He was crying, trying to turn and reach her but she was pushing him on. "Run," she called, as a man rushed up and seized her. "Run!" she shouted as the helicopter pounded air. "Run," she was mouthing as she went down. "Don't look back. Just run."

17

Don't Look Back

As the rush in Tahr's head began to clear, he saw the fret-work of leaves above him. He was stretched out on the forest floor. He'd been stumbling, he remembered that—struggling and staggering on until that choking feeling rose and swamped him. Now there were leaves and sky, and a warmth like sunlight spreading through his chest, although he was lying in the shade.

Someone was soothing him, with a firm and gentle touch. His first woozy thought was, *Mother?*. . . then *Shengo?* . . . then *Paris?* All this in a second, till he turned his head toward the figure kneeling over him. The *yeh-teh:* Geng-sun. Her hands were on his rib cage, easing the cramp inside him with slow kneading movements. It was matter-of-fact: she just knew what to do. As he looked in her eyes, the only message he saw was the ordinary human one of puzzlement and concern.

Could she have glimpsed what he'd had in his mind—that horrible flicker-book of memories from long ago? She gave no sign of it. He didn't want to think those thoughts again . . . but

165

simply thinking of them made dreadful pictures start to stir. He shut his eyes and turned his head away.

How had this happened? And what was he doing here, trusting this creature he'd have thought was a story just a week ago? What did he know about her? Did she even have feelings like a human? He knew that she could look at death—that heap of charnel in the village—and show no more reaction than he would to a pile of fallen trees. And yet here she was, caring for him just like one of her own.

Don't upset yourself, her hands and face, no, *all* of her was saying, in that subtle nonstop meaning-dance of hers. She left off the soothing and sat back, making a small crooning, deep back in the throat. It wasn't quite a lullaby, because it wasn't sending him to sleep, but leaving him calm and clear-feeling, like the best of meditations. As the bad thoughts rose in his mind, he could look at them straight, and they grew clearer, too.

Yes, his mother had loved him. Shengo had been right about that. Tahr had always known—his body had that memory inside it—that someone had pushed him away. Pushed him into the forest, where old Shengo found him. But *why* they had pushed him and *where*—away from what . . . all that had been a painful blur, till now.

When finally he sat up, he saw that Geng-sun had found more food—even a little *tsampa,* which he mixed with water. *Yes,* she nodded, *that makes it better to eat.* Then for a while they ate, and let the goodness flow into their bloodstreams.

Then the peace was over, for Geng-sun, at least. When she was at ease, Tahr noticed, those little voice sounds of hers were a running stream—the same, and always changing. Other times, there would be other notes in it, sometimes hard-edged, sometimes sadder. In particular, there was one sound, sweeter and rougher at the same time, which came in when she thought about her mother . . . and it made Tahr want to weep. He recognized it now—her mother song.

She was up on her feet and pacing, agitated. She needed to go. "Yes," he gestured to her. "Let's go on. Let's find . . ." How was he going to say "your mother"? He mimed "large" . . . and "kind" . . . spreading his arms wide, as if rocking. And she answered with one of those all-over looks and gestures. It had a little of the rocking in it, but something muscular, too—and then a sudden weakness, as the muscular went limp. Then her fists clenched: "angry" . . . Yes, she'd understood. Tahr felt like a student who'd managed his first word, stiff and stumbling, in a language where there weren't exactly *words* at all. She looked at him, and gave a brief, practical smile. Then they moved off, with her leading, him following as best he could.

Tahr didn't know which way he'd bolted from the empty village, but she seemed to, and she led them in a wide arc, keeping out of sight of the clearing so he wouldn't have to see. In a while he spotted a bent-down tree he recognized from earlier. Any moment, he would see the stream where they'd skirted the mud. And there it was. But when Tahr came up behind her, Geng-sun had dropped to a crouch, her body rigid and not a sound in her throat, not even breathing. *Danger,* all of her was saying. *Danger . . .*

The tracks went straight across the stream—broad pad prints, scuffed and sloppy where the mud was wettest, melting into water, but just by the edge one was perfectly preserved. As Geng-sun turned, her bared teeth might have been a gesture for the thing itself, though it was probably fear.

Dog . . . Not just any dog—Shikarri's brindled mastiff. And a little farther over in the mud were human bootprints, too.

Now Tahr knew how it was to be a hunted animal. *Run!* said his instincts. *Which way?* said his head. Geng-sun was crouched like a sprinter, with the same question written all over her. Which way had they gone, the hunters? They were surely on the trail, but how close? Why hadn't Geng-sun, with her brilliant hearing, heard the splash of dog through mud? She must have been in one of the houses when it happened, but that was a while ago. Why hadn't they been caught by now?

The woods were very still, and Tahr tried to listen as hard as Geng-sun listened. No sound, no clue. Would they even hear the voiceless mastiff, slipping through the bushes? It could be behind them (which way *was* behind?) right now.

Don't look back . . . Without a word or sign, Geng-sun went dodging through the forest. With his mind on his feet, on the uneven ground, Tahr could scarcely keep her in sight. But then she would halt, still as a tree or boulder, listening. As Tahr caught up, she would hush him—*Quiet!*—and listen again.

Don't think of those big paws pumping, that square heavy muzzle raking the ground for their scent. Don't think of the big white people at its heels, their way of wanting what they wanted, at all costs. Their fingers on their triggers.

Listen!

Every bird in the forest was loud, too loud, and the breeze in the leaves was doing it on purpose, as if even it was in the hunters' pay. Then faintly, beyond all these sounds, Tahr could make out the hush of a river. Geng-sun nodded that way.

"Wading," she mimed. "Cross the river." Of course, if they could do it, wouldn't water wash their scents away?

When they came to an edge, they went slithering down, clutching ferns, grazing themselves on stones, no time to stop and check if it was safe. Tahr reached the ground with a thump and rolled over on a beach of flat gray stones. There was the river, all right—quite shallow at first—then suddenly deep, fast, churning with the force of being funneled through the rocks above.

Geng-sun was wading cautiously out, but before she was knee-deep, she was fighting with the pull of the current. It couldn't be done. Tahr ran to the edge to warn her, but she was already wading back, and just at that moment a splattering rush filled both of them with fear. For a second they just cowered, waiting for the mastiff to come crashing through the shallows.

Instead, with a quacking like cruel laughter, three ducks flapped across the water and took flight downstream.

Tahr and Geng-sun stared at each other. That was one more signpost for the hunters, as sure as calling out, "They went this way." There was no crossing. Downstream was back toward the village. In the woods behind . . . the hunters would be coming. There was no way to go but upstream, though the slopes drew in and steepened to a gorge between rock faces that channeled the rush of water, zigzag, through its bends. In the spring, meltwater must come gushing, filling the gorge up and scouring it bare. Now, the narrowing beach of gray stones was wide enough—just—as far as Tahr could see.

There was no point in wading. All Tahr could think was, *Run, run as fast as you can.* And: *Don't look back.* He ran.

In the open, Geng-sun ran low, as if she could drop on all fours at any time. She was fast, and Tahr began to think that he would lose her when she paused, leaning against the rock to help him by. "Run on!" she gestured, as she held back, casting edgy glances back the way they'd come.

As the rock walls closed in, the rush of water echoed from all sides, filling Tahr's head like his own breathing. Now he had to concentrate: as the gorge took a bend, the water slewed right over to the rock face, and the stone beach narrowed into nothing but a few sloped steppingstones. Tahr looked back, and saw Geng-sun coming after, so he held his breath and jumped. Then he was on good dry beach and running, head down. He glanced back to see if Geng-sun was at the bend yet, and she wasn't, and as he turned forward, two men stepped into his path, from nowhere. He butted into one, and both of them grabbed him roughly, and two or three more of them were there—he was surrounded—and if he shouted, it was not so much in warning as astonishment. And hopelessness. *No,* he thought, *after all this, no, please, no.*

"Where d'you think you're going?"

"Who are you?"

Questions came at Tahr from all sides. Two of them locked his arms behind his back. But the words weren't hunters'

English or Shikarri's tight-lipped language, but in Tahr's own, though with the accent of a different valley.

A short broad man stepped forward, took a bunch of Tahr's robe in his fist, and pulled him close. He had a square, worn face that could be any age, and Tahr could see a little slanting scar across one eyebrow that made him look like someone squinting down a rifle sight. "What's the rush?" the man said.

Tahr looked round. These weren't farmers, though they looked as if they had been in the days before the war came to live in their valley. One, bare to the waist, wore a green flak-jacket, another an army cap with its marking ripped off; one had an ammunition belt strapped round his skinny waist. Even their automatic rifles looked too big, too black, not quite their size.

"I'm—I'm a monk. A novice. From over the mountains. My master . . ."

"His master, huh!" It was a new voice, higher, with a cold bite in it, and Tahr turned to see. "I know his kind. Parasites. We have too many of them." There was something chilling about this one, much worse than a scar. The man who'd spoken so harshly was young, with a smooth, pale face, scarcely a man at all. He couldn't have been more than a few years older than Tahr, with a wisp of moustache on his top lip, but the bitterness in his eyes was ageless. Most shocking of all, his accent was from Tahr's own home.

"At least he's running away," the square man said. "He's not stupid."

"My master . . . was killed," said Tahr.

"Killed?" Now they were listening a bit more closely.

"An accident . . . I was lost." It was hard to know how to go on, or what was best to say. *Don't mention Geng-sun,* Tahr thought, and without thinking he glanced back downstream. She wasn't in sight. Was that good . . . or bad? He didn't know.

The pale young man was watching him closely, and he'd seen the glance. "He's holding out on us," he muttered. "Don't waste our time, little boy. Who's after you?"

The sound of the river seemed to rise and fill his head, until he couldn't think straight. "I was captured," he blurted out. "But I escaped from them."

Tahr paused. He hoped this was enough, but he knew it wouldn't be. He couldn't stop now. "Foreigners," he said.

Now the air was quivering. The rebels were very close around him, four or five of them, but he felt others coming up behind. They were looking at him in a new way. "Foreigners? What kind of foreigners?" the older man said slowly.

"Several kinds. English . . . Americans . . ."

"Americans!" Someone clicked his rifle like an exclamation mark. "He has been with Americans!"

"They caught me," Tahr said.

"You were working for them," said another. "You were their scout! Their spy!"

"No! I'm running away. They're chasing me, with guns!"

There was a stirring among them. Everybody's eyes glanced back the way he'd come . . . all but Square-face. "Talk. Fast," he said, though his voice was very slow now. "What are these Americans? Special forces? The U.S. Marines?" Tahr shook his head. The man slapped him, hard. "Don't play dumb."

"They're hunters," Tahr said.

"Hunters!" It was almost a laugh. "What kind of fool comes hunting in a war zone?"

Then there were three or four voices, all raised together.

"No one gets in—not without permission."

"They're special forces all right, whatever this kid thinks."

"Thinks? He *knows* things." This was the pale one speaking. "Let me get it out of him."

"Not now." The square one stepped in, suddenly the leader. "Darwa . . . VJ . . . Take him to the cave. Leave him for comrade Gurung to look after."

"Why not me?" It was the young one. Darwa. Hearing a name from home gave Tahr a twinge. "I could 'look after him' better," Darwa said in a low voice. "I could get some answers."

"Later. If we have American visitors—well, we want our hardest fighters here."

Darwa nodded, satisfied for now. The leader pushed Tahr backward, and many arms grabbed him, binding his hands with harsh rope. Another length was knotted in a noose and jerked, like a halter, round his neck.

"Walk," said the man behind him. "You've been lucky so far. Just don't push your luck." And as the rebels melted into their positions in among the rocks, Darwa led Tahr upstream, along the narrow gray beach. In a while, the river slewed around another bend, and the sound of rushing water closed in round them. Once Tahr tried to look back. Darwa gave the rope a nasty jerk.

"Okay," said the other one, stopping without warning. "I hope you know how to climb, you monk-boy. Yes? You'd better!" and as the man chuckled, Tahr followed his look up . . .

up the cliff beside them. Unnervingly far up, a gnarled tree had found a foothold in the rock face, leaning out, its roots curved out beneath like clutching fingers. Balanced on the lowest of these, another rebel's face looked down. A moment later, he threw out a tangle of something, which hung in the air a moment, then, with a series of twists and jerks unfolded, unfurled, and with a final clatter lay flat against the rock face, all the way down. It was a ladder—two tightly twisted ropes of bamboo fiber, and the makeshift wooden rungs between.

"Now we climb."

"My hands . . ."

The rebels looked at each other. Darwa nodded. "Sure," he said. "Just remember, I'll be up above with *this*." He gave a tug on the noose. "You try anything, you know what happens."

"What if I slip?" Tahr said faintly.

"Ha!" The other one gave his short sharp laugh. "You'll be careful. I just know you will."

18

A Cage of Roots

Back in the village below Shengo's hut, the children would catch birds in the places where the trees still clung to the hillside. They would make little stick cages for them, but the small bright finches were not there as pets. They were a tasty snack or, better, worth a few coins from a passing grownup stranger. Once Shengo had bought one, because Tahr had liked it, and on the steep track back up to the *gompa* they had set it free.

If only Shengo could be here to do the same for him. The bars of Tahr's cage were the roots of the tree, which half hid the gap that they seemed to have opened between the rock ledge and the overhang, and which centuries of seeping water had hollowed to a cave.

Behind his back, Tahr felt another root, as rough and cold and damp as stone. He was tied to it, trussed up the way Geng-sun had been in the supply tent. "So the Wheel turns," Shengo would have said.

They'd left his mouth free—that was one thing. He could shout his throat raw, for all the good that would do. Who was out there to rescue him, anyway? Franklin and Shikarri? If there was a choice, he would rather be here.

Gurung didn't look like a cruel man, and there wasn't that cold edge of anger in his voice, as there was in Darwa's, when he spoke. Still, he wore a rifle like the rest, and Darwa had left him with a warning: "Don't feel sorry for him. I know all about his kind. Don't believe a word he says." Gurung was in charge of supplies, the one they could spare to stand guard when a fight was in the offing, and Tahr could see why. He had the face and the wind-tousled hair of a shepherd, and perched in the tree roots, he was always aware of Tahr—looking out and down, listening, sometimes glancing in at Tahr to make sure. Once a crow called, suddenly, from very near, and Gurung's trigger finger tensed for action. Then he relaxed and turned to Tahr with a peeved, embarrassed grin.

"Damned crows," he said. "Voices just like Americans."

"Do you . . . fight Americans?" Tahr said cautiously. Gurung's rifle had swung round, dangling on its strap, and it pointed somewhere vaguely near Tahr's head.

"We will if they come here," Gurung said, and meant it. "The government *loves* Americans. They show them on their TV every day."

"You've got TV?" Tahr glanced around him. "What—here?"

"No, idiot!" Gurung laughed. Then his face darkened. "We took out a police post last year. You know what? The men were in there with their boots up on the table, watching Jay Ree Springa!" He paused, waiting for some reaction. Tahr couldn't guess what it was.

"A program all about stupid people," Gurung went on. "Shouting, laughing, crying! All of it was stupid."

"You watched it? With the policemen?"

"Sure. Right after we had put some bullets in their heads."

There was an awkward silence. For a moment, Gurung's face had been a bowl of smiles; then it was suddenly tense, as if he had remembered Darwa's warning. He glanced out of the cave mouth, down into the gorge, and his knuckles on the rifle grip were tight and pale.

"I saw the village," Tahr said softly. "I was frightened. Did the people you are fighting do that? With the helicopter?"

"Huh!" Gurung's face was hard now. "Which village? There have been so many. All of us here, we come from one village or other. Different place, same story."

"Me, too," Tahr said it quietly, not even sure if he had meant Gurung to hear. But the man leaned forward.

"And your family?" The look on Tahr's face seemed to answer him. "I see." Gurung brandished his rifle. "You can join us. We will give you one of these!" Then he hesitated. "If you are telling the truth, that is. The comrades will decide." But he couldn't quite leave it at that. "You'll join us, won't you, if they say so?"

"I—I am Buddhist," Tahr said. "We are not allowed to kill."

"Hah! You'd better ask Darwa. He'll put you straight about that. He's the best shot we've got, young Darwa. Straight between the eyes—*zap!*" Gurung paused. "His family was Buddhist—and much good it did them when the helicopters came."

Suddenly, he whipped round, back on guard. Very faintly, over the sound of the river, there came a crackling sound like hot fat on a fire. Gurung was crouched in his lookout in the tree roots, with his rifle cocked. Echoing from rock face to rock face up the gorge, one shot became a dozen. For a minute, there seemed to be hundreds. Then, as suddenly as they'd begun, they stopped.

"What's happening?" Tahr said.

"Shut up. I should have been watching, not talking." Gurung's voice was harsh with uncertainty. "You made me do it on purpose, didn't you? Like Darwa said."

"No! I—"

"Shut up!" Tahr heard him stop in midbreath, and he raised the rifle, squinting down the sights. Tahr could see his body trembling with tension. Then, just as abruptly, Gurung breathed again. "They've got one!" He swung round to Tahr, his rifle dangling, clenching a fist in the air. "They've caught an American!" And he was standing on the tree roots, leaning out and waving, before Tahr could speak again.

For Paris, the tracking had been torment. Shikarri went first, at the heels of his terrible dog, with one of his scouts and Franklin close behind, and Gavin bringing up the rear. And Paris, of course. Her uncle had made it clear there wasn't an option. Whatever she'd started, by her carelessness or worse, she was going to be there for the finish. To put it another way, he was going to rub her nose in her mistakes.

There was more to it than that, though. Renaud had been right: Her uncle had a fixed idea, something that obsessed him, and it scared her a little. She'd always known he was driven by thoughts that ordinary, boring people didn't understand. That had always been the thrill of it, something rather grand. Now she wasn't so certain. All she knew was: It was too late to turn back now. And this was what she had wanted, after all.

When Franklin talked her out of school, he'd told the principal that this trip would be an *education*. He'd meant what he said. In his own way, Franklin always did. He'd been setting her tests ever since. She'd passed some and she'd failed some, and this was another. There was something in the way he told her "I've got faith in you" that gave her goose flesh.

The tracking had gone on. And on and on. Being alongside Gavin was a pain. It wasn't just that he disliked her, it was everything about the way he looked and moved. She could almost hear his tensed-up muscles like taut springs, a fighting mechanism just waiting to click into action. From head to toe he was that sort of man, and it made her flesh creep. As his boots came *thud-thud* up behind her, she found herself thinking about Tahr—the way *he* moved. Once she'd asked him what his master taught him, expecting a whole list of textbook things, and he'd said, "To do things—how you say it?" and he made a gesture with his hands that made her think, *Elegant . . . graceful.* "No mess," he'd said. "Simply doing." Suddenly, she understood that, now that he wasn't here. And she thought of her break dancer in the subway, and she thought: *Of course, that was the same thing,* though the two pictures were thousands of miles apart.

She wanted Tahr here. At the same time, part of her mind thought: *Run, Tahr, don't stop, don't look back, just run.*

So the tracking had gone on. The mastiff had picked up the scent soon enough and surged forward, hauling at its leash. They'd lost some time when the trail seemed to split, going uphill and downhill at the same time, but Shikarri was a hunter. Down on hands and knees, he quizzed the ground like a detective, then. . . . That way, he'd said: the downhill trail was fresher. So fresh, in fact, the dog was drooling with anticipation. Any moment, instinct told it, you'll get your teeth in the prey.

That was when Franklin had spoken. "Hold back." Shikarri had frowned. This wasn't his kind of hunting. But Franklin was boss, and Gavin had nodded, as if he saw the sense of it, too. To *catch* them would be only half of it. They could do that any time they liked. But for the prey to lead them back to more prey, to the other *yeh-teh*—that was the point. That was elegant, a very Uncle Franklin sort of plan.

I want it to be over, Paris thought. But "over" meant Shikarri got his hands on Tahr. Or the dog got there first. No, it mustn't be "over." It was just that Paris didn't want it to be "going on." So she bit her lip and let herself be dragged along with the others, as helpless as if the dog was the real master, and the rest of them leashed to it, following its hungry nose.

When they came to the deserted village, the dog went lurching from house to house, as if the trail led everywhere . . . and there was something else, too, stirring it up into a silent frenzy, till Shikarri had to whip it in that practical way of his, as matter-of-factly as driving a car. At the entrance of one of the houses he waved her away, and she was glad Uncle Franklin wasn't looking, or she guessed he would have made her go and see. Part of the education. Whatever was in there, she felt sure she didn't want to know.

She wanted this over—and not over. Wanted to find them,

to see Tahr . . . Wanted not to have them caught. The thoughts hit her in waves. What if Tahr and the *yeh-teh* weren't together? Maybe he was miles away, and safe, by now? And yet . . . the creature was a wild thing. Maybe it had turned on him once it was free?

Paris wanted to know—and wanted not to. She wanted not to be there . . . and she had to be.

An impossible quandary. What was going to solve it for her, even Uncle Franklin did not foresee.

When the first shot cracked out, at the entrance to the gorge, it could have been a stone slip, and the echoes came from everywhere. Just in front of her, Shikarri's scout went down onto his knees quite slowly, as if he was considering whether it was time to say his prayers. Then he keeled over sideways. "Down!" yelled Gavin, throwing himself full length, loosing a rattle of fire at nothing Paris could see. Just beside her was a flood-worn boulder, and she threw herself behind it, hugging her knees, willing herself to be small, small, with a horrid freeze of panic spreading through her veins. This was nothing like hunting. Something whanged off the boulder just above her. Very suddenly, her stomach clenched, and she vomited once, then put her face down and lay very still.

Like a short, sharp thunderstorm, the firing passed. Then there were footsteps, running, crunching on the stones. *Don't look up,* she thought. There was scuffling. Shouts. Then a terrible quietness. *Don't look. Don't look up.*

A voice above her shouted, shrill with adrenaline. Two curt words in no language Paris knew—an order. She opened one eye, just a slit, to see the barrel of an automatic rifle, steady in the air above her. *Play dead,* she thought. The young rebel, thin and pale, with a slight moustache, considered her a moment, then gave her a sharp kick under the ribs. She gasped. He shouted, and another two or three came running over. They stared for a moment at her—her and her puddle of shameful sick—then dragged her to her feet.

There were people lying on the beach—*sunbathing?* she thought in a dreamlike way. *In all their clothes?* Then her brain came into focus, and she recognized Shikarri's scout, lying with his knees still bent up under him and his mouth open, with a dribble of red coming out. Gavin was still full length, and he had made it halfway to cover, wriggling in commando style. His head lay sideways at a weird angle, and from shoulder to waist he wore a line of ripped red, like a sash.

She couldn't see Franklin. Over by the rock face, two men had Shikarri pinned. His rifle arm hung limp at his side, streaked with blood, and the dog lay like a dumped sack at his feet. But Shikarri was alive . . . and talking. One man had an arm crooked round his throat, and each time he jerked it tighter, the guide talked more—talking in a shrill voice, fast and scared.

But she couldn't see Franklin. There in the shallows lay his gun and his pack, and a couple of rebels were poking round it, knee deep. One loosed a round or two into the water, where it deepened and gained speed, but just for the fun of it, and he and his comrade started wading back ashore.

Back by the rock, there was a shout of warning, and she turned to see the heap of brindled fur give a heave and raise its head. A rebel brought his rifle down, butt first, in a blow that should have finished it, but didn't. The beast fell back and lay there whining, whining. *Put it out of its misery, please,* thought Paris, as her gut lurched and the whole beach swayed around her. Then there was only the rush of the river, and the far-off rattle—begging, pleading—of Shikarri's voice, then even that faded, and she passed out with a groan of relief.

Just how they manhandled her up the rock face, Paris wasn't awake to see. Once, she came to in the dark, and knew that she was blindfolded, and there were ropes trussed around her, round and round, cutting into her skin. Worst, there was no ground—she was swaying, pulled and prodded, yawing to and fro in midair, and she retched and slipped away again. The next time she was aware, there was cool, moist rock against her cheek. Her hands were still tied, and there was something rough against her skin. Her clothes . . . They'd stripped her— the thought made her wince—and dressed her up like them. Then she had a worse thought than embarrassment. If a rescue squad should come in shooting, they'd think she was a rebel, too.

The mouth of the cave came into focus, with its bars of tree roots and the dizzy space and drop beyond. And there beside her, leaning back against a tree root, was Tahr. *Tahr!* Shikarri was right: Tahr was one of them! Then she saw that he was tied up, too. "Tahr!" she whispered.

From his lookout in the cave mouth Gurung looked round. So, the girl had woken. . . . But it was Tahr's face he was watching, and the boy's expression did not flicker, not that he could see.

"Tahr, thank God, you're okay . . ." she was saying. "They've killed Gavin—an ambush—and Shikarri, they've taken him somewhere and . . . Tahr? Tahr, what is it? Are you all right?" The rush of words dried up, as her friend looked back without a smile or a greeting. All he did was turn toward the rebel, and for the first time Paris saw him, too.

Gurung said something in his language—quick, suspicious—and Tahr answered him, just as quickly, with a firm shake of his head. The guard spoke again, and this time Tahr nodded, thoughtfully.

He turned to Paris. "He is telling me to say this," Tahr said in a strange, tight, level voice. How could he keep his face so blank, as if he didn't even know her? "Because he knows little English. *He knows a little English.*" His eye caught hers a moment, like a flash of warning, and her heart leaped. It *was* Tahr, the Tahr she knew. And he had not just repeated himself. She got it. The rebel understood some English. "He says I am to say: I am not your people's servant now."

Another question from Gurung, and Tahr's answer, to and fro.

"He says," Tahr went on, "there is no use lying. They now know there was a member of the British SAS among you."

"Gavin? That doesn't mean—"

"Shikarri told them." Tahr went on as if she hadn't spoken. Now his voice went wooden, as if he was reading out a quote. "He has seen the error of his ways and has chosen to side with his own people, against the foreign aggressors." Every now and then Gurung would stop him and ask him to repeat, in his own language, what he'd just said.

"What happened to Uncle Franklin?" Paris burst out.

There was a mutter of translation. "He says the white-hair American abandoned the rest of you and ran away. But they will catch him."

"And . . . what about me?"

She could hear in the guard's voice that his answer was matter-of-fact. "Money," said Tahr. "He says, 'America will pay good money for a young girl. If they care about you.'"

Paris's mouth was dry. "And if not . . . ?"

She wished she had not seen the little gesture Gurung made to this. No words. It said it all. Then he added something.

"He says: When the government patrol finds your companions at the campsite, they will know that we mean what we say."

It took a moment, just a moment, to get what this meant. "Please," Paris said, "tell him: The people at the camp aren't SAS or whatever he's saying. I mean . . . Donald! And Harriet. Sheesh, she probably thinks that the rebels are *right.*"

She wished the man could hear it in her language. Then he'd understand.

"He says: The people in the villages who died—they did no harm, too."

She opened her mouth, but the man slammed his rifle butt hard on the floor. One word. Then two or three more. Tahr turned to her quickly.

"He says: Too many words. Shut up, or he will hurt you." And there was a long pause. Paris was hardly breathing. Something told her that she must not take her eyes off the man's face. If she looked away now, she'd be just a thing to him. A hostage, something with a market value, and if it didn't bring that price, they'd throw it away. While she could keep him looking at her, and could meet his eyes, she would still be a person. But he'd finished with her. Any moment now, he'd look away.

Once in a drama class at school, the teacher had told her that the hardest thing to do well was to cry onstage. That night at home, she'd practiced. It wasn't a thing she'd tried often—she'd never wanted to be *that* sort of girl—but she started now. Just a little at first, so the man wasn't sure, then louder, with just the suspicion of a real wet tear.

"Shut up!" the man said in his own language again. But not so harshly; he wasn't a cruel man. Maybe he had sisters of his own. And there was another reason now why Paris *had* to keep him looking, and she would try anything for it. Even if it made him come and hit her, he must not turn round.

At first, she'd thought the movement at the corner of her vision had been her imagination, but after a moment there it was again. She had to force herself not to look toward it—not to look at Tahr or shout out. She kept up the crying, looking up, pleading, at the man from time to time. He was flustered now, edgy, angry, as men are when women start crying and they don't know what to do. But just behind him, the silhouettes of the tree roots seemed to shift a little, freeze, then move again.

"Tell him I'm sorry. Tell him I confess . . . or anything!" said Paris, and Tahr suddenly got the idea, because he launched into a long speech—much, much longer than just "Sorry."

It was too much. "Shut up!" Gurung shouted, and got to his feet. And that was when the silhouette behind him swung in on its long arms and caught him a kick with a strong leg, right into the back of his neck. He buckled forward, and there

186

she was, over him—Geng-sun, flexing her fingers to lock round his throat.

"No!" It was only a word, but something in Tahr's voice made Geng-sun look up and hesitate. "No. Not a bad man," Tahr was saying, and his hands were working in a swift ballet of gestures. They seemed to get through, because the *yeh-teh* paused, and frowned, and looked at Tahr, then at the man again. He was motionless, and unconscious at the very least. Geng-sun kicked his rifle away, and it spun out over the edge and down toward the stream below.

Tahr and Paris were straining at their ropes now, and Geng-sun danced from one to the other, fiddling, tugging, but the knots had pulled too tight. Geng-sun tried rasping them against an edge of rock—not sharp enough—then another idea jerked her upright, and she scurried back into deeper shadows, where the roof sloped down to meet the floor. She seemed to know where to look, and a minute later she was back beside them, with a small triumphant whoop. In her hand was a sharp stone—no, an ax blade, though the wooden haft must have rotted away. With a frightening, swift *hack-hack* she sliced through Tahr's ropes, then Paris's—a centimeter from her bare wrist, but dead accurate. As the two of them shook their arms free, Geng-sun raised the ax head to the cave mouth, as if showing it the sunlight for the first time in many long years. Then she turned toward them, with a beam of pride and pleasure and a wide sweep of her hand that took in everything: the cave, the ax, herself. "Me," it seemed to be saying. "This belongs to my kind. This is ours!"

19

No Way but Up

Where did you come from?" Tahr hardly knew these days whether he was speaking words out loud, in his own tongue or in English, or in Geng-sun's way with hands, the angle of his head, his eyebrows, eyes, and shoulders.

He must have said it out loud, because Paris answered. "She came down . . . from . . . up there." She had edged to the cave mouth, steadying herself against the tree roots as she looked up. She swallowed. "Oh, geez," she said. Above them, the gray rock leaned out, glistening with wet, hung with fringes of ivy from the overhanging edges. Below them, the river swirled. Paris clutched the tree and closed her eyes. "Oh, geez," she said again.

Geng-sun looked at her mildly, puzzled, then swung past her, leaning out over the drop by one hand, pointing upward as casually as if they'd asked for directions on a city street. "Let's go," her look said.

Tahr was out beside them now. "No, no!" He shook his head, gesturing to Paris, then himself. Even a mountain goat wouldn't contemplate it. Geng-sun didn't seem to grasp the problem till Tahr mimed, "trembling" . . . "frightened" . . . "slipping" . . . "falling." He signed to the rope ladder. "Can't we go down?"

Geng-sun's "No!" had no words, but it came like a shout—a shake of her head, her eyes shut tight a moment, and a sideways chop of the hand. End of argument. There were some more gestures, but she didn't need to spell it out. Down there, somewhere, were the rebels—out of sight now, but they might be back any moment. Once down in the gorge, they would be in a trap. "No." Geng-sun wasn't arguing. She was telling them, with all the instincts of a sometimes hunter, sometimes hunted thing: "We go up."

"It's impossible. Tell her!" Paris whispered. But Geng-sun was answering her already—with a swift look to the coils of the ladder . . . to herself . . . to "up there." Her hands did a knot dance, indicating: "Take the end . . . and tie it . . . safe."

And so that was the plan. There was no other. Geng-sun was in action quickly, rifling through the spare supplies that the rebels had up there. Any scraps of food went in the hide pouch at her belt. All the weapons were gone, though there was ammunition—no use on its own. And there was a rope, the one they'd looped round Tahr's neck. Geng-sun made that small, quick startle movement Tahr had come to recognize as "having an idea." Uncoiling enough for her climb, she tied one end of the rope to the rope ladder, clamped the other in her big strong teeth, and then she was off, up, flowing from tree root to foothold to tiny cracks not big enough to take a finger . . . flowing upward as if her big bones had no weight. She threaded a way between overhangs and crumbling clumps of vegetation with the ease of a snake through grass, and she didn't look back. Tahr did not call after her. He knew that every muscle, every sense of hers was in the climbing, just the way every part of her was running when she ran or eating when she ate. Besides, he had a job of his own to do. He had to sell this plan to Paris.

When the rebels hauled her up into the cave, it had been so hard not to react. But if he had called out, as he wanted, if he'd even smiled, that would have been it for both of them. And yet Tahr's heart was thumping as he struggled to keep his face expressionless.

Had he been *glad* to see her? Yes and no; no and yes. No—because she was hurt and captured. Yes—because he'd heard the gunfire . . . and she wasn't dead. No—because she should be miles away, on the road to some airport, bound for her own world, not mixed up in this.

But in the end, Yes, yes. He was glad. He had tried to tell himself that it was for the best that they would never meet again. Then he'd tried not to think about it. But there was a sort of numb ache where the thought had been.

Paris looked younger now—a girl, not a woman. Hurt and shaken, she wasn't one of the gods. She was a girl a little older than he, from a country where the food they give them makes them grow up big and pale. That sprawling, swaggering ease of hers had gone, and her air of command. She was frightened.

At the first look up the rock, her whole body had gone rigid, and her head was shaking: "No, no, no." Now, as he explained what was going to happen, she relaxed a little—just enough to have a doubt. "Don't you think I'm better off with these guys?"

she said, glancing down at the unconscious Gurung. "I mean, if I'm a hostage, they won't want to . . . lose me, will they? Pop's got money—him and Franklin. . . ." Her voice trailed off, as the ambush played itself out again inside her mind. And she seemed to remember something from a year or two ago, about some hostage on the news. "I know what you're going to say," she said hopelessly.

Tahr looked at her. She was hesitating, and the more she hesitated, the harder it would be. "These men are desperate," he said. "They are angry and afraid. Very bad combination." There was a jerk on the rope, and the ladder started to unfurl itself and clatter up. Paris glanced at it and went pale.

"Your uncle," said Tahr. "We can find him, if he has escaped."

The rope ladder went taut, and after a moment there was a little hissing in the air, and the end of the spare rope snaked back down. Tahr caught it and gave it a firm tug. "There," he said, as if this was a plan they'd already discussed. "We tie this round you . . . so. Then she can hold you if . . ." He stopped. Just the word "fall" might be too much for her.

Easy. All she had to do was . . . trust the *yeh-teh*. With her life.

Tahr had looped the rope around her, more than once, just in case, and three or four extra knots at the end to be sure. "Now," he said gently. "You climb."

"Only if—if you climb, too. If you . . . talk to me."

"Talk?" Tahr said. "About what?"

"Anything. Please!" said Paris. "I just need to know you're there."

Twice she nearly blacked out—she almost wished that she could—and she found herself clamped to the ladder, her arms through the rungs and hugging it with all her strength. Eyes shut, she felt the rung against her cheek and it was all right, it would be all right as long as she could stay right here and never move again. Except her calf muscles were starting to ache and tremble. But when she tried to shift her weight at all, the rope ladder swung away and she froze and clung again.

Tahr was there, as he'd promised—just below her—and his voice came in a steady mutter, one of his chants in Buddhist language. As long as it was his voice, Paris didn't care.

She mustn't look down. She mustn't think about the obvious—that if the rebels came back now, they'd be dangling up there, helpless. Target practice.

"Please," said Tahr. "My hands are tired. You must climb on."

Once Paris's foot slipped, rolling off the rung. The rope around her waist snapped tight at once, as if Geng-sun could see her, which she couldn't, or could read her every movement through the twine. For a moment, she dangled, and her free foot lashed out. "Still!" said Tahr sharply as he caught it. He guided it back to its rung.

The last bulge in the rock face was the hardest, with trailing creepers and crumbling earth raining down into her face and eyes. The rope was tight against the rock, and she had to squeeze her fingers in behind it to get hold. She knew her knuckles were bleeding, but she could not feel them.

Tahr spoke again, in a strained voice. "You must go faster. Please."

Then Paris was over the overhang, with Geng-sun hauling her in, hand over hand. She lay full length, panting, with the feel of cold rock and crumbly lichen on her cheek. Already, Geng-sun was stepping over her and climbing down, right to the edge, reaching down to where Tahr must be. Dimly, Paris realized what Tahr had been saying all that time. He wasn't roped, climbing up behind her, and he'd had to wait each time she got scared, hanging on. . . . Now Geng-sun held the rope with one hand and reached with the other, and gradually Tahr's head appeared. He was gray with exhaustion, and the ledge was not in reach, not quite. . . . As his fingers slipped, Geng-sun's hand clamped his wrist and held him. It was only a second, but enough to give him strength. He clutched at the ladder again and dragged himself onward, and there he was suddenly, flat out on the ledge beside her like a landed fish.

With one swipe of the ax blade, Geng-sun severed the rope where she had lashed the ladder to a tree. It went clattering down. Then she dropped down beside the others, gasping.

The flit of a small bird in the bushes brought them to their senses. They were lying in the open, and so close to the edge that Paris could imagine them falling asleep and simply rolling over. More to the point, they were in full view of the hillside opposite, if anyone was scanning with binoculars. They had to move.

Under the shelter of some stunted firs, they looked at one another. Here they were, the three of them together, and they had to think.

"Uncle Franklin," said Paris. "I've got to find Uncle Franklin." That was the answer—it had to be. Franklin could make anything happen. He could get them out of this. But even as she thought it, Paris had a hollow feeling, like thinking back to when she was little and believed in Santa Claus.

"Naturally," Tahr said. He made a gesture to Geng-sun, which Paris recognized: a small mime of one of her uncle's expressions. She could see by the *yeh-teh's* reaction that she recognized it, too. Geng-sun's whole body tightened with anger and fear.

But the two of them were talking in that wordless way, and Paris felt a twinge of envy. "Hey, what about me?" she said, and as they turned to her, she realized she was doing it, too— pointing to herself, using her eyes to look the way she thought the camp must be. Almost in spite of herself, she spread both her hands palms upward, and her face said, "Please!"

Tahr thought a moment. "I will come with you," he said. "Just to the edge of the camp." Geng-sun was watching and listening, and she knew what he was saying. She struck the ground with the back of her hand, contemptuous, and looked away.

"Geng-sun says that I am stupid," Tahr said, mildly.

"Geng-sun?" It was the first time Paris had heard the word. "You mean . . . her? She has a *name?*"

"Not in words." Tahr tried to remember the gestures the *yeh-teh* had made, which brought to mind the way the snow lies in a gully . . . how it shrinks and dwindles . . . and the dripping of the water as it melts away. He did it slowly, fumbling for the English as he did so. Paris watched him, then "Again?"

and this time she mirrored him, doing the movements as well as she could. Then she looked up at Geng-sun. "Is that it?" her eyebrows said.

Geng-sun looked at her, and Paris wondered if she was about to burst out laughing, but instead she smiled and gently shook her head. "And you?" her gesture said.

"Paris." But Paris could see that sounds on their own were like birdsong to the *yeh-teh*. She looked at Tahr. "Help me." But what would a city in France mean to him? Or the fact that her parents had honeymooned there, and by the time she was born they weren't so happy, and Mom had insisted on the name "Paris" to make sure that Pop never forgot.

Her heart sank. "It's only a word," she said lamely.

"Never mind," said the *yeh-teh*'s expression. Then she stood and beckoned: "Come with me."

"To the camp?" said Paris. Geng-sun made that hand-slap gesture—"Stupid!"—but gently this time. At the same time she was nodding: "Yes."

"She is doing a very brave thing," Tahr said. "We must be careful. Very quiet. If the others catch us," and he indicated himself and the *yeh-teh,* "they will kill us, I think. Do you understand?"

Paris nodded, but as they started off, she realized that she didn't know whether he had meant the rebels or the hunters. Or the government soldiers in the helicopter. Maybe everybody was against them now?

Being quiet was harder than it should be. Right after the climb, Paris had been tingling all over, still afloat on a tide of adrenaline. Now, as they walked, the tide went out and all she felt was weariness and ache. She had lost any sense of which way they were going, and she trudged in Geng-sun's and Tahr's footsteps as they slithered and climbed. Fallen twigs reached out to trip her and she stumbled, swearing. Several times Geng-sun rounded on her with an urgent, silent "Hush!"

In between times a sick feeling rose inside her. It had all gone wrong. Everything that had seemed like a buzz— Franklin's important friends, the way they talked, the whole Ultimate Diners Club thing—was stupid, and the game was over. It had come to this.

Home, she thought. *I want to go home.* Wherever that might be.

Geng-sun was suddenly still, watching and listening. Tahr was beside her, peering. When Paris caught up, he drew her closer, too.

The campsite, down beneath them, looked like a small-scale model of itself. Toy tents in the folds of a rucked-up blanket of a forest. Any moment now someone would put the toy people in it—a toy Gavin, maybe, showing off a toy gun. The sickness rose in her again. Gavin was dead, a line of bullets ripped across his back. The scene in the gorge flickered in her mind, and the worst thing of all—*Why?* she thought—was that wet, bone-cracking thud and whine as the man felled the dog.

There was nobody moving in the campsite. There was no one at home. Paris knew that, just the way you know sometimes when you walk in through the front door that you're in an empty house.

What had the man in the cave said? "When the government

patrol finds your companions, they will know that we mean what we say." That was Tahr's translation. Maybe he was being tactful. Paris had heard the man's voice when he said it, and she shuddered.

Where was Uncle Franklin?

"I'm going down to take a look," said Paris. Tahr didn't argue, just gave her that patient unreadable look. "You don't have to come," said Paris, "I mean, don't. *Don't!*" As she started downhill he was just behind her all the same.

Now that Geng-sun wasn't leading, Paris found herself doing Geng-sun things. Stopping and listening. The stillness of the forest didn't feel normal—as if she'd never noticed it was full of tiny sounds, until they stopped. The next view she had of the site was when they were right beside it. Almost in the same spot that Tahr must have been, that first day when he stumbled into the campsite—when he wasn't "Tahr" yet, and there was no *yeh-teh,* and the whole thing was a big adventure. Worlds ago.

She had thought she might call out, cautiously. Maybe Harriet's name. But the stillness was too big. "Careful!" Tahr's voice hissed close behind her as she stepped into the open. *Yes, she should be careful,* she thought. But it was dreamlike: part of her was scared, part of her watching, as if all this *was* a movie after all. It was too much to take in. What the heck.

Crossing the clearing, she looked round her. This was where she had lived. How strange. All these little toy houses made of clever man-made fabrics. If they were abandoned, nature wouldn't rot them for . . . how long? Centuries? What were these people playing at? Maybe that was what Tahr thought when he first stumbled on them. Even he couldn't have guessed, that first day, at the craziness of the game.

First—Paris couldn't help it—she looked in her tent. She could see before she reached it that someone had been there—ripped the door flap back, scattering kit from inside. Most of it was gone, but she found a yellow plastic hair comb, trodden in the mud, and she picked it out vaguely, as if maybe nothing *really* bad had happened. Or as if somehow what had happened could be put right.

Tahr's tent . . . Ripped open, too, but there couldn't have been much to steal, except the bag he'd been lent to sleep in. Now Paris found a voice to call out, "Harriet? Donald?" It was a small voice, rather hoarse, and didn't sound like hers.

Renaud's kitchen . . . The worktables were tipped over, the boxes busted open. There was the canteen where the silver cutlery had been. Poor Donald—he'd been so *upset* to see the servants laying knives and forks in the wrong order. There was the empty case for Renaud's glittering knives. They seemed to have taken some of the bright copper pans and left others, as if they'd been enjoying the power of choice.

Paris wandered on, dreamily, from the kitchen to the dining tent. It seemed the natural thing to do.

Donald. Harriet. Franklin. They sat upright, waiting for their dinner. It was really the fact that Renaud was sitting down beside them, in his chef's regalia, that tipped Paris off that things were not quite how they ought to be. The etiquette was very strict for the Ultimate Diners, and for the chef to sit down with the guests was . . . well, *not done.*

Donald's head was tilted forward, Harriet's was sideways,

and Renaud had thrown his right back, with his mouth open, as if fast asleep. They had been pinned to the back of their chairs—the special almost-antique chairs that the porters had carried through the jungle—pinned neatly, with a cook's knife through the chest . . . though now Paris could see there had been other damage, maybe gunshots first, and the knives were just a bit of ghastly theater.

She hardly dared look to see what they had done to Franklin. And then Franklin spoke.

20

The View from the Edge

"Paris, my dear, . . . you are a little late for dinner," Franklin said.

Now that she looked, Paris saw that Franklin's clothes were torn and muddied, though he seemed to have found himself a tie from somewhere. The others, by contrast, were dressed in their best . . . and dead.

"Uncle Franklin!" Paris said. "I—"

"I know, I know—I was late, too. Unavoidably delayed. They seem to have . . . started without me." Just for a moment, Paris had been about to run over and hug him—in the way she hadn't done since she was a child. Now she was frozen. There was something in his voice—cool, controlled, almost casual. What he was saying might have been a joke. A joke? Not even Franklin could be that dry. It was as if he was really in his Malibu beach house, or his little pied-a-terre in Paris, or his stylish London mews—and broadcasting his voice by satellite link to the body of a wild and hunted man who bore some slight resemblance to Paris's extraordinary uncle.

"You're alive!" said Paris. "I thought you were . . . I thought . . . I didn't know what had happened."

"It's over," he said, as if he hadn't heard her. "The porters have run off, of course. Our . . . visitors have taken everything, including the radio transmitter. End of party. So . . ." He sat up and straightened his tie. "We might as well make an occasion of it. Are you alone?"

"Uncle Franklin . . ." Paris faltered.

"Ah, I see not." In the doorway, Tahr had stopped in mid-step, staring. Franklin gave him a glance, no more, then spoke to Paris. "Tell your little friend that, unaccountably, the meal is cold. Oh, do sit down," he said.

"Uncle Franklin, wh—?" To say "What's wrong?" sounded stupid. Everything was wrong, and more.

"Sit *down*," he said, with all the charm and certainty she'd ever seen in all the years she'd known him. "That's better. I want you—you of all people—to appreciate this moment with me. It is really . . . quite unique."

From somewhere in the debris of the rebels' looting, Franklin seemed to have found a candle, though the silver candlesticks were gone. It was stuck in a crack in the table, not quite upright, and now he lit it with a flourish and got to his feet.

"Ladies and gentlemen," said Franklin. "I call to order the final, positively the final, meeting of the Ultimate Diners Club. A toast!" With a wave of relief, Paris thought: *That's all it is— he's drunk.* But there were no bottles. In front of Franklin and each of the diners was a wine glass, or what was left of one. The rebels must have spared some time to break every single item, one by one. Franklin pushed the stem and the base of a glass, with just a shard of the bowl left, toward her. It had probably been priceless—worth as much as a farmer in the rebels' village could earn in a lifetime. They would know that kind of thing. They'd watched TV.

"To Nothing!" Franklin raised his empty glass. "A fine year. Pure vintage Nothing, Nihil, Nada, Sod All, Sweet FA." He swirled the broken edge of it close to his nose. "Ah . . . a saucy little hint of burning flesh and cordite. Serve chilled with a breath of endless snow." He raised it high. "To the next Ice Age. Let the yetis inherit the earth!"

His eyes were fixed on Paris, with an intensity that held her motionless. "The toast," he said. "That's better. That's my girl." He turned to the dead diners like a genial host. "You might be wondering, ladies and gentlemen, why I called this meeting when so many of you are . . . indisposed. It is, of course, on account of my niece Paris." He turned a very brief glittering smile on her.

"Uncle Franklin," she started. Paris had seen people drunk or stoned. She knew that this was something very, very else. "Stop it. Stop it!"

Franklin did not even pause. "You know me well enough, I trust," he went on, with a confidential look at Donald, "to know my feelings about the human race. I have never felt tempted to encourage it by adding to its numbers—which are already obscene. Still, a man wants to feel that something of him will continue, and I find that satisfaction in young Paris here."

"Uncle Franklin, listen to me! I could have *died* back there." Her voice dropped. "Uncle Franklin? I'm *scared*."

"In her," the speech went on, "I have seen something of my own originality of mind, including the gift of being exquisitely, utterly bored. She too has sampled what the richest state on earth can give her . . . and found it *banal.* Accordingly," he gathered his best toastmaster's voice, "I wish the world to know that Paris is, in every sense, my *heir.*"

Paris jumped to her feet. "Who are you talking to?" she yelled. "This is me. Me! Uncle Franklin, look at me!" That stopped him for a second.

Now, she thought. *Suddenly he'll blink and come to, like when someone's in hysterics and you slap their face.* "Do you know who I am?" she said.

He gave a wide, chill smile. "Oh, yes. A member of a dying species. As we all are. It's a pity your young Neanderthal isn't with us. She could have told us what it's like. To be skulking in caves. To be the last." Franklin chuckled oddly, and reached an arm toward her. She flinched.

"That's what *we've* got, you see," he said softly. "There are so few of us—just a handful in each age who dare look it straight in the eye. No cant, no pretty stories, no illusions. And for us, how exquisite: To be in at the *end.* The earth wrecked. Oceans poisoned, forests stripped. A busted flush. The edge of extinction." He was reaching out now with his eyes—that look with which he'd find her at a family party, in an airport crowd, which said: "You and me, *we* understand each other." It was so hard not to look.

"Oh, yes," he went on, "*we* know, don't we, there's no future? It's in the family. How do you think your grandfather made his millions?" He paused. "Did I never tell you that? Suffice it to say that when some madman starts the final nuclear war, your grandpa's name will appear on the credits. Paris, my dear . . ." There was a clinging softness in his voice. "I always dreamed that you'd be there to see it with me."

Paris was backing away.

"Do *I* know who you are? Do *you?*" he said suddenly, sharper.

"Sure. I'm that spoiled kid who wanted to make movies. That's all. Nothing special." Paris reached back with her hand and found Tahr's. It was what she needed, and he led her gently backward, not taking her eyes off Franklin.

"It doesn't matter," he called after her. "Run where you like—you'll never get away from me. Because I'm *part* of you. I've seen to that, all these years. It doesn't matter if I die. I'll always be inside you." The candle gave a flare and sputter as a stream of wax poured down. Tahr pulled at her hand, and they ran.

"We come back another time," Tahr said, when they were out of the campsite, on a little track into the forest. "Later he will be better, maybe."

Paris did not speak. In her eyes was the expression that she'd had looking over the cliff, but this time, Tahr thought, the drop she saw just went on down and down and down. . . .

"He is crazy now, maybe," Tahr said. "All those terrible things . . ."

"No, no," said Paris. "You don't understand. That's Franklin. Deep inside, I guess it always was. And I guess I kind of knew it, but. . . ." In her mind the scenes unreeled and unraveled. The alligator party. All the times Franklin had appeared, on the edges of the family, not saying much but promising the world, and more, and more. "Tahr, maybe that was what I *wanted.*"

"No blame," Tahr said, as he had once before.

There was a noise in the bushes, something heavy, clumsy, coming straight toward them, and as Tahr cried "Run!" there it was. The dog. *The dog that should be dead—it* must *be,* Paris thought. *I saw them beat its brains out.* The great mastiff swayed and lurched toward them, and as Paris turned to run, it was coming at them, and they heard it gaining, gaining. At the last minute, Paris turned and glimpsed it, and the image of it froze into her mind. That heavy bull-like head . . . a great raw wound down one side, the square jaw hanging sideways, one eye gone. Tahr threw himself aside, and Paris did the same, and the mastiff blundered on straight past them, blindly, with its nose down, as if the scent in its nostrils was the only thing existing in the world.

For a moment, they stared after it, then: "Geng-sun!" Paris said. And they followed it, although a minute earlier they'd been running from it for their lives.

They weren't the first to come this way. Maybe it was the porters as much as the rebels who had made such a thorough job of the looting. Either way, there was a trail of litter, as if they'd had their arms full and couldn't carry it all. There were bits of camping gear, shards of Renaud's finest crockery—cans of unopenable food, even—leading like a paper trail into the clearing where the porters' tents had been.

They were gone, of course. But the clearing wasn't empty. Tahr and Paris came to a stop, and stared.

There was one tree in the middle, and under it the dog sat, on its haunches, straining its muzzle upward like the dog in those old ads beside a gramophone. His Master's Voice . . .

Yes, its master: Shikarri swung gently, hanging. Hanged. Every now and then, the dog tried to heave up its weight and reach up on its hind legs . . . but one of them was lame, and it collapsed back, just touching the man's bare feet, so that he swung again. Pinned to Shikarri's chest there was a crude hand-lettered sign.

"What does it say?" said Paris.

"'Traitor.'"

Exhausted now, the dog lay panting, though its muzzle kept on lifting feebly. Faithfulness and the traitor. The dog and the man. Hadn't the two of them always seemed like two sides of the same coin? Paris made a small, choked, sobbing sound, and turned back into the forest, blundering and tripping, until suddenly she buckled over, her face in her hands, and simply wept.

Tahr waited by her quietly for several minutes before he dared touch her shoulder. She slapped his hand away. "Leave me alone!" she snapped. "I didn't ask to be here. I didn't want any of this." And she sobbed again.

"I'm sorry," Tahr said as it eased a little.

"No, you're not! It's your fault, setting free that stupid yeti creature. Oh, geez . . ." She blinked and looked up, suddenly calm. "I sound like Uncle Franklin, don't I?" Paris reached for Tahr's hand. "It's true, isn't it? I'm like Franklin. He's got inside my head. You heard what he said: 'I'm part of you.'" She stared into the undergrowth bleakly. "Maybe we should all die here. Him, me, his sicko friends. Then we can't do anyone any more harm."

"You will go home," Tahr said. "You will go home safe."

"Home? How? Go on, tell me: *How?*"

There was a quiet sound behind them—a low, bubbling, crooning sound—and there was Geng-sun, watching with a gaze so old and sad that Paris nearly wept again.

"Do you know what she's saying?" Tahr said as Geng-sun began to beckon, mixing complicated tones and gestures in the movement. "Her . . . and her mother . . . and—something like gathering in. As though there's lots of them. Her people. 'We will help you,' that's what she's saying."

"Why?" said Paris.

Tahr shrugged. "Why not? She looked after me."

Paris felt small and tired, and she bowed her head. "Okay."

Geng-sun led the way, first slowly, then with more conviction. Paris didn't even ask where they were going. To be going *somewhere*—that was all she wanted. To let someone else decide. And not to think of all the things she'd seen.

They climbed into a band of sparser forest, and the views started widening. Geng-sun was leading them on a contour, pointing now and then. The hillside went up steeply, over where the rebels' gorge must be—went up in tiers, with two, three ranks of outcrops, and it was between two of them that they were heading. The closer they got, the more Geng-sun was pointing, and Paris guessed what she was looking for. The shadowy ledge and caves. The shelters under overhangs.

Again and again, there was the broad sign she'd made with her arms before—like gathering the world in from all sides. "All of us. My people." Now it started to include the hills above: "our places." She was nimbler now, sometimes skittering from rock to rock or swinging round a tree trunk for no reason except that something was bubbling up in her. *Something,* Paris thought, *like home.*

And yet it was so quiet. Almost as still as it had been down at the campsite. Geng-sun was moving faster, ducking, hunting here and there. She was looking, listening, bending down to sniff the rocks, examining the ground like a detective. Then she was out of sight, and neither Paris nor Tahr could see where she had gone. They looked at each other, nervous.

"Trust her," Tahr said. *What alternative is there?* thought Paris. They sat down together and rested their legs.

From somewhere far beneath and behind, down in the valley, something rose. It wasn't the black smoke they'd seen rising from the burning village, when the helicopter came, but a brief whitish plume, already fading, as if something had flared up and not lasted long.

Tahr looked at Paris and guessed what she'd been thinking. She was. She was thinking of the candle on the table in the dinner tent.

Then Geng-sun was crouching with them, agitated, eager, though not even Tahr could work out what her flickerings of movement might be saying, not until he thought: *Relax. Breathe. Listen.* In the midst of the twittering, throaty sounds Geng-sun was making, he caught one tone running through it, getting stronger, stronger—one he'd heard before but never so urgently. Her mother song.

21

Mother Song

Tahr had never seen a man possessed—but Shengo had, or maybe that was just another story that he'd heard, about the Bon priests over the mountains who would call up the spirits of the forests and the stones, lending them their bodies, speaking in the spirit voices, in a language no one understood. Paris had seen much stranger things, of course, in the horror videos she wasn't meant to watch. Whatever possessed Geng-sun now was a kinder thing than that, but still a shock to Tahr and Paris. For the first time since they'd known her, Geng-sun seemed not to see them at all. She was gazing this way, with a wild hunting look, and she seemed to look right through them as she sensed or scented something, something near, something so big and important that nothing else mattered.

Tahr caught Paris's scared look.

"Her mother, I think."

Geng-sun was hunting, down on hands and knees among the boulders, running off this way or that, then stopping with an anxious little cry as the trail went cold on her. Then she'd come back to where she'd lost it, scanning for the clue, the scent, the feeling in the air that said *Mother. Mother.* At last she seemed to get it, stronger this time, and she was running, in and out of the sparse trees, uphill at first, then following a contour around.

"Shouldn't we leave her to it?" Paris said. "I mean, what if her mother . . ." It seemed silly to say: *What if her mother is mad at us?* Even if they could use words and spoke in English, how was she going to explain: It was Gavin who shot you, honestly, not me.

"Trust her," Tahr said, and didn't wait to argue. Geng-sun was already almost out of sight, but there was no question which way she had gone. As they followed, the slope grew steeper, and there was a line of cliffs above them. Just out of sight below, another dropped away. The slope was narrowing, with moss and wiry shrubs among the boulders, no trees, only splashes of gray or white or yellow lichen on the stones. From the foot of the rocks above, screes fanned out, and any false step would send loose stones scudding down, right to where the hillside stepped off into space. Each time one slipped and clattered, Tahr froze, uselessly, and held his breath, as if he could stop the force of gravity. They were out in the open now. The last thing they wanted was noise to tell the rest of the valley where they were.

When the noise came, it was not a falling stone. Geng-sun had stopped, abruptly. She lifted her head and gave the loudest cry Tahr had ever heard her make—a high, hard chatter, like hammering stone very quickly on stone. Just a second or two and it was over. Silence . . . and the scattered echoes of it came back from across the valley. She cried out again, her eyes fixed on the cliff above them, where a shadowy break might be the entrance of a cave.

She waited twice, not moving, then started climbing. Compared to the sheer face of the gorge, this cliff was leisurely. It was broken by gullies and cracks, and just above them was a corner of rock that was opened like the pages of a book. To wedge yourself into the crack and go up step by step felt safer than walking on the scree, and Tahr was halfway up already. Paris followed. Whatever was going to happen next, with him seemed the safest place to be.

The moment Tahr reached the cave, what he thought he knew about the *yeh-teh* changed. He had thought they huddled in caves for shelter, much like animals, or like him and Shengo in the Snows. One glance said he was wrong. The rebels' cave in the gorge had been nothing—just a bivouac, an overnight stop, not a home. As he stood upright, the cave mouth opened in and back, sloping downward, and a pool had gathered in the center—black, except where a bar of light fell from the crack above it. Every now and then, the stillness of the pool would shiver as a drop fell from the ceiling, and the bar of light would flex and bend.

The cave was a hall—higher and deeper than any building Tahr had seen. Maybe the *gompa* Shengo told of, with its hundred monks, might have been like it. Around the edges, in each alcove and recess, were the living quarters—not quite huts, not quite tents, but wickerwork screens of branches woven together, stouter palisades of hewn logs here and there, and wooden frames on which patchworks of decaying hides were stretched and dry.

Decaying . . . Yes, the first thing Tahr saw was the grandeur. Then he saw the emptiness. As surely as the human village in the forest, this was an abandoned place. Not abandoned all at once, though. Some of the huts seemed sound, just damp and cobwebbed. Others had crumbled into firewood long ago. He imagined the emptiness of it slowly growing, year by year, as a smaller and smaller band of *yeh-teh* moved down from the mountains, and one family's hut after another was let go.

And now?

A village of one. And there was Geng-sun, in the shadows, not quite kneeling—more like fallen forward onto a pile of discarded furs. And clutching them, clutching them. As he came closer, Tahr saw that she wasn't motionless but throbbing quietly with tears, just like any person—not a member of a different species, but a cousin, after all.

The mother must have crawled here for shelter, injured, hoping to find others, maybe, following a memory from long ago. She'd curled up in what furs she could find, and it looked as though she had managed to make a small fire, but at some point it had burned down, and the effort to fetch wood had been too much. She lay on her side, with her knees up, as if hugging her pain. That was over, at least.

Paris was beside Tahr now. She didn't speak. After a while, he began to look round, careful not to disturb Geng-sun. There wasn't much in the shelters, though he saw tools—an ax, still with its handle, and scrapers, and thick, smooth needles made from bone. There were hides and furs, carefully piled in an alcove. They might need those later. Now he wanted to do something for Geng-sun, to offer her *something,* however little use it was. Then he found the wooden bowl, deep and wide enough to hold in two hands. Maybe she'd be thirsty. After filling it from the pool, he laid it by her, within reach.

Geng-sun looked at the bowl as if she didn't remember straightaway what water was. Then she cupped a little in her hands and began to wash her mother's face.

So the ritual began. When they offered to help, she neither accepted nor pushed them away, but she seemed happy for them to be alongside, watching. Paris flinched a little when Geng-sun peeled the furs back, and she saw the ugly wounds left by the bullets. *They're so much tougher than us,* thought Paris, amazed that the mother had survived at all. How long it had taken her to crawl uphill to shelter, bleeding, Paris didn't like to think. How long had she been there, gazing out, too weak to move, with just the thought of her daughter somewhere in the hunters' hands?

They were tough, but the wounds had festered. There were flies. As Tahr looked for firewood in the ruined shelters, Paris became water carrier. She fetched her bowl after bowl, and Geng-sun went about the washing—weeping softly, but practically, deftly, as if she'd learned what to do, maybe watching her mother as the others died, and she became the last of them. The *only-one.*

When the washing was done, the mother's body lay out straight with the best of the furs across her. *Just like Shengo,* Tahr thought, as Geng-sun gently traced the ocher lines and spirals on her mother's arms and feet and face. With the last of the reddish mud, she sketched a circle round them on the cave floor, then worked back around it, joining the breaks in it, making it whole.

How strange, thought Tahr: The circle made him feel safer, even when he thought, far down below, he caught the helicopter sound. The usual twinge of fear went through him, but it was like remembering a bad dream, or a story of another world. Right now, inside the ocher circle, they were in the only real place, the same place Geng-sun's ancestors might have been ten thousand years ago.

But the ritual wasn't quite ready yet. "Wait," signed Geng-sun, and as Paris and Tahr watched from the cave mouth, she went shinning down the hillside. The light was sinking, and the air was cooling, but neither of them said, "Let's go back inside."

"I've never seen anyone dead, except my grandma," Paris said. "I mean, not until . . . all this."

"I am sorry," Tahr said, "about your friends from the camp."

"I wouldn't say 'friends,'" said Paris. What she wanted to say was: Even with everything she'd seen today—Shikarri, Gavin, Donald, and the rest—she'd never *seen* somebody dead the way that they were seeing Geng-sun's mother. But she couldn't find words for it.

"They took me to look at Grandma in her casket," she said instead. "Someone had put all this *makeup* on her. Weird. All you could see was her face. And they'd put a kind of frill around it, like a cake."

Geng-sun returned with an armful of ferns and sprigs of bushes—even a few late flowers. She began to arrange them round the body, scattering the petals on it like a pale blue snow. Then, unexpectedly, she dug into her waist pouch for the food she'd pilfered from the rebels' cave, and as the light drained from the valley, they sat looking out and ate and drank together. Behind them, the cave was filling up with shadows. Geng-sun went in and set about cracking a spark from two worn flints, and cupping her hand, she coaxed the little pile of firewood by her mother's head into a crackling glow.

As the flames went up, the roof of the cave seemed to stretch up as high as the night sky outside. Shadows from the wooden shelters stood up taller than they, in the background, and nothing was still in the firelight except for Geng-sun's mother's face. Paris joined Geng-sun and Tahr beside her, sitting cross-legged, and she couldn't look away. The angle of the light picked out and hardened everything that was Neanderthal about the face. The heavy nose, the slanting jawline, all the sheer tough bulk of her was . . . more so. The brows seemed to jut more, and the eyes were unknowable caves. Paris glanced at Geng-sun and saw how her features were a softer, not-quite-finished version of those same, like children of any race before they harden into *us* and *them.* Tahr, too . . .

He was looking at the faces. Turned to the firelight, all of them were masks. If Paris looked at him now, he thought, would she see what was inside of him? That he was happy, strangely happy, to have her there beside him? Shengo's training had failed. As a monk, you were supposed to practice nonattachment—not to want things so that you cling to them. You had to learn to let things go.

He looked at her—another mask face, with its sharp, thin lines and its colorless skin. Maybe that was how all the gods were: frightened children, holding god masks to the light. And when she was frightened, she needed him there.

Geng-sun was kneeling now, with a gentle rhythmic moaning more like singing than she'd ever done. For once, her hands were still and saying nothing; she leaned over, gazing into her mother's eyes. It was as long and hard a gaze as when she and Tahr had met each other, met each other's thoughts for just a moment, in the supply tent that first night. What was she seeing now, in the eyes of the dead? Or was she trying to tell her mother something in the same way, one last time?

After a long while, she sat back and motioned to Tahr. His turn. So this was part of the ritual—that everyone should do the same. He knelt there, half afraid of what he'd see. The *yeh-teh*'s eyes were like Geng-sun's but older, bloodshot, and now with that cloudy, flat look that said "dead." Only as he moved back and sat did something flicker through his mind. It was nothing to do with the *yeh-teh*—just a fleeting sense, again, of his own mother, urgent and frightened by the smell of burning, pushing him away. He thought how Geng-sun had been clinging to her mother's body. Would a little boy, as he was, have turned his back and run away from his mother? Unless, that is, there had been someone with him, someone he trusted? The scene was still a blank to him, with sound and smell and feeling and an odd sense: No, not quite alone.

Paris faced the mother's eyes for a moment, willing herself to, just for Geng-sun's sake, then looked away. The vigil started. Sometimes Geng-sun made her song sounds, sometimes Tahr took a turn with his muttering chant. Paris wished there was something she could do, but what? A small speech Geng-sun wouldn't understand? A hymn, when she'd only ever been to church, bored rigid, for a brief spell when her mom tried out religion years ago? A pop song with some soppy lyric about love? The best she could do was try and sit still with them, trying not to yawn, not to shuffle when her back hurt and her legs had to be stretched.

She was doing quite well, for quite a long time. Then she leaned her head in her hands, closed her eyes for a moment, and before the moment was over, she had crumpled gently forward, asleep.

When she woke up, the cave was quiet. Geng-sun was motionless, sitting with her eyes closed. And Tahr? He was at the cave mouth, gazing out into the night. Paris went over shyly and sat beside him. In all this sadness and darkness, it seemed the natural place to be. She moved closer, till they felt each other's warmth, then put an arm around him, and he put an arm round her. They kept staring out into the night.

"Is—is that okay?" she said. "I mean, you Buddhists aren't meant not to touch or something?"

"It's okay," he said, and for a long time neither of them spoke at all.

"Is it real," she said at last, "that mind thing? When she looks into your eyes?"

"I don't know. I . . . saw something, I think. I felt things . . . only once or twice. And only when I try to think like meditation, with the mind clear . . . and when her thought was very, very strong. But it is hard. Maybe it is easier when they do it with each other."

"Was that what she was doing just now?" Paris dropped her voice. "With her mother. Her mother is *dead.*"

"How can we know the way they think?" Tahr sighed. "But Geng-sun told me something while you were asleep. I think she had a kind of . . . no, not dream—a 'leading,' like my master used to. Or maybe she remembered her mother telling her a story. I think it was an old one that the *yeh-teh* have told for a long time." From deep in the valley there came the faint sound of the river, like a shifting of the trees.

"She says there is another place. A safe place for the *yeh-teh*. That is the story. She has never been there, yet."

It did not come easily. Again and again Tahr would trail off or come to a halt with "Maybe that is what she meant." But the feeling was clear. Her kind were gone now, gone from here. But there was a place, a strong place in the mountains. Somewhere they did not have to live by hiding and stealing. When he'd asked "Where?" she had just pointed up, up over the horizon. In a pass between three mountains was a . . . Now her hands had worked at filling in the feelings: signs of coldness, and of building something, heaping up a great wall. Walls and roofs—a fortress, a fortress of ice. Inside the walls, high spaces, higher than this cave, and fires that burned all winter in the halls of ice. Food, drink . . . and many *yeh-teh,* all together, safely, because there were strong guards posted, keeping watch. The Ice Fortress . . .

In the world down here, she'd signed—and every part of her had shown the feeling—she was the last, the *only-one.* Up there was where she must go.

As Paris stared out, maybe a cloud had shifted, or the little moon had just come up behind them, out of sight. What she saw was a thin edge of pale light up and over the tops of the heads of the valleys, as if a glacier had crept a little closer: the touch of that moonlight on the ever-present Snows.

22

A Slingshot at an Eagle

A thump in the air shook them awake, out of separate dreams. It was as if a bolt of thunder had dropped from the sky and gone rattling down into the valley bottom, several tiers of cliffs below. Right down into the rebels' gorge. A wave of small-bird panic rippled outward in the hazy dawn light.

Tahr's dreams had been of running, and he was glad to get out of them, but his heartbeat was still on the run. What had the sound been? Another sharp thud . . . and echoes walloped to and fro. Before they had finished, Tahr could make out the spitting of small-arms fire, and he knew that the drone of the helicopter had been there, too, in his dream.

By the time Paris had opened her eyes, Tahr was out on the ledge. Scrambling up, he could see almost into the deepest folds of green beneath them, where the gorge must be. There was no smoke—there was nothing to burn, after all—but a slight haze of whiteness rose above it, thickening the morning mist.

And the helicopter. And the sound of firing. Once Shengo had talked about tear gas, thinking of his soldier days. Tahr had laughed. "You mean it makes you sad, so you can't fight?" Not unkindly, the old man had put him right. It meant you couldn't breathe or see; you felt you were going to die and panicked, so you ran into the open. There they shot you, Shengo said.

The squall of gunfire didn't last long. Trapped in the gorge, the shots and echoes clattered to and fro. Who could tell whether both sides were firing, or just the soldiers, as the others came stumbling out of their cave? Tahr could make out the helicopter, hardly moving, with the blur of its blades like a dragonfly's wings. Now it inched along the gorge, as if examining it in detail, and every now and then came gunfire, sharp above the thud of rotors.

"What is it?" Paris called up. "What can you see?"

Tahr shook his head. He knew what he was looking at. He didn't know, though, why he seemed to feel the thud of it inside him like a dull punch. Why should he care about the rebels—hard men, hurt men, driven to violence by violence— bound helpless on the Wheel of it? That's what Shengo would have said. They had offered him a gun, as if it was an honor, but it was a threat, too. They wouldn't be happy till he'd used it. He could kill or be killed. And now he'd helped their precious hostage to escape. He thought of the bare feet of Shikarri, dangling, and the TRAITOR sign around his neck.

"What's happening?" Paris called again.

Of all the rebels, he found himself remembering Darwa, the thin, bitter Darwa, who had spoken in Tahr's own tongue. And there in his mind was the ghost of a shadow of his broken dream. Not *one* child pushed into the forest—*one* little child who would surely have cried and clung to his mother—but if there were *two?* If there was another child, a little older, whose hand he could hold when Mother cried "Run!" to them. "Run!"

For a moment, Tahr stared into the dark deep waters of his dream. Then it was gone, leaving him with a question he couldn't get hold of, starting, *What if... What... What if?*

There was no time to ask it. Far below, the iron dragonfly banked in its sinister, elegant way, and climbed a little. At the same time something prickled in Tahr's nose—a waft of a sweet smell from inside the cave. Paris had already turned to face it. "Look," she said as he scrambled back down. "It's like incense!" With arms thrown open, like a final offering, Geng-sun was heaping the last of the leaves and twigs onto her mother's fire. The sweet herb smell of it rolled outward, drenching her and the body, cleansing the air of the cave.

Smoke... Tahr ran straight toward her, shouting, "No! Not now!" Geng-sun looked round, first astonished, then enraged. The last dignified act of the ritual, and Tahr was acting like a mad thing—as he'd done once before, at the waterfall. "Stop it!" Tahr grabbed for the twigs. Geng-sun swiped him aside—not quite a punch, but from an arm as strong as hers it sent him sprawling. The last armful of crisp shrubs went on, and smoke rolled out of the cave.

She stood up, suddenly limp and used up, the ritual done. She turned in Tahr's direction with an angry, hurt look.

"Danger!" he gestured, getting up slowly so as not to scare her. "Outside ... Come and look ..." She came, keeping her distance. Only when she saw Paris running in toward them, shouting something in those human sounds, did Geng-sun feel the "Danger!" for herself.

"It's coming!" Paris was calling. "Get back inside. They've seen the smoke."

"No—outside!" Tahr was running outward, and the two of them collided, not sure for a moment whether they were wrestling or holding each other. "They have tear gas," Tahr said. Paris nodded. She'd seen the videos. Commando assaults that start with tear gas and stun grenades.

"Sure," she said. "Where's Geng-sun?"

By the time they turned, Geng-sun had gone. *Back into the shadows,* thirty thousand years of instinct told her. *Whatever happens, caves are safe.*

Tahr ran back in, shouting. But she'd vanished in some inner recess. At the cave's lip, there was Paris. For all her long-limbed size, she looked suddenly fragile and uncertain. He ran back to her.

The helicopter throb was louder. When they looked out, it was almost on a level with them, but still over the middle of the valley, as if it had stepped back for a long view. To take aim. Then, as they watched, it tipped its head and came slicing toward them. "Over there!" Tahr pointed to the crack they'd scrambled up. But Paris wasn't moving.

"It's no good," she said, her eyes on the helicopter. It was coming, coming fast. "I could wave. If I wave, they'll know I'm . . . white. These are from the government, aren't they?" She stepped forward, with her arms up, through the smoke. From behind, Tahr saw her, like a puppet silhouette—in torn shorts and the shirt the rebels gave her. Fourteen: She was about the height of grown men hereabouts. Then the first shots cracked into the rock behind her.

Maybe it was Geng-sun's smoke that saved them, swirling just enough to spoil the marksman's aim. The helicopter pulled out in a tight curve, angling round to sweep back at a closer angle. At the shots, Paris had stood there, frozen. Now Tahr grabbed her, pulling her toward the corner crack. If they could just get out of sight . . .

For a moment, as they squeezed in, the hammering noise of the machine relaxed a little. Playing with them, letting them feel the relief. Then it swept along the cliff toward them, and the sound was like a solid thing, beating the rock with its fists. They shrank back as it hung right there alongside, and they stared into the cloudy, bulbous windscreen, with a glimpse of a goggled, earmuffed, masklike face. But he couldn't have been looking, because there was a mortar whump as a tear-gas canister went into the back of the cave, and the helicopter slid on by. It hovered there, watching the cave mouth, waiting for the panic, the surrender. Or that's what Paris guessed. She waited a minute, then poked her head out of the crack to make sure.

It made sure. The gunners hadn't been certain what they'd seen behind the smoke, and one of them glanced back, and he caught the movement. Then he opened fire.

The first round that he loosed was just a gesture. The angle was wrong, but it would keep them pinned down in the crack, these rebels. And the helicopter rocked a little outward, swinging the fuselage, angling the gunner's hatch to best advantage.

Paris closed her eyes. There was nowhere to bolt now, and her limbs had gone like a rag doll's. She found Tahr's hand and pulled him closer, as if that would make some difference. *I just don't want to be on my own,* she thought, *when the bullets hit.* Tahr's eyes, though, stayed open. The sounds and the fears of his old bad dream moved in toward him slowly. It wouldn't let him get away this time. And Paris held his hand tight, tight.

Don't let go.

That was it. The small child in the forest, years ago . . . Of course he wouldn't leave his mother—unless someone was holding his hand. And he saw *two* children, one a little older than the other. "Run!" their mother cried. They ran . . . and then the thunder of the helicopter hit them, and they panicked. They were only children, after all. "Don't let go!" the little one wailed as the elder slipped his grip and ran the other way.

"Never trust anyone from our side of the hill." Who'd said that? Darwa. Was that why he was so hard on himself and everyone? But there could have been a hundred families, in a hundred villages, the whole world over, just the same. And they *were* only children.

There was the pilot's mask-face, and in the crack of the hatch, the marksmen, ready, taking aim.

Something cracked off the glass. It wasn't big, but big enough to shock the pilot, and the helicopter seemed to wince, like a live thing. It was enough to send the first spray of bullets raking up the cliff. *Crack,* again. Tahr glimpsed it this time: Stones were falling—no, someone was throwing them, as futile as a slingshot at an eagle. One of the gunners let off a round, up at something Tahr couldn't see. Then the rockfall came in earnest.

Whether the stones had been waiting, a last-ditch defense of the cave prepared by the Neanderthalers over centuries, or a serendipity of ice and scree had left them there, Tahr would not know. But a cloudburst of rocks arced out over the lip of the cave. For a moment, it was in the air between the rock face and the helicopter, and the firing went astray. Then, just as the last few crashed down, one last boulder, the biggest by far, trickled over the lip. Too heavy to fall far out, it clipped the shoulder of the rock and looped out at a crazy angle. For a long, slow moment, Tahr could see it in midair, and one of the marksmen swung round as if he could shoot it out of the air. Then it went over him, over the cockpit—*Missed!* thought Tahr—and into the half-transparent whirlpool of the rotors. There was a *crack!* as if one of the titans from the Wheel of Life had grabbed a blade and snapped it over his knee.

The helicopter shuddered. Then it tilted outward, farther, farther, and suddenly lost its grip on the air. It went straight down sideways and into the hillside with a slow, terrible crunch. It balanced for a moment, strangely quiet; then something gave way, and gravity took hold, rolling it onto its back like a cat to be stroked, and then on, crunching the one unbroken rotor, and over and over again, to the edge of the bluff. It let go with a kind of sigh, as if glad to be done with it, and there was a silent moment of its free fall, then the final muffled crash below.

Paris and Tahr dared not move until the dangerous smells

began to drift toward them—prickling gas from the cave, a whiff of scorched fuel from below. There was a tightness in his chest, but it was only the gas. No, he hadn't gone breathless. The fear had not stopped him. The thing that had clutched his lungs from time to time was gone.

"Look!" Paris pointed upward. There on the skyline was Geng-sun, arms raised with that same defiance they'd seen when she'd raised the ax head in the rebels' lair. They waved and waved.

As Tahr and Paris climbed, still trembling, they were a little surprised not to see her scrambling down toward them, on this rock that was like a stroll in a meadow to her. When they reached the top, they saw why. Geng-sun was stretched back on the bare rock, not far from the crack in the roof of the cave, where she must have climbed. She was hurt. Tahr saw the red patch spreading in her rough skirt, just above her knee. She was huddling round it, touching the wound as if she could not quite imagine where it had suddenly come from—this pain, this blood.

She'll be okay, thought Paris. *They're tough . . . aren't they?* Geng-sun was struggling now to get herself upright, and she swayed and would have fallen if Tahr hadn't been beside her. There was a look in Geng-sun's eyes that Paris didn't want to face. *Hurt . . . Hopeless . . . End of everything . . .* But Geng-sun blinked it away. One hand was leaning on Tahr's shoulder, but the other was already pointing: "On, on . . . Up . . ."

"Not now," Tahr said. "You're hurt," and signaled "resting" and "sleeping."

"No!" she made the karate-chop sign sideways. No argument. Pushing Tahr away, she started walking, wincing with the pain but walking. "Go now!" she indicated. And Tahr got the meaning from the way her eyes looked upward, and the hands mimed something falling, falling deeper, coming this way . . . Snow. "The winter, coming. Can't wait. Go."

Tahr looked at Paris, and she looked at him. "You—you can wait here if you like," he said.

"What?" she said. *"What?"*

"Better you stay here," he said. "Only needs one with her. I can help alone."

"Like"—Paris then said a word she hadn't taught him—"you can. I'm coming."

Geng-sun was looking from one to the other. They were speaking tightly, with words only, but when she saw the smile that went between them, then she knew. She was going to the Fortress of the Ice, the Fastness, and she wasn't going there alone.

23

Tongue of Ice

Three orange red fingers moved in silhouette against the skyline. Their fur capes, gathered and stitched into hoods, gave them the look of being tall and hunched, with a ridge of hair on pointed heads. If anyone had seen them in the distance, he'd have said: "Look, yeti!"

They had brought all they were able to carry from the cave. Tahr had done what he could, or what Geng-sun would let him, with her wound. An arrow, a stab from a spear, a slingshot blow—those things made sense to her. But bullets that had come from the sky? She recognized that torn flesh, though, as the same that killed her mother, and a shadow of fear came into her eyes. Paris forced herself to watch as Tahr bathed and mopped the bleeding. When he tried, and failed, to find the bullet, Geng-sun howled, and Paris looked away.

They did their best with a bandage, and once the blood was out of sight, the *yeh-teh* seemed to put it from her mind. Before they left, they braved the sour, stinging air in the cave to scour the deserted shelters for anything that might help them on their way. None of the ax heads were still attached to serviceable handles, but Geng-sun took one all the same, and a stone scraper with an edge like a knife. There was the haft of a good spear, though the head was missing. Still, it made a staff to walk with, and Geng-sun was going to need it. At first, Paris and Tahr had helped support her, but she had waved them away. In normal times, she would have been twice as fast as them. Now she seemed to make a bargain with the pain, and with the spear she would not slow them down.

Most important were the hides and furs—where they were going, every wearable scrap would help, and when they found a niche with crudely stitched but sturdy boots of hide in several sizes, it felt as though provisions had been laid on especially for their journey. For a minute, Tahr and Paris had played dressing up, like children.

"Look," said Paris suddenly. She stomped her wide feet and pulled up the *tahr*-hair hood. "This is just what yetis look like—I mean, in cartoons, back home."

"You have *yeh-teh* in America?"

"I don't think so." Personally she'd always thought the stuff about Bigfoot was a joke—good for horror stories, but actually *believing* it was for nerds. "But everybody thinks they know what a yeti looks like—big fat hairy ape things, big footprints . . . and the head sort of comes to a point. Like this!"

They had laughed at each other, then noticed Geng-sun waiting at the mouth of the cave. She had not interrupted, but she was leaning back against a rock, in pain. At last, she insisted: They must start *now*. There might not be time.

———

The three silhouettes came up onto the skyline, clear against the gray white cloud behind. From below, they would have been there for a long time, as the slope curved smoothly, treeless, over boilerplates of lichen-crusted rock. Small birds standing lookout on stones would chitter away, and once they alarmed a flock of blue sheep that had watched them approaching for half an hour, as still as the rocks, then dissolved and poured away like water. The three were out in the open now, for anyone to see. But who could be watching? Not long ago, it had seemed everybody had been after them—the rebels, the hunters, the helicopter . . . Suddenly all the dangers had canceled each other out and left the three of them alone, with an even stranger feeling. No one in the world knew where they were. Apart from maybe Paris's parents—though from what Tahr had heard, they scarcely sounded like a family—there was nobody who cared.

Geng-sun decided when they would stop and get their breath back—not as often as Paris would have liked up in this thinner air. She hadn't been in the mountains long enough, and there was a flickering ache in the back of her head. The sweat they'd worked up started chilling as soon as they stopped, and Paris wasted effort taking her furs off and putting them on again. Tahr had gone very quiet, not wasting his breath on talking, and she couldn't guess what was going on inside his head. Probably being *one-pointed,* the way he'd told her Buddhists try to do—just thinking about what you're doing. Or not even that: just *doing it.* Paris only wished she could.

She lapped up a still moment, gazing back over the valley.

On a clear day they would be seeing snows all round them. Paris would have the kind of view she'd wanted when they first stopped in the forest, the kind tourists pay a thousand dollars for. She wondered which ridge, back beyond the valley, Tahr and Shengo had come over, from his home. Maybe he was looking for it, too.

Paris glanced at Geng-sun. She looked weaker. Catching the *yeh-teh* in profile, Paris thought: *She's not so ugly after all.* Or rather, she was, but. . . . Down in the human world below, every feature that was different about her would say "backward." Up here, they meant nothing like that. Paris had seen her use those strong teeth as a tool, as subtle as fingers when she picked apart a knot, as strong as a clamp when she carried the rope ladder. Now, as they gained height and felt the breath of ice around them, Paris wished she had a nose like that to warm the air. And there was something—could it be *dignified?*—in the way Geng-sun stood and moved, at least before the bullet made her limp. And even now, just in the way she sat.

Tahr had it, too, that quality. What kid of his age back home ever looked so calm, so . . . *in possession of himself?* She reminded herself that he was older than he looked, but still. . . . What would he look like in a few years? She thought of the men round here—the wiry porters, none of them muscular or macho, hoisting packs as big as themselves. She could see Tahr as a slim man, like the dancer in the subway. Even now, he sometimes looked like a dancer preparing, waiting for the time to dance.

Paris wondered: *Were the yetis Buddhists, too?*

"On," gestured Geng-sun, pulling herself to her feet. She leaned on the spear a moment, then led on.

They'd been laboring toward the skyline for hours. Now at last it relented, and there they were over the top into a scooped-out side valley littered with boulders that might have been as big as houses or as small as footballs—the eye couldn't make sense of distance or perspective. White on gray, streaks of snow stretched down out of the greater whiteness that went up on each side, getting steeper and more jagged as it vanished into cloud. Tahr and Paris could feel the mass of the mountains closing in around them, though they could not see.

Geng-sun was suddenly lighter, moving forward faster. Wasn't this what she had told them: a pass between mountains? *Three* mountains, she'd said . . . "Don't stop now," she gestured. "Still a long way to go."

They took one side of the valley to avoid the clutter of rocks that glaciers had scattered in the dip of it. So they climbed. Time passed, but nothing in the landscape seemed to move around them. There was still the same distance on all sides, before the same landscape blurred into cloud. And still Geng-sun pointed onward, where the valley came out of the mountains, where there had to be a pass. They stopped from time to time to eke out the food they still had. Tahr glanced at Paris and thought once again: *What is she doing here? I should have made her stay back in the valley. Made her? Who could stop her when her mind was made up? Not even her terrible uncle.* Paris had insisted, and—was he being selfish?—Tahr had agreed. He told himself: *If she wanted to leave now, I would let her go.*

Something had changed in front of them. Where the valley narrowed in toward its head was a line of blue white. Gradually, the line became a wall, and they saw where the glacier flowed down to wedge itself into the valley with its tongue of ice.

"Is that it?" Tahr tried to ask Geng-sun. Was that what she'd meant by the Fortress of Ice?

"No. On. Beyond." They were going to have to cross it. Paris looked into Geng-sun's eyes. Just once she wanted to do that spooky thing it seemed that Tahr did, and *see* what Geng-sun was thinking. She found herself imagining things vaguely, but they were cartoons. Disney, not Geng-sun. All she saw in Geng-sun's eyes was weariness and pain.

Then Geng-sun was looking past her, back the way they'd come, and her eyes narrowed with alertness. Tahr was on his feet, too, squinting with her, and gradually Paris made out something . . . was it? . . . in the light and dark of snow and boulders. Way back, as far as the cloud let them see, there was something moving. One lone figure. Moving this way, on the far flank of the valley. Following.

Even with her ordinary eyesight, Paris could see that it wasn't an animal. It walked on two legs. Geng-sun, with her mountain vision, knew at once. "One of your kind," she signed, and there was a flash of panic in her eyes. Tahr and Paris stared at each other, but Geng-sun grabbed them. Shook them. "Move on," she was saying. "No talk now. Move on."

They were nearing the edge of the ice. Unless the follower crossed the valley now, the tongue would be between them, as it piled into the valley bottom. If it did cross the valley, it would lose ground. They glanced back, but the figure had dropped out of sight among the boulders . . . then there it was, coming, still on a contour—not gaining but not losing ground. If they could see it, it could see them, and it saw where they were going. It knew that in the end the mountain walls closed in and they'd have no choice but to cross the ice.

Not yet, though. They followed the edge of ice uphill, until the slope steepened to broken cliffs, impassable. Now there was no choice.

There was a steady coldness flowing out of the glacier into their faces, and they folded their capes up to their eyes. Close to, the ice looked hardly different from the ground they'd been walking on—pitted and dirty with grit—except here and there it broke. As they moved out onto it, they saw what these breaks meant—each one a sheer crevasse, going blue gray, getting darker, going down.

Geng-sun led on, using her spear as an ice pick, threading through the bands of rucked-up ice, watching for the sudden glassy patches underfoot. Slip there and you'd slide helpless, slowly, and no one could save you. It was slow work, getting slower, as their way led them into more and more contorted patterns in the ice flow. Ice boulders piled up against them . . . until Geng-sun turned with a bleak look. It was no good. They would have to turn back. Find another way.

Not quite back at the edge of the ice sheet, they spotted it—a band of dirtier ice, good for friction, that led up the stream of the glacier for a while, to the lee of an island of exposed rock. That was solid ground, smooth, sprinkled with fresh snow, good for walking on. If they could reach the rock, they would be halfway over, with a good view of the way to come. They kept their heads down and climbed. Each time they looked, the whaleback of safe rock was closer. Closer. It was no good thinking. In this time-frozen place, all they could do was watch their feet and climb. Then Geng-sun stopped abruptly.

In its meter-a-year rush downhill past the rock, the ice had sheared a crack, a blue green crevasse no wider than a man was tall. Tahr and Paris came to the side of the crevasse and stopped. Geng-sun hung back, whimpering slightly. Softer snow turned the edges to overhanging lips, and here and there the sides had crumbled inward, wedging slantwise blocks of ice across the drop. Over these the snow had settled and frozen, and been snowed upon again. One was near enough the surface to step down on it—a snow bridge—if they dared, and walk across.

Then they looked up, and the figure sat there, looking down from the rock, calmly waiting.

It was more wrapped in rags than they were, as if it had looted scraps of clothing from anywhere, maybe even from the *yeh-tehs'* cave. It, too, had wrapped a cloak round its face like a hood. From that bit of personal shadow, it was watching. For one moment, something in Tahr's heart leaped: *Could it be Shengo, come to save them?* Then that mad thought faded, as the figure laughed.

Franklin. That was the way he'd laughed back at the campsite—world-weary, out-of-this-world, as if he alone had suddenly spotted that the whole thing was a farce, a joke. On the echoing ice sheet, it sounded like the laughter of the gods.

Paris gave a little cry beside Tahr as Franklin peeled back his hood.

The suave, sophisticated Franklin was gone. They might have been looking at his savage ancestor—the same set of the head, the line of the nose and forehead, but framed by a straggle of hair and blood-and-dirt-caked stubble. Whether the blood was his own, Tahr did not like to think. The hands were hidden under the ragged cloak. Could he still have some kind of weapon? But Franklin was only looking at Paris.

"Well met, my dear . . ." He hardly raised his voice, but it carried in the stilled air. In spite of herself, Paris felt it entering her brain. "You didn't think you could just walk off like that, surely?" The brief smile was stranger than the laughter. "I mean, where else could there be to go?" With one part of his mind, Tahr wondered: *How does this man do it?* Even here, he made it seem as though all their days of running just converged on this one point, this bridge, and there was nothing else they could do.

Paris stared, her mouth half open. *Don't look at him,* Tahr thought. *Don't speak.* She might tell him, he suddenly realized, she might tell him about the Ice Fortress. "Don't!" Tahr whispered.

"Ah," said Franklin. "So we have a little secret, do we? Just where *are* you going, you and your two little pets?"

That smile again. For a moment, she met his eyes, and felt his willpower in them, like a deadly undertow.

"A private party?" Franklin purred. "Tell your Uncle Franklin. You know you've got no secrets from me. . . ."

They were so still, Tahr fancied he could feel the glacier moving.

"Won't you join me?" It was not a question. Franklin came to the edge of the bridge, holding out his hand. "That's my girl," he said as she took one step closer. And another. "You know we're two of a kind."

"Paris, no!" Tahr said, and she hesitated.

Franklin had moved nearer, testing the snow crust. It squealed, as fresh snow does, but held his weight. "You can bring your little friends, if it amuses you. . . . *Whatever* amuses you, I can fix it."

As if her feet were not operated by her own mind, Paris took one step more, onto the snow bridge; Franklin's hand was out toward her, almost within reach.

"No one's going to get hurt," he said soothingly. "Just in case you think I have . . . *designs* on your Neanderthal. I've *just had* a better idea." He smiled. "Oh, that's very amusing . . ." His chuckle multiplied along the ice. "When your little pets grow up, you can extract their DNA, and—"

"Shut up!" said Paris faintly.

"Touchy, aren't we?" he said in his most honeyed voice. "Think about it. Special people like us, we don't have *families*. But you can engineer yourself a species!" He was reaching forward now, and as if operated by a wire, her hand began to lift toward him.

"You're . . . crazy," she said. "Twisted. Shut up!"

"Oh, I've shocked you. Sorry. I speak purely as a scientist. You still have some of your parents' hang-ups—*so* conventional. Very well . . . You can give them a nice little wedding. A white wedding, on the ice!" The thought of it seemed to tickle him; abruptly, he began to laugh. This wasn't his dry chuckle but a hollow belly laugh. He laughed as if it was the best joke of his life. His Paris, playing weddings with her pets, just like a little girl! He laughed. He threw back his head, and his body shook. The laughter echoed back up from the crevasse, as if the glacier had got the joke and it was laughing, too, laughing till its sides began to ache and wheeze and creak. And then the bridge was crumbling, folding inward into nothing, as if it had never been anything more than frozen air.

"Paris!" She was quite still, her whole body rigid, as the snow went sliding from beneath her feet. At Tahr's shout, her trance broke and she tried to turn, with her feet going one way and an outstretched arm the other, and Tahr grabbed it, falling flat, spreadeagled in the snow. Next moment there was a hand on his other hand, and Geng-sun was there, too, stretched out, holding . . . For a moment Paris's feet kicked on the edge, kicked, got a moment's purchase, gained a little, slipped again. Tahr pulled, and Geng-sun braced him, Paris thrashed again . . . and came up wriggling, clawing, as the crumbling slowly stopped and she lay face down in the stinging snow.

Behind her, the snow bridge was gone. It had made no sound that she remembered. In her panic, she couldn't have heard a thing, of course, Still, she couldn't stop herself imagining that she'd heard her uncle, heard him laughing all the way down.

24

The Fastness

On and upward. Franklin had said it: Where else was there to go?

They waited a while as Paris stared at the lip of the crevasse. She crept a little nearer, till she felt the ice creak, and she stepped back. *No.* Once she had thought she would follow her Uncle Franklin to the ends of the earth, but she was not going to follow him *there.* She'd had a glimpse of the ice depths. Blue green gray, they went down out of sight, getting darker as they went. She stared a while, as numb as ice, and then, to Tahr's relief, began to cry.

Arms folded round her. First, Tahr's arms. Then Geng-sun's wrapped around them both, and from a lammergeier's distance they would have looked like a single animal, a mound of reddish hair. They held on partly for the comfort, partly for the warmth. The day had passed its warmest without the low cloud showing any sign of lifting, and now it would slowly get colder. The coldness in the ice didn't feel like the absence of heat but like a living thing, a power of nature, locked inside the glacier and reaching for their bones.

At last, Paris looked up. Geng-sun was shivering, too, her big jaw clenched against the pain. It was worse, and it was draining her. "We should move on," said Tahr, trying not to sound frightened, and they did.

At the head of the whaleback of rock, where it parted the glacier, there was a safe way over. The crevasse had been only at the lower edges, where the ice sheet pulled away. On the rock they rested for a moment, trusting their feet. Through the powdery snow they felt the warmth of rock you never notice till you try to live on ice. Here Geng-sun shared out the last of her pouch of supplies. But it was enough, she assured them. They would be there soon.

From the high ground of the rock they could see how the glacier flowed—in all the streaks and twists and channels of a river, only motionless, unchanging to the human eye. It made their eyes go mazy to stare at it, but Geng-sun was working it out. There was a way through, and she was fixing it in her memory—a map that would be inside her through the laby-rinth of dips and turns. She led forward onto the ice, using her spear to test each drift of snow, backing off more than once where it crumbled into the emptiness beneath. So they came through.

The other shore rose in the mist now, startling white. As they approached it, Geng-sun turned to Tahr and Paris with an odd expression. "Do what she does," said Tahr. "Narrow your eyes in the snow. Or else it makes you blind." He looked up at Geng-sun, and Paris could see he was worried. Truly worried. "How far now?" his look said. "Not far," came Geng-sun's answer . . . as it had for most of the day. A gentle smile crept over her face, but she pushed it away. She was so tired. It could be the end of her, and them all, to let herself relax too soon.

After the ice, it felt like a blessing to sink their feet into snow. It was almost warm, thought Paris. You could lie down in it like a duvet. But Tahr was by her. "Walk." Paris threw herself back at the slope, and slipped and sank as on a sand dune. Then she did what Tahr did and followed the single line of footsteps—wide, flat yeti footsteps—that Geng-sun was making for them through the snow.

At last, the slope relented. There was a movement in the cloud, too, as a wind sprang up, and something in Tahr thrilled. The wind was coming from in front of them, over the pass. Even before it thinned the mist, he knew this was it. *The gap between three mountains,* if you counted the two that straddled the glacier on the one side. And the wind that blew from over it seemed to have a different smell.

All the way up, Geng-sun had been dragging, going slower, as the pain and exhaustion pulled her down. Now, for a moment, speed and strength came back to her and she was forging forward ahead of them through the almost level thigh-deep snow. She made straight for the saddle of the pass, and they hung back waiting for her call. If there were armed guards on this stronghold, they had better see her first. She would have to explain what she was doing, bringing with her members of the deadliest species on earth: the human. For the first time, Paris felt a worry, and wondered why she had not thought of it before. Why should Neanderthals accept them? Why should they take Geng-sun's word that they were friends?

They waited, huddling closer. All Paris could see of Tahr, or he of her, was a slit beneath their hoods and, somewhere in it, narrowed eyes. Even speaking would let out precious body heat, and the cold would press in tighter. Now and then, the mist thinned and they looked around. Smooth, unbroken snow stretched on this side, and on the other . . . the same. Both ways it seemed to rise evenly. Only in front of them was the ground dead flat, as if there had been a lake here once, before the cold. Tahr saw it in his mind's eye, with a fringe of reeds around it freezing, crisping, snapping in the wind. The Lake of Ice.

And they could not see the fortress. Beyond the flat, the ground sloped down, gently at first, then dropping out of sight. They looked round, scanning the slopes of the three peaks. All were unbroken. Not even the shadow of a ditch or rampart buried under snow.

Geng-sun was quite still, looking this way, looking that. She went to and fro across the lake, hunting for the special angle that would show her the secret way in. She quested up the slope to one side, came back, labored up the slope on the other side, almost out of sight. . . . At last, the cloud lifted, just enough to show the blank tremendous sides of the mountains. There was nothing that could be, or hide, a fortress. *Yet if I close my eyes,* Tahr thought, *I can see it, as clear as Geng-sun saw it in her mind.* It was like a great *dzong* out of Shengo's stories, part monastery, part castle, built with buttresses of ice. He saw it as if he'd been there, in some other life.

Geng-sun came back slowly, staring at them with no expression, no gestures at all. Tahr tried to meet her eyes, and for a moment it was like looking into a deserted cave. Then she looked away. He reached out to touch her, but she drew back.

"Nothing . . ." Geng-sun's hands said it all, lifting spreading fingers, lifting something fragile . . . then with palms turning inward, slowly, as everything crumbled and dissolved away. Her head sank, gazing down at the snow where that nothing had gone.

"Come back with us," Tahr said, in words and gestures. Or rather, not back, but onward. Over and downhill, out of this killing cold, while there was time.

"No!" It wasn't an angry hand chop this time. It was tired, and final. In the same movement Geng-sun turned away. She was climbing the snow slope. Tahr called out and took a step to follow, but she spun round, raising her hands in threat and anger. "Off, off!" She jabbed the spear toward him, chasing him away.

"Please . . . ," signed Tahr, and Paris joined him, copying his gestures. "Please," she called out loud. Then the *yeh-teh* lunged at them, moving with more strength than she had all day. One hand pointed on, down and over the hill—just long enough to get the message. Then she was baring her teeth and lashing at them with that stone-edged screeching, and they stumbled backward. Still she came at them, swiping with the spear, until they turned and started to run. Each time they slowed and looked back, she loomed up and brandished fists and weapon, still there on the skyline, as if she had become a sentinel on the Fastness in her story, after all.

The next time they looked back, the cloud was twisting back in streamers. On the skyline there was nothing. Then, up the smooth white slope to one side, they saw a small red brown speck, climbing.

Tahr looked at Paris. Her face was red as blisters from the snow and wind. "Oh, God," she said in a small voice. "I can't feel anything. Hold me, I think I'm cold."

Tahr held her firmly, for only a moment. "We must move. Move fast. Your arms and legs and hands, move all of them. Make blood flow."

Paris sighed. It was so much effort. Later . . .

"Now!" Tahr shouted, louder than she'd ever heard him, and her dreamy spell broke. "Do what I say, you stupid . . . tourist!"

"What?!" her eyes flared.

"Good!" Tahr cried. "Shout at me later. Now just follow." And he locked her arm in his and towed her downhill, till gray rocks took the place of the snow.

Afterward, neither of them could say how long they stumbled, slithered, blundered down. Looking back up to the pass from the sheepfold, they saw the mountainside crisscrossed with bands of sudden rockfall, any one of which could have done for them. Sometimes Tahr wondered if they had fallen and died, and this was another life, reborn in this highest thin green pasture, with a shepherd staring at them, disbelieving, not unkind. No, it couldn't be another incarnation, because they were both the age they'd been, and just as sore and cold and aching.

The shepherd led them gently to a tiny hut and stoked a fire, heaping up his blankets round them. Then, as Shengo would have done once in another hut, another valley, he began to make tea.

"You are lucky," he told them later, in a dialect Tahr could make out now and then. It seemed to be next morning some-how, and in the middle of thinking that, Tahr fell asleep again. The sleep that pulled both him and Paris under wasn't calm, and there were slow, terrible dreams beneath it, pulling past like monsters frozen in the ice. When they woke again, the shepherd looked relieved. He rubbed both of Paris's hands and told her: Flex your fingers. When she found she could, he smiled. "Lucky," he told Tahr. "People lose toes and fingers up there." He had a little warm broth for them now, and later hard bread. Tahr wanted to say, "No, we must help you," but as he tried to stand, his legs gave way, and the man tucked him back into the blankets, gently, like a feverish child. Paris lay in the warm and the dark, in a place with no name, and was con-tent to let it hold her. And she slept, and healed a little, and slept more.

A day or two later, when they could both stand and walk, the shepherd sat down, serious. "I must go down tomorrow," he said. "It's already late." They must come with him.

"I can help you," Tahr said. "I know sheep and goats." He tried to tell him the joke with his name, but it did not work in this dialect, and the man shook his head. Then he smiled. "Maybe you are some use," he said. "But her?"

Now the two of them had turned to Paris, and looking at them, Paris saw a man and a boy who was nearly a man, two foreign faces as you might see in a TV documentary . . . look-ing at a gangling, awkward Western girl who had no place here. Hadn't Tahr called her a "tourist"? She'd meant to scold him for that, but it felt so long ago.

245

"He says there's a place in the valley," Tahr said, "where the trekkers come. The last for the season may still be there. He will take you."

She began to shake her head, but his look stopped her. *No!* she wanted to say. *You can't! Come with me! You can live in America, Mom or Pop will fix it. . . .* The jumble of words was too much. *Tahr,* she wanted to say, *I thought you liked me.* She shut her eyes tight. *What am I meant to do without you?* When she opened them again, his eyes were still on her, steadily. There was something in them that made the thousand words they could have traded now a waste of breath.

She would go. That was the truth of it. She had no option. Her parents were waiting. He, of course, would stay. He would be sad. He loved her.

All the words in the world, in all the languages, would only say that. None of them could change it. That was all.

Next morning they helped the shepherd close the hut up for the winter. Paris looked at Tahr. "I've been thinking," she said. "About Geng-sun . . ." She couldn't help glancing uphill, but the Snows were untouchable, too far away even to think. "If she was the last one . . ."

"Yes?"

"Then—then it was over already, wasn't it?"

"If she was the last." Tahr followed her gaze up the mountain. He tried to imagine Geng-sun like the mystic lamas in old Shengo's stories, forging through a blizzard in their own heat shadow, so the snowflakes melted just before touching their skin. He tried to see it, but he couldn't.

Was hers the life "on the edge"—the words Shengo had used when he launched them on their journey? Or was that Tahr's life, growing restless in their *gompa?* Or Paris's, under Uncle Franklin's spell? Or did Shengo mean his own death, after all?

Where was "the edge," anyway, if the Wheel of Life kept turning? Wasn't every point as much the edge as any other? Maybe that's what the old man had meant: his final joke?

"I think she *was* the last," Tahr said to Paris.

"Does it make any difference to all that . . . being Buddhist? I mean, reincarnation and all that?"

Tahr shrugged. "Still we die," he said simply. Then he hugged her, tighter than he'd ever done before. "But I am glad you did not. Stay alive, in your America, and think of me."

Later that day, they reached the little terraced hamlet where the shepherd's wife peeped out among a happy mess of children. The man explained a little, where these strangers came from, and sent Tahr into the hut to greet her. There was a mule round the back, and that would do for Paris. No, Tahr couldn't come down to the station, the man said, as if he had guessed how much harder the leaving would be among Western people. The least Tahr could do, he said with mock sternness, was help his wife a little, what with their new baby.

In the warmest, darkest corner of the house, but looking out through the small slit of a window, the shepherd's wife sat with the tiny wrinkled baby at her breast.

"How old?" said Tahr shyly.

"Two weeks. But he is strong."

Already Tahr was working backward in his mind. How many

days since their ordeal on the mountain? How many more since the rebels in the gorge . . . since he came to the hunters' camp? How many days since the waterfall . . . since Shengo?

"Have you a name for him?"

She smiled. "Not until the Hundred Days. Then we'll know he is staying with us." As if she had said too much, the baby twisted in her arms, screwed up its tiny face, and squalled.

Once, when Tahr was much younger, he'd asked Shengo, "Why do babies cry?"

"Because they wake up in this life and look around, and find they're still here—turning on the Wheel!" Shengo had said, but he'd said it like a rather wistful joke. "They must do it all again! But then . . ." And he'd given Tahr that rare sly twinkle. "But then . . . their parents love them. So what can they do?"